The Chimerical Quest

The Chimerical Quest

by
René Pujol

translated, annotated and introduced by
Brian Stableford

A Black Coat Press Book

Visit our website at www.blackcoatpress.com

ISBN 978-1-61227-488-1. First Printing. March 2016. Published by Black Coat Press, an imprint of Hollywood Comics.com, LLC, P.O. Box 17270, Encino, CA 91416.

TABLE OF CONTENTS

Introduction 7
THE BLACK SUN 13
THE CHIMERICAL QUEST 83

Introduction

La Chasse aux chimères by René Pujol, here translated as "The Chimerical Quest," was originally published by Éditions des Portiques in 1932. That edition seems to have been moderately successful, being reprinted twice. The novella that precedes it in the present volume, "Le Soleil noir," translated as "The Black Sun," was originally published in *Lectures Pour Tous* as a three-part serial in March-May 1921 (the various sources that give the date of its publication there as 1929 are incorrect).

René Pujol (1878-1942) was a journalist who branched out after the Great War into the production of popular fiction and theatrical sketches, also writing librettos for comic opera, sometimes using the pseudonym René Pons. He went on to work prolifically as a screenwriter and director in the cinema during the 1930s. He ventured into the realms of speculative fiction several times in addition to the two stories included here, initially in stories written in the early 1920s for the children's periodical *L'Age Heureux*, but more notably in three feuilletons published in the popular science magazine *Science et Voyages*, "Le Secret de la Sunbeam Valley" (21 parts, 1927-28, with Henri Bernay), "La Planète invisible" (25 parts, 1930-31), and "Au Temps des brumes" (17 parts, 1931).

After publishing *La Chasse aux chimères,* Pujol wrote no more speculative fiction, although he did write five more novels before his increasingly prolific cinematic career monopolized his time. Those later volumes were in the mildly humorous and slightly cynical vein of crime fiction that had featured in most of his earlier book publications. The tone and manner of those books is reproduced in *La Chasse aux chimères*, but it acquires extra satirical bite by virtue of its association with a speculative technology that has the potential to change the world completely, if the world will consent to be changed.

"Le Soleil noir" is markedly, although not completely different, very much darker in tone and more coldly cynical—evidently a result of being written in the immediate aftermath of the Great War.

The five years following the end of the Great War bought forth a glut of catastrophist fantasies, partly as a reaction against the fact that virtually all fiction published during the war was obliged to be relentlessly upbeat, as a calculated instrument of maintaining morale, and partly because of the realization, rammed home in no uncertain terms by the experience of the war, of exactly how vulnerable civilization was to the possibility of complete collapse, and how people might really be expected to react and behave under tremendous stress and the possibility of imminent annihilation.

"Le Soleil noir" is not the most extreme of the cynical studies of catastrophe published in the aftermath of the war, but it is one of the most stylishly laconic. It makes an interesting companion with J. H. Rosny's classic "La Force mystérieuse"[1], which was published in another popular magazine, *Je Sais Tout*, not long before the outbreak of the war in 1913. Although the plots and fundamental attitudes of the two stories are similar, and their development equally conscientious, Pujol's clearly bears the traces and scars of the real catastrophe that had occurred in the interim. It was an unusually sophisticated work for the rather downmarket *Lectures Pour Tous* to publish, and might have been accepted, or even commissioned, with "La Force mystérieuse" in mind, as the editors tried to reposition the periodical at the higher market level of *Je Sais Tout*, but whether that is the case or not, they never published anything else nearly as corrosively downbeat in the magazine thereafter, and might have instructed the author to bring it to its rather abrupt conclusion.

Partly because it is too short to make a book, "Le Soleil noir" went unreprinted until a version appeared in the fanzine

---

[1] tr. as *The Mysterious Force*, Black Coat Press, ISBN 978-1-935558-37-8.

Altaïr in 1984, so it is not nearly as well-known as some of the other works of a similar tripe published in the same period, such as Henri Allorge's *Le Grand cataclysme* (1922)[2] and Ernest Pérochon's *Les Hommes frénétiques* (1925)[3], but it does not suffer by comparison with those works and is one of the finest examples of its subgenre, perhaps the deftest of all in the delicacy of its touch and the subtlest in terms of its depiction of psychological reactions to unexpected and uncomprehended disaster.

La Chasse aux chimères, by contrast, deals not with disaster but golden opportunity, starting from the hypothesis that a modern scientist might discover the secret for which the ancient alchemists sought so long and hard: a method of converting lead into gold. Because the method is scientific rather than magical, it is laborious, unable to produce unlimited quantities of gold without great effort, and it is also a process whose minor technical hitches need ironing out if it is to be adapted to an industrial scale—for which reason, its inventor requires the initial capital to build a factory and time to refine its production to the point at which it will become truly prolific: a point at which it will inevitably become socially problematic for a world whose financial system is still firmly based on the gold standard. That political problem is not, of course, insoluble, although it threatens to become so because the inventor who has developed the alchemical method is an idealistic anarchist who wants to give his secret away to everyone as soon as he has perfected it, so that anyone will be able to make gold.

As with "Le Soleil noir," *La Chasse aux chimères* develops that story with an unusually deft touch in its development of the various central characters involved with the project—some involuntarily because of their existing relationships with

[2] tr. as *The Great Cataclysm*, Black Coat Press, ISBN 978-1-61227-026-5.
[3] tr. as *The Frenetic People*, Black Coat Press, ISBN 978-1-61227-118-7.

the inventor and others avidly because of their determination to profit from it in spite of his eccentricities—and in its depiction of their psychological reactions to gradually but inexorably changing circumstances. Although it has the same lightly humorous aspects as the author's crime novels, the artificiality of that humor becomes much more apparent, and its underlying dark cynicism much more nakedly obvious, as the hypothesis is extrapolated into a political context and the feverish insanity associated with the Californian and Klondike "gold rushes" moves gradually closer to the story's surface. That complexity, as well as the novel's greater ambition, makes *La Chasse aux chimères* Pujol's masterpiece, so far as his prose fiction in concerned.

By the standard that had been set in the first third of the 20th century by ever bolder ventures in the *"merveilleux scientifique,"* *La Chasse aux chimères* is a modest and relatively quiet story, the heart of which is not so much the potential transformation of the world by science as the analogy between the not-entirely-chimerical quest of the alchemists and the similarly problematic, but perhaps similarly soluble, quest for personal fulfillment via *amour*. In that respect too, it has a significant affiliation with "Le Soleil noir," in which the eponymous black sun, in the process of devastating the world, puts enormous stress of the narrator's idyll of love. In *La Chasse aux chimères* that pressure is inverted, Jacques Gellé's wealth and dandyism distancing him remotely from even being able to think in idyllic terms, but both stores submit the fundamental ideology of *amor omnia vincit* to a searching and scrupulous proof. For that reason, they make an interesting pair, an intriguing collectivity, and a distinctive component of the evolving patchwork of interbellum *roman scientifique*.

The following translation of *La Chasse aux chimères* was made from a copy of the 1932 Éditions des Portiques edition. The translation of "Le Soleil noir" was made from a scan of the relevant pages of *Lectures Pour Tous* (which are not available on *gallica*) made for me by the collector and bibliographer Jean-Luc Boutel, whose excellent website "Sur l'Autre Face du Monde" is an invaluable mine of information about the development of French speculative fiction; I am very grateful to him for his kindness.

Brian Stableford

THE BLACK SUN

1

Jane was pretty. Nevertheless, the sentiment she inspired was not so much admiration as a keen interest, so intelligent was she divined to be, incapable of vulgar thoughts and miscalculations. She had magnificent eyes whose exact color was unknown; their irises were tinted with blue and green, and speckled with flecks of gold that augmented their brightness.

That day, I was contemplating her in silence. I was taking pleasure in detailing her delicate features while she leaned over her embroidery. Sometimes, she bit her lip lightly, and then pushed back a rebellious curl that was tickling her ear. I smiled tenderly at my fiancée. My happiness was complete.

Jane had been in my house since the previous day, with her father and mother, Monsieur Jérôme Sterneballe and Madame Amélie Sterneballe. Christmas falling on a Friday, the businessman was having "a long weekend." They had closed their shop for three days—for my future father-in-law kept an optician's boutique in the Rue Sainte-Catherine in Bordeaux, and they had come to spend their vacation under my roof.

I was in charge of the school at Roque de Thau, near Blaye. I loved that region, between the placid waters of the Gironde and the vineyards that produced a justly reputed wine. The commune being small, I did not have many pupils, and my work was not difficult. Fond of my métier, I was passionate about shaping the young souls confided to me.

"Where's Papa?" Jane asked.

"He's finishing painting the wine-store door."

If I dare express myself thus, painting was Monsieur Sterneballe's Ingres violin. The honorable optician spent his leisure time covering with multicolored layers anything that seemed to him to be worthy of his brush. Every time he came to see me he brought his pots of paint. It was sufficient to count them to know how many days he intended to devote to me. Thanks to him, as much as to the old woman who served as my housekeeper, a "Carabosse" of whom I had only ever known the nickname, La Barboque, my house was a jewel of neatness.

It is no bad thing to have laborious distractions. For my part, I profited from my hours of liberty to cultivate a piece of land situated behind the school, and no one went past my enclosure without complimenting me on my vegetables or my fruit trees.

"One day," said Jane, "Papa will paint himself—you'll see!"

I started to laugh at the idea that the long, thin figure of Monsieur Sterneballe might be ornamented by tattoos. The worthy man was approaching sixty. Commercial cares had marked his physiognomy with two deep wrinkles that, departing from the base of his nose, gave the illusion that his cheeks were crumpled like crepe. As for his forehead, it was striped from one temple to the other by three rigorously parallel furrows whose extremities were lost in hair that was still thick.

"You're teasing," I told my fiancée. "You'll be cruel to me if I become too old."

"Oh, I'll be very peevish," she replied, laughing.

"Then you'll have changed a great deal."

"We continued to chat merrily, while maintaining the beautiful fire that was blazing between two cast iron andirons.

The bells were ringing for the end of vespers and, a few minutes later, we heard children chattering in the road.

The previous evening, we had gone to midnight mass. It had been bitterly cold, with a sharp north wind that drew tears. When we returned we had huddled around the table to have supper.

"Would you like a game of chess?" I proposed.

"Good idea. A game, and a return match."

I had just set up the chessboard when someone knocked. It was Léonce Mistouflet, one of the Baron de Lansac's tenant farmers.

"A thousand apologies and beg pardon," he said, shaking my hand. "I'm disturbing you, Monsieur Dantenot."

"Not at all, Monsieur Mistouflet."

"Yes, I'm disturbing you. You're being polite, but it doesn't alter the fact..."

"No matter…what can I do for you?"

The fellow was not embarrassed. Before felling some oaks to sell the wood, he wanted to consult the official land register in order to determine the limits of his forest. He had come on the afternoon of Christmas day in order not to lose an hour of the working day.

"I know that everything is shut," he said, "but you're so obliging, Monsieur Dantenot..."

"A secretary of the Mairie ought not to spare his trouble," I replied. "Come with me; it won't take long."

I picked up my cap and we left. The weather was splendid. It was as warm as spring. I made that remark to my companion.

"Don't talk to me about it," he said. "That old devil of a sun is lashing out today. One would think it were May."

And he lamented the irregularity of the seasons, affirming that nature had been more reasonable once. One had hot weather in summer, cold in winter and rain in autumn, as regular as a musical score.

I listened to him with a distracted ear, for I was in a hurry to get back to Jane. I unrolled the plan, on which I pointed out to the farmer the part that interested him. He ran his rugged index-finger over it slowly, the fingernail as hard and yellow as horn.

"Yes, that's it, yes…I see…it's there. So, Féraud comes as far as here? That's curious... Anyway, thank you, Monsieur Dantenot."

"No trouble, Monsieur Mistouflet."

"I won't hurry going back to the farm. It's not right to be sweating in December."

I went back with him as far as the house. The village was almost deserted. Père Fouessart, who was suspected of being a centenarian, was smoking his pipe in his doorway. We exchanged a few cordial remarks.

"I put myself in the sun to soothe my rheumatism," he said, "but it was so hot that I came back into the shade."

"With these satanic seasons," Mistouflet said to him, "one no longer knows which foot to dance on."

"Oh," the old man replied, philosophically, "it's been a long time since I danced on either foot."

"Joker!" said the farmer. Addressing me with gravity, he added: "I'll be frank, Monsieur Dantenot. All these upsets that are ruining us come from the telegraph. These electricities, these waves, as the newspaper says, are troubling the sky. They claim that it's progress. Progress? I bow my head—but what good will progress do when nothing germinates any longer?"

I kept quiet. He seized me be the shoulder in a familiar fashion.

"You who are studious, Monsieur Dantenot, you ought to write articles about that. Too many cannon shots were fired during the war, and now we're being poisoned by airplanes. And the clouds? No one even thinks about them, the clouds! If I were something in the government, I'd have all the inventors shot."

"*Au revoir*, Monsieur Mistouflet."

"Bonsoir, Monsieur Dantenot…and thank you for showing me the register."

Jane was waiting for me with impatience. We started playing, pushing the pawns after mature reflection, because we were both serious players.

The contest had been seriously engaged when Madame Sterneballe came into the dining room. The good woman was scarlet.

"Oh, my children," she said, letting herself fall into a chair. "I can't digest my lunch. I have the vapors, and they're choking me..." She rolled her anxious eyes and fanned herself nervously with her handkerchief.

Jane hastened to run in search of melissa cordial. I made a circuit of the room several times, making vague remarks, which is the usual fashion in which men make themselves useful.

Madame Sterneballe was suffocating. Her plump, short hands were trembling.

"I was in the drawing room," she said, "reading the feuilleton. I suddenly felt my temples becoming moist...and a ball forming in my stomach..."

Jane handed her a glass, which she emptied in brief draughts, while continuing to talk.

"In order not to alarm anyone I went to sit down outside...but it didn't pass... I'm streaming from head to toe. Oh, my God...! What's wrong with me? A congestion?"

"Don't be alarmed, Madame," I said to her. "Everyone's complaining about the heat today."

Jane looked at me with a mocking expression. She thought that I simply wanted to reassure her mother, and doubtless judged that I lacked imagination. Madame Sterneballe was of the same opinion, for she shrugged her shoulders and repeated: "Heat in December? You're not thinking, Roger!"

Monsieur Sterneballe appeared in his turn. He was even redder than his wife.

"Well!" he said. "What does this comedy signify? I can no longer stand the heat!"

"You too!" stammered Madame Sterneballe. "Then I'm not ill?"

"It's the sun that's ill. It thinks it's April!"

I went out immediately. As soon as I had crossed the threshold I was astonished to feel the caress of a veritable summer breeze. I went to consult the thermometer. It marked twenty-eight degrees. I took out my watch. It was half past three.

"What do you think of it, Roger?"

It was Monsieur Sterneballe, who had rejoined me. I spread my arms and let them drop to indicate my ignorance. We advanced into the middle of the courtyard in order to examine the sky.

An elongated cloud, pink and gray, was floating at the zenith, and the sun was resplendent in the occident, where it would soon disappear. Nothing in particular attracted our attention. It was a superb day, and nothing more.

The almanac told us that the sun would set at three fifty-six. When it had sunk beneath the horizon, the temperature gradually dropped. The twilight was, however, exceptionally beautiful.

After dinner, we perceived that the fire had gone out. It was definitely not cold, and it wasn't relit.

We did not accord an extraordinary importance to what had happened during the day. We talked about the whims of nature, Indian summers—in brief, we exchanged banalities, the same ones people must have been emitting on the same subject in all the houses in the village. We did not stay up very long, because we had gone to bed late the day before.

I dozed off into a dreamless sleep. A kind of oppression woke me up. I propped myself up on my elbow and, having taken a deep breath without experiencing the slightest pain, acquired the certainty that my discomfort came from having too many bedclothes. I therefore cast off the eiderdown and went back to sleep—but not for long, for the same sensation forced me to open my eyes again. Irritated, I leapt out of bed, opened the widow and leaned on the sill. I stayed there for some time, breathing I the slightly cooler air delightedly.

Myriads of stars were resplendent in the firmament. The moon was silvering the roofs of houses. Dogs were responding to it, as if to invite one another mutually to redouble their vigilance. The sound of the flow of the Gironde reached me, as faint as the rustle of the willows in the Avenue du Port. Everything gave an impression of tranquility and absolute security. I went back to bed without reclosing the window. I thought it original to sleep in the open air, so to speak, at the end of December.

2

I got up at daybreak. It was already after seven. No one was moving yet in the house. I went down to the garden in order to dig over a patch of ground that I wanted to sow. I had only been working for five minutes when I was sweating as if it were the middle of summer. I took off my jacket and the pullover I wore outside, rolled up my shirt-sleeves, and continued plying the spade vigorously.

Fradinotte, my neighbor, went past driving a cart full of dung. He called to me over the garden wall.

"Hey, Monsieur Dantenot, is the soil good?"

"Not bad, not bad..."

"In any case, it's not last night's frost that has hardened it. If this goes on, the vine shoots are going to sprout, and the first cold snap will cut them down."

"Damn! That would be annoying."

"It's what we call a false spring. Let's hope everything will sort itself out. It's not warm weather we need, but a thick carpet of snow, to destroy those accursed insects! Hup, Bourrin! Hup!"

And his donkey pulled away while I went back to work.

"What an admirable man!" said Jane, suddenly, who had just arrived. "Come in quickly. You deserve the nice buttered toast I've made for you."

I readjusted my pince-nez in order to see my fiancée better. Every time I saw her she seemed to me to be more exquisite.

Hazard alone had allowed me to make her acquaintance. Monsieur Sterneballe was not my optician, but having noticed a pince-nez in his window whose frame seemed to me to be solid, I had gone in to buy it. An enchantress served me: that

19

was Jane. She had admitted to me since that I had been ridiculous. I no longer knew what I was saying, and made a mistake in the number of diopters. Those who have been in love will comprehend the disturbance in question, which infallibly reveals the sincerity of the heart.

I went back the following Thursday. I bought another pince-nez, and that second conversation with Jane only reinforced my sentiment.

I have never been very bold. Every week, regularly, I went back to Sterneballe's with the formal intention of declaring my love, but as soon as I went into the shop, my courage vanished, anguish gripped my throat, and I went away having bought another pair of spectacles.

During the Easter vacation, I went to change my lenses five days in succession. On the last day, Monsieur Sterneballe emerged from his back room.

"Jane," he said, "your mother's asking for you. I'll take care of Monsieur."

When the young woman had disappeared, he looked me full in the face, with a gravity that was not devoid of sympathy.

"Monsieur," he said to me, "You're ruining yourself on lorgnons. You're a great breaker of lenses and a famous executioner of frames. You'd be better off addressing yourself to a wholesaler."

Nonplussed, I attempted a weak smile while darting a glance at the door, mentally making my preparations for flight.

"I wouldn't be sorry to know who you are," continued Monsieur Sterneballe, deliberately cutting off the route of my retreat.

As I was incapable of articulating a single word, I handed him my card.

"Aha!" he said. "You're a schoolteacher? I have a young cousin in the educational corps…Philippe Escarpit."

"He was in my class!" I exclaimed, in a stentorian voice.

Thank you, Philippe Escarpit. I never told you so, but you rendered me a sterling service. I spoke about you emotionally, I felt an extraordinary affection for your person. You abruptly became my best friend, my brother. I enquired after your health, your aspirations. I learned with immense pleasure that you were about to get married. Ah, family life! The wife sowing beside the lamp...the children playing on the carpet...the grandparents generously dispensing the advice of experience...

I was so enthusiastic and eloquent that I nearly reduced the good Madame Sterneballe, who had come to join her husband, to tears.

Regretfully, I finally took my leave. Monsieur Sterneballe accompanied me to the threshold of his shop. There, he said to me: "*Au revoir*, Monsieur Dantenot. I'll expect you tomorrow, since you're on vacation. And henceforth, don't feel obliged to buy spectacles in order to chat to my daughter."

In losing his best client, he was gaining a son-in-law...

"This is for you, Monsieur Greedyguts."

I bit into the enormous slice of buttered toast, which I washed down with a cup of milky coffee. Madame Sterneballe gave me honorable competition, for she had a good appetite.

At about nine o'clock I was scanning the newspapers that the postman had just delivered, when I was summoned. Monsieur Sterneballe was standing in front of the thermometer, shaking his head pensively.

"Twenty-eight degrees!" he said. "It's climbing visibly."

"That's odd," I said. "We had the same temperature yesterday evening."

"We're passing that, my dear!"

Gradually, the level of the red liquid rose in the tube of the thermometer. The ascent was slow but regular. In a quarter of an hour the level reached twenty-nine degrees, in half an hour, thirty.

"Fantastic! Fantastic!" murmured my future father-in-law. "Your instrument isn't out of order?"

"I don't think so. Let's go and consult the one at the Mairie."

"*Cristi!* What a heat-wave!" sighed Monsieur Sterneballe.

The thermometer at the Mairie was fixed in the upper corner of the panel containing official notices and parliamentary speeches deemed worthy of display, which no one bothered to read. The said panel, facing south-east, was, in consequence, in full sunlight.

"Twenty-nine degrees and three tenths!" exclaimed Monsieur Sterneballe.

The Maire, Monsieur Nattechoux, was signing a few documents. He came out on hearing voices, to inform us that his amazement equaled ours. He uttered a few unnecessary observations on meteorology, and then took the *Petite Gironde* out of his pocket. The great Bordelais daily contained an article thus conceived:

We had the benefit on Friday of an ideal evening. The day had been rather sullen until, at about three o'clock, the solar rays increased in strength. Our fellow citizens, who were very numerous in the streets of the city center, where they were admiring the sumptuous window-displays in the large stores, observed that the temperature changed rapidly and agreeably. Even after the disappearance of the sun, a warm breeze was blowing, and the majority of strollers took off their overcoats and mantles with satisfaction.

Interrogated on the phenomenon, one of our most eminent astronomers at the observatory in Floirac attributed it to an abnormal atmospheric current. According to him, a veritable wave of sirocco, born in the confines of the Sahara, has crossed the Mediterranean and made its influence felt over the major part of Europe. That explanation would seem plausible if the same temperature—twenty-eight degrees—had not been registered at the same time in Madrid, Paris and London.

As on the previous evening, we examined the sun. It had an unsustainable glare, and the purity of the sky was absolute.

The intensity of the radiation was no longer augmenting with the same intensity. At eleven o'clock, the thermometer had scarcely passed thirty degrees. I ceased keeping watch on it after that, because we had a marriage to celebrate.

The nuptial cortege did not take long to appear. Behind a violin scratched by an idle fiddler, the spouses and the guests were bathed in sweat. They hastened to arrive in order to take shelter from the burning rays. The women especially, wrapped up in their winter clothes, overloaded with woolens and furs, were in torment. The bride's godfather was walking bare-headed, and had confided his top hat to his god-daughter.

The ceremony commenced with the reading of the contract. While I pronounced that standard phrases that I knew by heart, I observed the assembly, whose members seemed weight down by fatigue.

"Monsieur Robert-Émile Dufraison, do you consent to take for your legitimate wife…?"

My gaze was obstinately attached to the bride's godfather. The old man was experiencing an undeniable disturbance. He was opening and closing his mouth like a fish out of water, and his eyelids were rounding out immeasurably.

"Mademoiselle Ernestine-Gabrielle Tardivaud, do you consent to take for…?"

The godfather was as red as a poppy. Suddenly, he collapsed, delivering a rude blow of the fist to his neighbor's nose. There was a frightful tumult, an indescribable disorder. The women were all talking at once; a few children were crying; the men were interrogating one another. I had never seen such chaos.

"Air…! Air…!" I said, in a comminatory tone.

People drew apart slightly, and I laid the invalid out on the floor. He was completely inert, but his pulse was beating fairly clearly. At hazard, I was about to carry our respiratory movements, when Doctor Caffier came across the Place de la République. He leapt down from his cabriolet, fitted the safety-chain to the wheel, cleaved through the crowd authoritatively, and crouched down next to the old man.

"It's sunstroke," he said. "Roll back his sleeve—we're going to bleed him right away."

I obeyed, while he selected a lancet from his medical bag.

"Sunstroke!" people repeated. "Sunstroke in December! Oh la la! Sunstroke!"

The vein traced a little blue line on the white skin. With a swift gesture, Monsieur Caffier plunged his lancet into it. I saw half the blade disappear into the flesh and went pale, without letting go of the poor man's arm.

A drop of blood pearled at the edge of the little wound. That was all. The wound remained open, but no other drop appeared.

"Hmm! Hmm!" said the doctor without concealing his apprehension.

He made a second cut with the lancet, deeper and a little higher up. This time, I did not perceive a single drop of blood. He leaned over the sick man, stuck his ear to the chest directly over the heat, then got up and said, in a low voice: "He's dead."

The silence was absolute; everyone heard the words. Ernestine-Gabrielle Tardivaud fainted, uttering a terrible cry. The men took off their hats with a unanimous gesture. An old woman—I learned subsequently that it was the dead man's wife—screeched, in an extraordinarily shrill voice: "It's not true…it's not true…"

It was true, however. The man had died. The sun had just claimed its first victim.

Tears flowed and lamentations rose up. I was in haste to rejoin my future father-in-law, on whom that tragic scene had made a deep impression, but I was obliged to assist Monsieur Nattechoux to draw up, under the dictation of Doctor Caffier, a kind of witness-statement, to the bottom of which he added his signature, and to wait until the cadaver was taken away— with the result that it was one o'clock when we set off back to the school, and Jane and her mother were beginning to get anxious about our tardiness.

In the afternoon, the heat became torrid. The ardor of the sun was such that we dared not budge from the apartment. The thermometer, which I had taken into the kitchen—which is to say, into the shade—rose to thirty-five degrees. We closed the shutters and lowered the blinds, and Monsieur and Madame Sterneballe had a fine siesta.

Jane and I were not thinking about sleeping. Very close to one another, looking into one another's eyes, tenderly holding hands, we were making marvelous plans and building castles in Spain.

3

Jane, Monsieur Sterneballe and I left early the next morning, at sunrise, to go fishing for shrimp.

The harbor of Roque de Thau is very narrow. Upriver of the landing-stage where the paddle-steamers operating as ferries between Bordeaux and Pauillac put in, a canal had been dug into which the barges and lighters come; when those small boats are loaded with barrels they take advantage of the tide to go slowly up the river.

Beyond the landing-stage, marshy meadows constitute the shore of the Gironde. Reeds grow in the mud and rattle their long leaves in the slightest breeze. On the seaward side, the Île Verte and the Île-sans-Pain bar the horizon with an emerald line. Further away, in front of the old citadel of Blaye, Fort Paté crouches in the middle of the muddy water, and in clear weather the other side of the estuary can be vaguely made out.

All three of us coiffed in vast straw hats, for the day promised to be as hot as the preceding one, we went to cast our rudimentary nets. I had fabricated those instruments myself, by fixing canvas sacks to barrel-hoops. A cod's head and some sheep-bones served us as bait.

The fishing promised to be excellent. In twenty minutes we had caught nearly half a kilo of shrimp, which were competing with one another to leap out of the basket in which we had imprisoned them. Monsieur Sterneballe was proud of having caught an American perch that measured about five centimeters from head to tail. He was already glimpsing a monster fry-up.

In the meantime, the wind got up. At first it was an imperceptible breeze blowing from the west, but its strength increased with great rapidity. The river became wrinkled, and then veritable waves unfurled toward us. My hat blew away, and I had to run after it at top speed to catch up with it.

A furious squall bent the reeds; such a whistling filled our ears that we almost had to shout to make ourselves heard.

"There's going to be a storm!" howled Monsieur Sterneballe.

The sky, however, remained absolutely pure.

We packed our baggage. An instinctive fear drove us toward my home. It was not rain that we feared, since there was not a single cloud in the sky, but we needed to feel a roof over our heads. We succeeded quite easily in getting out of the meadow where we had installed ourselves in order to fish, but once we were on the road, the wind was lashing us sideways, and we only advanced at the cost of great effort.

Jane clung to my arm, laughing nervously. Monsieur Sterneballe talked continuously, and I heard intermittently the words: "...tornado...tempest...worse than the equinox..." I made no reply, occupied as I was in protecting my fiancée.

We were emerging from the Avenue du Port when a frightful gust assailed us. I had the presence of mind to lie down on the ground, and I dragged Jane down with me as I fell. I felt a sharp pain in my knee, but did not pay overmuch attention to it.

Monsieur Sterneballe was literally lifted from the ground. I saw him oscillate, trying to regain his equilibrium, take two or three enormous strides, and, as if launched by a catapult, was hurled head-first into the wall of a fisherman's hut build on the roadside.

Leaving my fiancée lying in the dust, I crawled toward my future father-in-law. He was squatting on his haunches, seemingly stunned, with an enormous bump on his forehead. I asked him if he was hurt, but he was content to protest that he did not understand it at all.

Reassured on his account, I turned toward Jane. She had succeeded in dragging herself along on her knees, and was soon beside us. We went around the hut in order to get to the eastern side.

When we were in shelter, we were shaken by an uncontrollable hilarity. Nothing about our adventure seemed tragic. The sun was still resplendent.

The cyclone reached its peak. We only truly had the impression of danger when we saw a poplar snapped clean through near its base.

Then a willow was uprooted and transported fifty meters like a wisp of straw. A runaway horse went passed at a gallop, an empty trap rattling along at its heels. In the blink of an eye it reached the barrier of the railway crossing. It slipped on a rail and collapsed. After kicking all four feet it succeeded in getting up, and continued its hectic course toward Bribazac and Villeneuve.

A loud crack terrified us. Monsieur Sterneballe jumped to the right, and I drew Jane desperately to the left. At the same moment, the hut collapsed, noisily. Its wooden roof flew away and came down in a nearby field.

"We can't stay here!" shouted Monsieur Sterneballe.

Putting our arms around one another in order to oppose the greatest resistance to the impetuous wind, which was suffocating us, we headed toward the school, stumbling at every step. We had the good fortune to reach the goal without any further accident.

Madame Sterneballe's expression brightened at the sight of us. A pad of cotton wool soaked in phenol was applied to Monsieur Sterneballe's bump, and his head was wrapped in an immaculate turban.

Something warm and sticky was trickling down my leg. It was blood. When I lay down on the road I must have knelt on the shard of bottle-glass or a trenchant flint, because I had a deep cut underneath the knee-cap. It needed a serious bandage.

Jane, luckier than us, had not suffered any injury. She had lost most of her hairpins, and magnificent blonde tresses were flowing over her shoulders. Oh, that sumptuous mantle! I could not weary of admiring it.

In the haste of our flight we had abandoned our nets, and, as one can imagine, our straw hats had abandoned us, but the famous basket of shrimp was still there. We decided to boil them for lunch.

The fury of the atmosphere did not abate. The old house moaned, the wind growled and blew under the door, like a malevolent beast. The windows were shaken, as if someone were trying to open them, and we heard the shutters on the first floor slapping the façade furiously.

I went upstairs to fix them to their hooks, and did not succeed without difficulty. The gusts were as hot as the breath of a forge. Dust was swirling furiously, drawing in its rotation pieces of paper, bits of straw and hay, and detritus of every sort. And above the demented atmosphere, the blinding sun continued to describe its immutable parabola.

In the company of Monsieur Sterneballe, I absorbed the formidable aerial turmoil for a long time. The wind was not blowing in a regular fashion. The principal current was from west to east, from the ocean to the land, but bizarre whirlwinds were forming here and there, the force of which was vertical, from top to bottom. In my courtyard, for example, a tin-plate trough, from which my chickens and guinea-fowl came to rink in ordinary times, rose ten meters into the air, fell back almost in the same place, and immediately repeated the same ascent.

After the midday meal, La Barboque left us to go to vespers. We saw her drawing away prudently, moving along the walls—which was not a superfluous precaution, for the roadway was strewn with tiles and slates dislodged from roofs.

When we had drunk the coffee, I read aloud from the *Petite Gironde*. Naturally, the meteorological bulletin was on the first page, and contained more precise information than the one the previous day. Nevertheless, the commentary was sparse. The specialists were limiting themselves to recording the facts, and reserving their judgment.

The heat-wave had descended on all five continents of the world. The rise in temperature was proportionately less in the tropical zone. On the other hand, the northern regions had passed without transition from the harshest winter to the most clement summer. Christiania, Viborg, Archangel and Omsk had never known such days. The thaw of the Siberian rivers had begun, and ships were signaling by wireless small icebergs off the coast of Iceland. A telegram from the Klondike said that the torrents of the gold country were threatening to inundate the majority of the claims. There was no information from Patagonia or the Antarctic region.

One American astronomer, bolder than his colleagues, attempted to give an explanation of the phenomenon. He spoke of an "excitation of solar incandescence due to causes of a mysterious nature" and left it at that. Another, a Dane, signaled the appearance of a monstrous sunspot, ten times larger than that of 2 February 1905, but confessed that the spot in question, observed on the equator of the star, had only been visible for a few minutes on 25 December. Already, an Englishman had categorically denied the claim, and, supporting his assertion on the anterior observations, demonstrated that although sunspots were modified with a disconcerting rapidity, they also disappeared just as suddenly. He affirmed that the gaseous eruptions that had taken place in that epoch had not been much more powerful than those once studied by Julius Mayer and Helmholtz, and that the protuberances were not abnormal. He then recalled that, every eleven years, the sun is the theater of crises that, although taking place two hundred million kilometers from Earth, are not without effect on our more modest globe.

Agreement was only unanimous on one point: all the scientists predicted the imminent return of the cold.

"We don't know much more than we did before," said Monsieur Sterneballe, when I finished reading. "I don't know whether or not the cold will be back soon, but what's certain is that the heat is increasing."

He was not mistaken. We were crimson and we were stifling. It seemed to us that we were in an oven, breathing fiery air.

I had the idea of watering the parquet copiously. The evaporation, very rapid, procured us some relief. We continued to throw water on it, in spite of the lamentations of Madame Sterneballe, who swore to the great gods that we were going to make the floorboards rotten.

That Sunday promised to be a mortally long day. The growling of the hurricane prevented us from thinking clearly, and a strange melancholy began to take possession of us. Jane attempted to sing in order to dissipate the sadness, but Madame Sterneballe asked her to stop, and all four of us remained dismal and preoccupied, waiting.

I received a visit from Monsieur Nattechoux, who was alarmed by the prolonged tempest. Considering me as a serious and sensible man, he had come to ask me what he ought to do.

"Do what?" sad Monsieur Sterneballe. "You don't, I suppose, have the pretention of being able to vanquish the elements?"

The Maire of Roque de Thau scratched his head in perplexity. "Obviously not...but within the limit of our forces...it's necessary to make some sort of plan..." Changing the subject, he said: "The wind has pulled my vines out of the ground."

That news appeared to consternate Madame Sterneballe, who usually had scant interest in agriculture. Monsieur Nattechoux addressed himself to her.

"It's ruination, Madame! The poles have been torn up and the stocks completely dislodged." With an energetic gesture, the countryman concluded: "My duty as the principal municipal magistrate is to comfort my administratees."

"Well said!" said Monsieur Sterneballe,

30

Sensing approval, Monsieur Nattechoux no longer hesitated: "Will you come with me, Dantenot?" he asked.

"We'll go," said Monsieur Sterneballe, spontaneously.

The ladies protested; they did not want to let us go out. I affirmed that we were taking absolutely no risk; the Maire insisted on the imperious character of his duty, my future father-in-law made a moving speech about the role of educated men, and Jane and her mother gave in.

It was not a banal departure. Under the leaden sun, buffeted by an infernal wind, we walked slowly, lending one another our arms like three drunkards, the Maire raising his thin face proudly; Monsieur Sterneballe affecting a solemn expression and me limping on my left leg.

The extent of the disaster terrified us. The closer we got to the river, the more the effects of the tempest were aggravated.

Trees that were still standing were very scarce. Save for the lowest fields, the vines were no more than tangles of branches. The embankment of the railway had protected a small area of the plain, but what subsisted was insignificant. The catastrophe was complete and irreparable.

Monsieur Nattechoux gazed fixedly at the earth. The man was suffering. Better than us, he understood what the destruction of the vineyards signified. It would require several years of labor before anyone could pick a single grape...

The postman came to meet us, tottering like us. He shouted in Monsieur Nattechoux's face: "It's not working anymore!"

"What?" shouted the Maire.

"The telegraph!"

And, with his head tucked in his shoulders, he headed for the railway station.

Mademoiselle Tournemire, the post office receiver, was smiling and relaxed. While chatting, she polished her fingernails with sustained application.

"It's not working any more?" asked Monsieur Nattechoux, repeating what the postman had said.

"No, completely dead," said Mademoiselle Tournemire, lightly. "See for yourself. I'm going to call..."

Very elegantly, she activated the Morse key.

"Nothing," she said. "Silence. But it's not surprising. This stiff breeze has knocked down the telegraph poles."

"Ah! The stiff breeze...," sniggered Monsieur Sterneballe.

Mademoiselle Tournemire pouted delightfully. "Some squabble, isn't it? Do you have a headache, Monsieur?"

"Yes," said Monsieur Sterneballe, outraged by such insouciance.

"As soon as communications are restored," Monsieur Nattechoux instructed, "send the postman to inform me."

"Yes, Monsieur le Maire. But the workmen are so slow that we'll probably be cut off until the end of the week."

When we had set out again, Monsieur Sterneballe's indignation burst forth. "That silly girl is insupportable," he said. "The sky could fall and she'd go on polishing her nails."

"She's young," said the Maire sententiously. "She doesn't reflect on the consequences. You, Monsieur Sternecanne, you reflect."

"Sterneballe," my father-in-law corrected, immediately. "Indeed, I'm reflecting...do you know whether the train from Bordeaux has arrived?"

"It isn't time."

It did not arrive that evening, however, because of the rupture of a viaduct in the vicinity of Bordeaux.

4

Almost the entire population of the village was on the waterfront, fixed in the grim and silent resignation that is quickly acquired in grief.

The Gironde had the appearance of an angry sea. Meter-high waves were crashing upon the bank with such force that the ground shook and a watery spray rose up above the foam.

The pontoon of the landing-stage no longer existed; the swell had broken its moorings. The gangway was still there, oscillating in mid-air like the arm of a gigantic crane. It certainly would not be there for long, for its worm-eaten tie-beams were giving way and splintering.

In the canal, it was worse. Two lighters, the *Étoile 124* and the *Guillaume-de-Rosa* were colliding repeatedly; at each impact the hulls resonated lugubriously. A dozen men, clinging to the end of a cable, were hauling obstinately, with the efforts of the damned, but the river paid no heed to those pygmies.

We watched the destruction of the two boats, our hearts sinking. The *Étoile 124* was lifted up in such a way that her prow came crashing down on the deck of the *Guillaume-de-Rosa*. A wave then caused her to fall back heavily, and the water followed into her black belly, where a hole was gaping. That produced a frightful gurgling, and the *Étoile 124* sank to the level of her rail. She did not sink completely—the canal was not deep enough for her to be able to disappear. The *Guillaume-de-Rosa* was then broken herself, falling like a battering-ram upon the wreck of the other boat.

A clamor rose up from all mouths, for the barrels forming the cargo rolled off one by one, cracking and tinting the canal with bloody reflections. One man was struggling like a madman in the hands of several others. It was the owner of the *Guillaume-de-Rosa*, who wanted to kill himself. His comrades held on to him, but they had the appearance of executioners ferociously prolonging the torture of a victim.

The crowd flooded back in disorder toward the landing-stage. We followed, almost dragged along involuntarily, and were obliged to brace ourselves in order not to be pushed too close to the edge.

Less than a hundred meters away, a boat was struggling against the wind and the current. It was probably from the Île Verte, and was trying to land. For people were steering her—or rather maintaining her, for they were visibly incapable of maneuvering.

Curiosity maintained us motionless. Monsieur Nattechoux's fingernails dug into my arm, and Monsieur Sterneballe was moving his lips actively, like a priest reciting his breviary.

An old fisherman was gesticulating in a disorderly fashion. He was so far forward that the water was up to his knees. Making his hands into a loudhailer in front of his mouth he shouted words that no one could hear.

The men on the boat were harassed. They replaced one another at the oars, but their skiff was waltzing in such a way that one might have thought that they were rowing in the air. One of the two was repeatedly catching crabs. The inevitable occurred. The boat seesawed slowly and turned turtle with an almost mechanical precision.

Everyone fell silent. The old fisherman came back to firm ground, his fists in his pockets, like a man whose work was concluded.

The four unfortunates splashed, disappeared and reappeared, like novice swimmers in a fish-pond. They were so close that we could make out two black dots—their eyes—in the white oval of their face. We knew that they were going to die.

"Let's go...let's go...," stammered Monsieur Sterneballe.

We set off without letting go of one another, Monsieur Nattechoux, Monsieur Sterneballe and I, like three friends at the exit from a play. The intensity of the tempest was diminishing. It was after four o'clock; the sun was no longer shining. It was a great relief no longer to feel its rays. My skin was dry and hot, as in the aftermath of a bout of fever.

Monsieur Nattechoux did not communicate his impressions to us. He was not sad; only one word could translate his state of mind: he was stupefied. In his distress, he blew his nose on a tricolor cloth; it was his mayoral sash, which he had been carrying in his pocket.

He left us at our door.

"Bonsoir, Monsieur Corneballe," he said.

"Sterne…Sterneballe," said the optician, with a hint of irritation. "Buck up, Monsieur le Maire. Days that follow one another don't resemble one another."

"Fortunately," said Monsieur Nattechoux.

"He's a good fellow," said Monsieur Sterneballe, when we were alone, "but he hasn't invented the coffee-grinder. Did you notice that he always gets my name wrong?"

Jane and her mother were embroidering peacefully in the dining room. Madame Sterneballe scrupulously described her real and imaginary illnesses, and finally ceded the floor to her husband. The worthy man, as talkative as her, started to re-count in detail everything that we had seen. When he finished his story, night was almost complete.

I wanted to call La Barboque to light the lamp, but Jane stopped me,

"Let me do it," she said. "Your housekeeper isn't in her normal state."

"What's wrong with her, then?"

"Hmm!" said Madame Sterneballe. "I believe she's been hitting the wine bottle too hard."

"La Barboque? That's not her habit."

"Listen to her singing…"

In the kitchen, La Barboque was mistreating the crockery, and howling a refrain: *La fille alla-t'au bois/Larirette, larifla!*"

"I can't tolerate that," I said, indignantly, while Jane suppressed an impulse to laugh.

Standing in front of her oven, La Barboque was striking a saucepan conscientiously with a metal spoon. She did not even hear me come in.

"Well!" I said.

She turned round. She had daubed her face with soot, and in that black mask, her eyes sparkled like carbuncles.

"Monsieur," she said, "I know all that. If I'm cooking a bar of soap, it's because the catechism is important. But no dandy is going to lead me by the nose!"

She came to me, claws forward. I seized her by the wrists in order to defend myself, but she allowed herself to be mastered meekly. She was as cold as marble."

"Bang!" she said. "You can't stop rabbits from jumping on the rubber."

La Barboque was not drunk. The sun had driven her mad.

I am not very impressionable; even so, anguish penetrated my heart. I scarcely had the strength to take the poor wretch to her nephew's house, and I took refuge in my bedroom without having anything to eat.

The wind had dropped completely. The constellations strewed the sky with twinkling fireflies. The blue darkness of the night invited dreams.

But what was the significance of the heat that was gripping me, irritating my lungs and forcing me to forget the winter?

Silence was the master of nature. Mystery was floating therein. Exhausted by the emotions and exertions of the day, however, I did not have the courage to try to investigate it.

I went to sleep thinking about Jane, our imminent union, and the happiness that awaited us...

I didn't know...

I didn't know...

5

The pain of my wound woke me up. It was still dark, but an indecisive glimmer brightened the orient and gradually caused the stars to fade. The angelus rang, with little irregular and feeble chimes that encouraged the supposition that the bell-ringer was still half-asleep.

Under my window, a cock crowed. I saw him singing, his chest thrust out, his feet apart; then he listened, until a response reached him, and seemed satisfied. Around him, the hens were actively pecking the ground, and seemed to be exchanging reflections on their finds.

Not a cloud in the sky; the air was absolutely limpid. It was another day of beautiful weather that was announced, a day of heat-wave.

The aurora was as red as the reflection of a titanic furnace. The last stars went out, and the sun appeared above Fradinotte's house. All the colors changed, becoming vivid. The occident remained tinted ultramarine by the fleeing shadow. The blinding disk remained tangential to the ridge of the roof for a few seconds, and then rose into the sky.

There was movement on the ground floor. I went downstairs to drink milky coffee. By tacit accord, we avoided mentioning La Barboque. Madame Sterneballe, wrapped in a white apron, had already wrung the neck of a chicken that she was planning to fry on the stove with potatoes and onions.

Monsieur Sterneballe was anxious. It was the first time in thirty years that he had not been in his shop at the habitual hour.

"There are no trains, of course," he told me confidentially. "There are no boats, I'll give you that…but I can't resign myself, even so…I'm annoyed…it's impossible for me to think about anything else. I can hear the neighbors gossiping—people in commerce are so malevolent. They'll believe that I'm rich enough to take vacations like a State employee. Not to mention that Monday is the best day of the week for us. All the people in the area will go to Bordeaux to get what they need. What will my clients think when they find my iron shutter lowered? I like you, Roger, but truly I regret having come to Roque de Thau…"

I listened to him with patience and deference. It's better to let people of a certain age talk. If one interrupts them, it annoys them and makes them angry.

"You're making too much bad blood," Madame Sterneballe told him. "Me, I'd be consoled if it weren't as hot."

In this story, the question of heat is sempiternal. The word recurs constantly at the end of my sentences, but I can't do otherwise. The temperature was rising incessantly; we were living in a steam-bath. It was in vain that we sought to procure ourselves even a semblance of freshness. We had given up watering the parquet, because the evaporation eventually saturated the atmosphere with humidity.

Monsieur Sterneballe wanted to open the windows; Madame Sterneballe preferred to keep them closed, and I agreed with her. It was a little less stifling inside than outside.

The absence of trains naturally deprived us of mail. I was put out by that, because I looked forward to my morning paper impatiently. I needed news, gossip. I understood that a cataclysm of an unprecedented kind as menacing the solar world, but the worst that I supposed as far from the truth.

As I found out later, the hurricane on 26 December had not simply devastated France. The entire atmosphere was in revolt. In the valley of the Rhône, framed by the Cévennes and the foothills of the Alps, nothing had resisted. The tempest had overturned the express trains, undermined tall buildings, scythed down the trees. Entire villages were no longer anything but ruins. All the coastal areas had been swept by tidal wave. The dyke at Cherbourg had been demolished; the ships at anchor in the port of Saint-Nazaire had been smashed against the quays.

The Eiffel Tower had held firm, as well as the pylons of the big wireless telegraphy station at Croix d'Hins; by contrast, the antenna of the German station at Nauen, which had told so many lies during the war, no longer existed. It was, therefore, via France that the old and new continents were still in communication.

The American telegrams were frightening in their laconism. The region surrounding the Great Lakes was no more than a desert. In New York, the skyscrapers had been decapitated, and the tons of materials that had fallen around them had struck countless victims. Several quarters of San Francisco no longer existed. In the Rocky Mountains, landslides had caused serious damage in several cities.

South America, Australia, Africa and Asia were mute, and their silence was more terrible than the most terrible news.

The British Admiralty did not publish any list of maritime losses, nor did the Veritas bureau. The telegraphists of the semaphores however, were not unaware of the number of shipwrecks. For twelve hours, uninterruptedly, they had received the tragic signal: S.O.S...S.O.S...S.O.S... It was by launching those three letters into space, thousands of miles around them, that ships in perdition requested help. One could not hear those desperate appeals, converging from all the points of the ocean, without experiencing an atrocious sentiment of impotence and terror.

A large number of boats escaped destruction, but they were not the transatlantic liners, the leviathans; they were the nutshells, the cod-fishers, the broad and flat coasters. They danced, ripping their rigging, but did not sink. The fashion in which the others agonized will forever remain a secret.

The dispatches of the last hour—the qualification was all too exact—announced cataclysms of every sort. Formidable torrents poured down from the Alps, the melting of the snows occurring suddenly. The dykes gave way in Holland and the Belgian lowlands, where immense plains were submerged. Everywhere, a number of mortal congestions caused by the heat were recorded. In the beginning, the sun only killed with a kind of discretion. It was the skirmish before the hecatomb.

Such was the beginning of the reign of Fear.

Monsieur Sterneballe was the most clear-sighted of the four of us, because he had nothing to do other than observe. Madame Sterneballe was occupied with the housework, and Jane and I with our future. We were choosing furniture in catalogues, discussing the styles!

My future father-in-law interrupted our tête-à-tête. He took me into the courtyard.

"Roger," he said, "I'm frightened."

I wanted to reply with a joke, but his face was so distressed that I kept quiet.

"Frigh-ten-ed!" he repeated, stressing the syllables. "The strength of the sun is increasing by the minute..."

"The increase can't be indefinite."

"How do you know?"

"It's never been seen!"

"What has happened in the last three days has never been seen either. We're in December! In December, it ought not to be, it *can't* be, so hot!"

"At the Equator, however..."

"We're not at the Equator! And even at the Equator, we'd have reason to tremble."

"Because the sun is in effervescence," I said, lightly.

"Precisely, Roger. The sun is our master, it can roast us as a cooking-fire roasts a vulgar chicken."

"Bah! It's been tranquilly playing its role for millions of years..."

"You can't deny that some phenomenon has exaggerated its ardor! Your cabbages, the cabbages of which you were so proud, are no more than yellow balls, fuming and rotting. The fields? Not a blade of green grass! I'm wondering, anxiously, whether our organism can resist for much longer."

He leaned over to repeat, in a low voice: "I'm wondering..."

I revolted. "What! You think that we...?"

To my unfinished sentence he replied by nodding his head affirmatively. And I felt incapable of protesting, for his conviction impressed me.

A glance around the courtyard reassured me. The weather was fine. Cocks and hens were pecking the ground here and there, plumping themselves up with pleasure. The sky was almost white, by virtue of the brightness of the light.

"You're a pessimist," I told him.

"I am since this morning. I've put the thermometer outside again. Do you know what it did, the thermometer? It burst. Now, it's graduated up to fifty degrees...it seems to me that that's a figure that justified my pessimism."

Raising his two clenched fists over his head, he said: "What's going on up there? What's happening...?"

We took some prudent measures to give us the illusion of security. Our apartment was a greenhouse, for the heat came in through the windows but didn't go out, so we nailed thick canvas over all the embrasures. The result of that padding was a relatively cool demi-obscurity.

Jane amused herself somewhat poking fun at her father. He didn't care. He made an inventory of all the receptacles, from the buckets and pitchers to the most modest pots, and we filled them the pump. That small task was extremely difficult, because the iron of the handle burned our fingers.

When we had finished, we seemed to be emerging from a steam-bath.

"Now," said Monsieur Sterneballe, "we're ready; we have no more to do than wait."

But several distractions were reserved for us. Blisters that soon formed on our skin made us itch intolerably. Madame Sterneballe supported that torture poorly—which, fortunately did not last long. The blisters disappeared, leaving a large number of little scarlet circles on our bodies.

Then came the flies. They arrived in swarms, slipping through the cracks in the doorways and windows and coming down the chimney. With great sweeps of dusters we made relentless and joyful war on them. They were gradually vanquished, and hundreds of shriveled strewed the floor.

Lunch was sad; my artificial cheerfulness did not fool anyone.

We started a game of lotto thereafter, but it lacked enthusiasm. Madame Sterneballe went to sleep over her cards. She woke up suddenly with a start.

"Fifteen! I've got it!" And after an attentive examination: "I beg your pardon. I haven't got it."

A visit from the curé, Abbé Escatafal, revived us.

"Can you guess what I've come to tell you?" he said, sitting down.

"Frost!" I said, gaily.

"Alas, no," he replied. "Monsieur Nattechoux is dead."

The Maire of Roque de Thau had left for his property at Gauriac. He had been found lying face down on the road, in a pool of blood."

"Congestion...hemorrhage...," said Monsieur Sterneballe. "He was already having trouble yesterday...he was mangling proper nouns..."

"There's panic in the village," the Abbé continued.

"Do you think that it will get even hotter?" Jane asked.

"I don't know, Mademoiselle. As the Scriptures say, the designs of the Almighty are impenetrable."

"You're being tragic," I said. "All this will sort itself out. It's sufficient to have a little logic to..."

"There's logic intervening!" riposted the curé. "It has nothing to do with this affair! Extraordinary events are manifest, a prodigious upheaval is occurring, and you talk about logic! That's pride, Monsieur Dantenot. Human logic is probably not universal logic. The laws of your physicists and your astronomers are based on hypotheses that I defy you to verify. We want to know everything, to explain everything, to regulate everything, but we don't know the most elementary things...you're protesting? Tell me, then, what flame is...! You remain silent, naturally. That won't prevent you, in a little while, if it gets hotter, from affirming that it's because of this, and if it gets cooler, that it's because of that... I've studied, like you, and I'm not so categorical. Logic? Today is not its reign. In the meantime, I'm going to go around the houses to comfort the inhabitants..."

"The wisest thing would be to return to the presbytery," said Monsieur Sterneballe.

"No, Monsieur," said Abbé Escatafal, "I have a role to fulfill. In the thirty years that I've been exercising my ministry it has never been difficult. I'd be unworthy of the soutane if I showed reluctance at the first danger."

We never saw him again. He must have perished like Monsieur Nattechoux.

6

The temperature increased incessantly. My apartment resembled the coal-bunker of a steamship.

Madame Sterneballe was suffering more than the rest of us. I calculated that if the increase of the heat continued, our organism could not resist until sunset. Strangely lucid, I foresaw that our last moments would be frightful. Even so, I risked a joke.

"It's the ruination of the coal-merchants."

I was talking to the deaf. Jane and her mother, overwhelmed and exhausted, seemed to be asleep. Monsieur Sterneballe never left the window. Through a gap in the curtain, he watched the shadow of the house advance further and further toward the road. But the sun wasn't disappearing rapidly enough.

To fight against an enemy, even if defeat is inevitable, is a consolation, and even a distraction, but there is nothing more depressing than passive resistance to a torture. I bit my fists because I was unable to offer Jane any relief.

Monsieur Sterneballe did not manifest any madness. Suddenly, we saw him steep several napkins in a pitcher.

"Compresses!" cried Madame Sterneballe.

We applied them to our burning foreheads, and savored a moment of indescribable wellbeing. Confidence returned.

At about three o'clock, Madame Sterneballe had a brief fainting fit. A drop of ether reanimated her, but I understood that she was at the end of her resources. In any case, we were all the color of brick, and it was evident that our collapse was only a matter of minutes.

Alone in my house, I had not made a gesture. My sensations were bizarre. When one comes home from hunting, in snowy weather, one installs oneself voluptuously beside the fire. One gets too hot, one almost burns. It is sufficient to step back to be more at ease, and yet one says there, heels on the andirons, torpid and somnolent. I was in exactly that state.

"Oh, how will I feel!" said Jane, in a plaintive voice.

Monsieur Sterneballe contemplated her sadly. I got up and I drank a draught from a large glass of water.

I was ready to fight, but against whom? Against what?

I learned later that the disorganization of Europe commenced that afternoon. All public services had been functioning until then, all the factories were working. It had not occurred to any government, or any employer, to stop the social machine because the weather was hot. Every man was therefore left to his own initiative, and resistance was more or less prolonged in accordance with his environment or his personal energy. Curiously enough, the ministries did not shut down any more than usual. On the other hand, trains stopped in the middle of the countryside, no matter where. But no traveler survived to tell the story of what had happened...

A noise of hooves attracted my attention. I perceived one of my best pupils, little Florimond Lestaque, who was galloping while weeping. The poor child had doubtless just witnessed a horrible scene and was fleeing at random.

I wanted to call out to him, but I did not have time. Before arriving at my door he fell as if he had received a sledgehammer blow on the back of his neck.

"What's that?" asked Jane.

Swiftly, I replied: "Nothing...nothing at all..."

Monsieur Sterneballe came toward me. He looked at the little cadaver, lying under the terrible sun.

"Our turn will come," he breathed in my ear.

"No," I said, clenching my fists.

He thought I had a means of delaying the final outcome. His face cleared. He pointed to the two women.

"Them first," he said.

But seeing my eyes fill with tears, he turned his back on me.

"Imbecile!" he murmured.

He had never been rude in my regard.

The howl of a wounded dog, a prolonged and heartrending plaint, suddenly broke the luminous and sinister silence. The beast went past, flat out, suffering without understanding why. It was a large and sleek sheepdog, with a long tongue hanging down. It swerved, and without paying any heed to a thread of barbed wire that tire its flank, it succeeded in slipping through the ventilation-shaft of a cellar. Its muffled moans became more lugubrious, and it fell silent. It seemed to me that the ventilation shaft was the maw of a monster that had swallowed it in order to abridge its suffering.

Delirium afflicted me, to my great satisfaction, for it attenuated my physical sensibility. Multicolored lights danced before my eyes. The state in which I found myself is difficult to describe; it was compounded out of an indifference in the face of death and a clairvoyance that left me under no illusion as to my fate.

The head of the dog reappeared in the ventilation shaft. It immediately went back into the shadow. Then a sense of reality returned to me. The cellar made me think of other cellars more spacious and more tenebrous. I started capering like a madman.

"The quarries! The quarries!"

I shouted those words, clamored them, sang them.

"The quarries! The quarries! The quarries!"

Without lifting a finger, Madame Sterneballe said: "It's like La Barboque!"

"Make no mistake!" I replied. "I have all my common sense. Let's take refuge in the quarries of Le Mugron!"

Like an echo, Monsieur Sterneballe repeated: "In the quarries of Le Mugron."

Le Mugron is a hill, a calcareous cliff that roses to the south of Roque de Thau and extends as far as Rigalet. People extract building stone from it, with the result hat a large number of runnels have been excavated in it. It was of those tunnels, those profound quarries, that I had just thought. How cool they must be!

"Let's go! Let's go!" said Monsieur Sterneballe.

But I had recovered all my reason.

"We won't reach Le Mugron like this," I said. "If we don't take precautions, the sun will kill us."

"That's true," said Monsieur Sterneballe. "Roger, you've saved us! We're going to shelter under umbrellas."

"That won't be sufficient," I said. "Let me think, let's not rush..."

The obeyed me with a child-like docility. Under our hats we rolled up damp sheets. But it was important to protect our bodies as well as our heads. I found nothing better than pouring a bucket of water over Monsieur Sterneballe's shoulders. His wife did not consent to an analogous treatment without jibbing.

"At my age!" she said. "I'll catch a cold!"

While she was arguing, Jane doused her copiously. She screeched like an osprey, and finally resigned herself. We soon had every appearance of survivors of a shipwreck. Our garments stuck to our bodies, and we spread a veritable rain at every movement.

"Let's go," I said.

I went out first. I had not taken ten steps when I doubted the success of my plan. The ground burned our feet. A thick mist was disengaged from our cloths. We advanced in a flameless conflagration. We had less than a kilometer to travel to each the entrance to the first tunnel. I don't know how much or how little time it took to cover that distance. The soles of my shoes were like hot irons. Monsieur Sterneballe was moaning.

We finally got there. Our clothes, completely dry, were irritating the skin. We dived into the black hole of the quarry.

The gallery descended at a gentle slope. We plunged on into the darkness. The further we went, the cooler the atmosphere became. We breathed in life greedily, dilating our lungs. The nightmare was over.

We embraced one another with intoxication, unable to see one another. At the end of the tunnel, the orifice was like a little blue dot.

7

If the first hour was exquisite, it was necessary for us to admit thereafter that our change of domicile had been effected too lightly. In the precipitation of our departure, we had not brought any food. We also lacked matches, and Monsieur Sterneballe only had a tinder lighter that could not give us any assistance. Sitting side by side on a long stone, we dared not move any further away from the exit, for the quarries of Le Mugron comprise several levels. We might have fallen and broken our necks.

The entrance to the tunnel became gradually darker, for night had to be descending over the earth. We were not too hot, but we were hungry and thirsty. Anguish was strangling us. I had difficulty chasing away the thought that we were buried alive. An insipid odor of mildew assailed us, similar to that which expands when gravediggers lift up the stone of a tomb. Then too, we were anxious because we did not know what was happening outside.

We wanted to talk, conversation being, in that darkness, the most reassuring manifestation of life, but we could not find anything to say. Jane, who was pressing against me, was trembling like a leaf. From time to time, Madame Sterneballe uttered deep sighs.

"We were wrong not to have eaten a more substantial lunch," said my future father-in-law. "I feel a ferocious appetite."

"Me too," said Madame Sterneballe. "I could eat no matter what."

I replied to them, dully: "I'll go look for some food."

I immediately repented of having pronounced that sentence. I waited for protestations, but only Jane replied: "Mightn't it be dangerous to go out?"

Monsieur Sterneballe reassured her, too affirmatively for my liking: "It's not as hot at night."

I was annoyed with him. He ought to have forbidden me to sacrifice myself. I felt safe on my stone, beside the woman I loved. Our suffering was still benign. Why not endure it for one more day?

"Bring something to drink," said Madame Sterneballe.

That order scandalized me. But my fury gave way to dejection when Jane added: "Hurry up, Roger. The sooner you go, the sooner you'll be back..."

I kissed her rapidly in the darkness. My kiss was lost in her hair.

"Adieu," I said, in a tremulous voice.

A hand palpated my side—that of my future father-in-law, seeking mine in order to shake it effusively.

"Would you like me to come with you?" he asked.

Madame Sterneballe immediately protested: "Don't leave us alone in this gulf?"

"All right, all right, I'll stay," said the optician, without insisting. "Let me tell our young friend what it's necessary to do."

I no longer had the initiative for the dangerous operation. I was about to risk my carcass benevolently—why had I been so talkative?—and Monsieur Sterneballe, abusing the authority of age, wanted to direct me from his place, as strategists behind the lines direct armies.

"Take my big square basket. Do you have tinned food?"

"No," I riposted, outraged by such a perfect indifference to the risks I was about to run.

"Pity. Get the ham, then..."

"And the rest of the chicken," said Madame Sterneballe.

"There's half a cheese in the larder," Jane recalled.

"Perfect," said Monsieur Sterneballe. "Don't forget the bread. We French don't know how to eat without bread. Hurry, Roger—a prolonged absence would make us anxious."

I had a desire to weep. Those people, who comprised my entire family, were only thinking about their stomachs! They were sacrificing me lightly in order to be able to satisfy their hunger.

I could not stay at the expense of my self-respect. I left.

The adieux were conventional. I kissed Jane a second time, at the invitation of her mother. That was the last favor accorded to the condemned man.

My knee was hurting badly. I limped up the slope that led up to the orifice. The heat increased at every step.

So much the better! I thought, at the peak of my indignation. I'm going to collapse immediately. That will teach them!

It would have taught them absolutely nothing. In any case, I didn't collapse. Breathless, slightly suffocated, I understood that I could resist. I paused on the threshold of the tunnel. My silhouette must have been cut out in the opening, against the sky, perceptible to Monsieur Sterneballe.

I waited for a cry, an appeal, in order to retrace my steps. I did not hear any. So I launched forth, vomiting imprecations.

The stars had never been so numerous or so scintillating. Their tiny lights danced in space. Bolides traced long phosphorescent streaks.

Crickets were singing.

I was scarcely sensible to the beauty of nature; nevertheless, it reassured me. I gradually got used to the heat, which must have been about forty degrees.

I went as rapidly as my myopia permitted. Before reaching the first house I made out a large heap in the middle of the road. It was a cow, already bloated, its legs stiff. A little further on there was another body, that of a man. My hair prickled. That macabre encounter took away all my valor. If I continued, it is because vanity is more powerful than cowardice.

The village was dark, peaceful and welcoming. I introduced myself to my home with an artificial assurance. If I had not found the matches in their usual place I would have fled.

Everything was in order, and yet I was groping. It took me five minutes to discover Monsieur Sterneballe's square basket. With a perfect docility I stuffed into it my ham, half a loaf of bread, two or three pieces of chicken and the cheese, all pell-mell. I added three bottles of wine, the end of a sausage and a few apples that were sitting on a shelf.

The clock chimed eight. The first stroke froze me to the spot. Then it appeared marvelous and comforting that the clock had tranquilly continued its work, as if the duration of time mattered more than events. I went back up with a kind of piety, and it was to the clock that I addressed my adieu as I left.

It was, in any case, a false exit, because, in spite of Monsieur Sterneballe's recommendation, I had forgotten the candles. I took two packets, and headed for the quarry

As I approached the dead man lying in the road I experienced a veritable terror again. I turned my head away and passed by rapidly on the verge. The dry grass crackled underfoot. That reminded me about the excessive heat. In reality, my mission had not been very difficult, but in remembering the details, I convinced myself that I ha jut accomplished an extraordinary exploit. I was in haste to arrive in order to recount my odyssey.

As I set foot on the rounded platform in front of the quarry I experienced a joy as great as that of a pursued badger reaching its sett. I lit a candle and went into the tunnel. It was about two meters high and as many wide. The walls were yellowed, perfectly dry, and the ground was constituted by a thick layer of stone dust, known locally as "perruche." I was very satisfied. In a loud voice I asked: "Where are you?"

My phrase echoed in the distance. Someone replied: "Yoo-hoo!"

The most eloquent sentence could not have charmed me more; I had recognized Jane's voice.

"I'm intact," I went on, thinking that it might interest them.

"Have you got something to eat?" demanded Monsieur Sterneballe.

"Yes, glutton," I said, but as I pronounced the latter word with a measure of discretion, my future father-in-law did not hear it.

All three of them were still sitting on the stone. The light of the candle cast great moving shadows over their features. They laughed, and that made me think of the dead man lying on the road.

"There's the blessed basket!" said Monsieur Sterneballe.

He set about taking inventory of the provisions. I poured a few stops of stearine on to the ground and the candle remained upright.

"It all went well?" said the optician. "I had to reassure the ladies..."

So, during my absence, he had transformed my perilous adventure into a pleasant stroll! It was with the laudable intention of "reassuring the ladies," but it vexed me profoundly.

"I'll wager that you haven't brought a knife!" said Madame Sterneballe.

I made a movement of annoyance.

"How are we going to cut the ham without a knife?"

"I'm a birdbrain," I said. "Would you like me to make another trip?"

"Of course not! We'll do without, that's all."

The bread was broken into four hunks of approximately equal size. The division of the chicken was less equitable. My share consisted of a part of the carcass, which I gnawed philosophically, while Madame Sterneballe tore apart an entire wing.

"No notable incidents?" asked Monsieur Sterneballe, his mouth full.

My good humor returned at that question. Without urgency, in a casual manner, I began my story.

I am still amazed by the embellishments that I took pleasure in adding to it. To hear me, I had only progressed with extreme difficulty, sustained by the imperious desire to discover alimentary supplies. I had found three dead cows, a semi-carbonized man and an agonizing dog. I made much of the dog.

"What a spectacle! The unfortunate quadruped was whining..."

But Monsieur Sterneballe was battling with the ham.

"It's resisting! It's resisting!" he said.

In fact, the ham, thickest and compact, was formally refusing to be divided. Madame Sterneballe recommenced her jeremiads on the subject of the knife. I then discovered a folding pen-knife in my waistcoat pocket, whose timid offensive against the tough meat permitted me to finish my story.

The golden halo of our candle rendered the darkness around us more impenetrable. The light isolated us in the middle of the gallery as in a closed room. We chatted insouciantly, for a fault—or a virtue—of human beings is to forget their troubles when they are no longer experiencing them.

If we avoided making plans for the future, it was because we estimated that our situation was temporary. We did not think we would be inhabiting those catacombs, which had to be singularly favorable to rheumatism, for long.

"Do you think that the human race will perish?" Monsieur Sterneballe asked me, in a light tone." And without waiting for my response, he added: "The disorder must be serious in the cities. People must be killing one another recklessly, because the troublemakers are always on the lookout for an opportunity to turn society upside down."

"I think, on the contrary, that the sun will have put everyone in accord, even the Bolsheviks and the bourgeois."

Later, I was to learn what had happened. The tunnels of the Paris Metro and the London "Tube" were filled with a tumultuous crowd. Deaths by asphyxiation and crushing were multiplied. In certain places the crush was such that the cadavers remained upright between the living, advancing and recoiling with them in accordance with the eddies, with a lugubrious impassivity. The sewers had been much sought after, and the victims there had been numerous.

Existing social inequalities had rapidly disappeared, to give way to others. The privilege of strength had been imposed. Powerful muscles and automatic weapons conferred an undeniable superiority on their possessors. It was not rare to see a scholarly professor or an influential politician behaving respectfully before a dock-worker he would have scorned a few days before.

Monsieur Sterneballe lamented the possible pillage of his shop in Bordeaux. While he waxed lyrical in his lamentations, Madame Sterneballe started snoring without discretion, which was a fashion of sounding the curfew. We decided to look for a sufficiently comfortable place to spend the night. I therefore picked up the candle, and we moved away, carrying the ham.

The gallery turned abruptly to the right and divided into two tunnels. I followed the wider one, which plunged into the depths of the hill. A few beams and stays reminded me of the possibility of collapses. The sound of our footsteps was amplified in the sepulchral silence. We were overwhelmed by all the shadow; we said nothing.

Suddenly, all four of us came to a halt, like a squadron in response to its leader's command. We had just heard something: a bizarre cry, strident and quavering, deformed by the echoes, and also by our fear.

We waited for another cry, but a heavy silence had fallen again. I was incapable of taking a step, either forwards or backwards, and my companions were no more sure of themselves than me. What mysterious being was troubling our retreat?

Three hammer-blows struck on a plank resounded violently. We looked at one another fearfully, ready to panic. But the cry resounded again under the vault, and we realized this time that it was the whinny of a horse.

Twenty meters further on, a door sealed the tunnel. As it was maintained by a simple peg, I opened it.

A fairly sizeable chamber had been hollowed out in the friable stone. The chamber served as a stable, a feed-store and a depository for tools. Quarrymen's picks, shovels and saws were stacked up in one corner, near a heap of straw and several bales of hay, which embalmed it.

The horse, a dappled pony, was attached to a bar of its empty manger. It extended its quivering nostrils toward us, and delivered several kicks to the partition of its stall. It had eaten all of its litter that it had been able to reach, and it was hunger that was causing it to whinny. It had probably not had any care for two or three days.

Jane caressed it amicably. It placed its large head on my fiancée's shoulder.

"It's blind," she said.

The animal's eyes were only two milky globes. Its infirmity rendered it more sympathetic. I gave it a copious ration of hay, which it started to chew incontinently with its long yellow teeth.

"We'll call it Coco," said Jane.

A copper plate was nailed to the snaffle. I read: *Fourtané Auguste, owner*. But we were never to make the acquaintance of Fourtané Auguste.

Ever practical, Monsieur Sterneballe scattered the straw. Ten minutes later, we were sleeping in the obscurity of a dreamless slumber. That was truly our best night, in the course of that period of frightful and exhausting emotions.

8

It was at dusk that I emerged from our subterranean refuge for the second time. Monsieur Sterneballe had come with me as far as the orifice. He was sprightly until the moment when the heat became unbearable for him. Then he wished me *bon voyage* and quickly went back into the tunnel like a snail into its shell.

When the fire follet of his candle had vanished, I felt my heart sink. I sat down on the threshold to accustom my organism to the ambient temperature.

My horizon was rather limited. To my right bristled a wood whose trees were completely denuded of leaves. To my left, some distance away, the river was flowing toward the ocean. In front of me, the roofs of a hamlet were outlined against the sky. The landscape was familiar, and yet it seemed to me to be different. I soon understood why.

Nature had lost its habitual coloration. Everything had become ruddy black, like a heath after one of those fires that, passing at the speed of a galloping horse, only burns the grass and brushwood, the leaves and twigs, leaving the pines upstanding like specters.

The road extended its ribbon. I walked with a long stride in order to arrive before dark. The Shepherd's Star was shining in the sky; the Great Bear designed its trapezium.

The dead cow and the cadaver of the man made les impression on me than the previous day, but as I penetrated into the village I shivered. Everything evoked flight, precipitate abandonment. The doors were ajar, the houses dark. The walls gave off an ardent heat, like the walls of an oven.

At home, I stripped the sheets from my bed. I was afraid of dying, of dying alone. I nevertheless remembered Madame Sterneballe's reproaches, and I collected knives and forks. There was no hurry, but I was as nervous as a traveler at risk of missing his train.

I knocked on the grocer's door; a yapping replied. I knocked again in order to hear the dog again. It replied to me, and I went in. It ran forward madly, bumping its muzzle against my wounded knee and drawing a cry of pain from me.

"Madame Ferry, are you there?"

She was there, but silent: the silence of eternity. I only saw her when I had a candle in my hand. She was collapsed on her counter, her arms extended, as if to defend her cash register.

What I did then was purely mechanical. I transformed myself into a burglar. I emptied the shelves of the shop, taking possession of sugar, tins of sardines, a small tub of herring, a lump of lard, two boxes of biscuits and six liters of wine, and I wrapped that precious merchandise up in my bed-sheets.

I hoisted the heavy bale on to my shoulder like a peddler's pack.

I set forth on the way back, but stopped several times to catch my breath. Suddenly, the dog crossed the road a few paces in front of me, and I understood that it was accompanying me. That witness to my burglary embarrassed me. I threw stones at it, but in vain. It attached itself to my heels, prudently maintaining itself out of reach. My poor eyesight prevented me from following all its movements, but it sometimes whimpered, as if to say to me: *Let me be your slave...I shall love you...no one but me is alive on this earth of desolation...let's join forces...*

Near the quarry it barked with a full voice and someone whistled to it. Monsieur Sterneballe was waiting for me at the orifice of the gallery. A human shadow appeared.

"I'm heavily laden," I said, cheerfully, "but I won't be obliged to return to the village tomorrow. The ladies aren't too impatient?"

To my great surprise, a nasal voice replied to me: "I don't know, Monsieur, to what ladies you're referring. What village do you mean?"

"Who are you?" I replied.

"If our interrogations overlap," the unknown man remarked, "We'll talk for a long time without learning anything. First, I want to know where I am. Oh, you have light—so much the better!"

I had just lit my candle in order to identify the individual. The unknown was a short man about fifty years old, his face lost in a bushy beard, with prominent blue eyes. He had little hair, as I observed when he politely took off his hat. His thin body was adrift in an ample frock coat that had emerged from the hands of a good tailor but was presently dirty and torn.

He submitted meekly to my suspicious examination.

"You asked me who I am?" he said. "That's a legitimate curiosity. I won't offer you my card, because it's not a time for ceremony, and in any case, I've mislaid my wallet. I'm Onésime Cynécarmieux, astronomer at the Observatory at Floirac. Do you know the Observatory at Floirac? Three domes surrounded by beautiful trees, resembling three white mushrooms in a lawn. What poetry, Monsieur! But perhaps I'm keeping you?"

That loquaciousness stunned me slightly.

"What do you want with me?" I said, still on my guard.

"Nothing, Monsieur. I'm a man in need of everything who dare not ask for anything. Do you understand that? I believe that I'm emerging from a bout of hot fever. I have vague memories...I was watching the sun, Monsieur...and *crack!* a rift in my intelligence. It's not pleasant. I remember a prolonged journey…extremely prolonged…to the point that I have bloody feet…literally bloody…and here I am, dazed, but in full possession of my mental faculties. Where am I?"

"Roque de Thau."

"In what part of the Gironde is that place situated?"

"Near Blaye."

"No," said Monsieur Cynécarmieux, firmly.

"What do you mean, no?"

"You won't make me believe that I've come all the way to Blaye on foot. It's risible, Monsieur. I walk like a woodlouse. To Roque de Thau, me! If it weren't the end of the world, I'd make a communication to the Académie des Sciences."

"What make you suppose that it's the end of the world?"

He put the tip of his index finger under his right eyelid. "My eye."

"Your eye?"

"My astronomer's eye, stuck to the objective of a telescope. I know what I know.

"Very well, Monsieur," I said, "but you've left me in the heat for a long time, when it's infinitely cooler in the quarries. Ask me for the information that's useful to you, and make use of it!"

Monsieur Cynécarmieux clicked his tongue. "The heat is making you irritable," he said. "That's normal. I have no more information to ask of you. I know where I am—that's already a great deal. In a few hours when I die, I'll think that it's in Roque de Thau."

"Make arrangements not to die," I advised him.

"A delicate arrangement, Monsieur…actually, I don't know your name…a delicate and superfluous arrangement. I repeat to you that it's the end of the world."

"That's possible," I said, "but I'm stubborn in living."

"You're not wrong, Monsieur…but I, although as stubborn as you, am obliged to die. I'm frightfully ill and I have no shelter. Phoebus has miraculously taken pity on me, but tomorrow morning, he will expedite me *ad patres*, in Roque de Thau."

"This quarry is as much yours as mine."

"Thank you," he said. "I feared being indiscreet. But I'll make you a confession devoid of artifice: I'm dying of hunger."

"Ah!" I said, vaguely.

"I even have a weakness in that regard; if not, I would have had the pleasure of making your acquaintance. You're scowling, Monsieur I-don't-know-your name. Don't worry—I won't deplete your provisions. You're free to leave me in the claws of famine."

"I'm not as devoid of compassion as you might suppose," I said, sulkily.

"Be careful—I might take you at your word."

The strange fellow had the effrontery to joke!

"I'm not a parasite," he went on. "Tappers give me the creeps. However, I'm ready to be a parasite, a glutton and perhaps a drunkard. Messer Gaster is a tyrant whose orders one doesn't dispute for long. In consequence, no surprise: if you offer me something to eat, I'll accept."

"I offer you something to eat," I said.

"I ought to refuse," he replied. "I'm ready to die, and I'll draw away from it only to catch it up later. It's puerile, Monsieur…what is your name?"

"Dantenot."

"You're really going to give me something to eat?"

"Yes."

"Then don't let me languish any longer."

"Follow me inside…there are people waiting for me."

"You're not alone? Your comrades might not be as magnanimous as you."

"Come on—this heat is crippling us. I'm with my fiancée, her father and her mother."

"I'm ashamed to be introduced to them in this state."

He was trotting behind me like a rat.

"Bloody feet!" he said. "But I'll forget those miseries, since I'm going to satisfy myself before bidding farewell to the world."

"I forbid you to talk in that fashion to the people you're going to see," I said, dryly. "Madame Sterneballe is already sufficiently alarmed..."

"I shall observe the formalities, Monsieur Dantenot. You're energetic? So am I, damn it! It will be amusing to struggle against destiny..."

Monsieur Cynécarmieux plunged into the quarries, blowing hard, in the manner of a seal.

"The first breath of fresh air I've had!" he said, "It's good, it's comforting. I'll take it in liters, cubic meters. You're my good genie, Monsieur Dantenot. It's building stone that's extracted here, isn't it? I'm no geologist, but I know a little about it, all the same. Oh, the geologists! Not a morsel will remain of their Jurassic, Hercynian, etcetera, rocks. All that will be igneous rock...simply igneous. Are you taking me far, Monsieur Dantenot? Apologies, but I have bloody feet."

The candle lighting the Sterneballes' refuge appeared as a yellow dot in the darkness.

"That's it?" asked Monsieur Cynécarmieux. "Oh, I'll be able to eat...eat..."

His nasal voice had tender inflections. He sniffed noisily.

"I'm weeping...veritably, I'm weeping...it's hunger that's making me weep. It's a physiological emotion..."

Monsieur and Madame Sterneballe were wondering anxiously what the arrival of that phonographic voice signified. Instinctively, they had placed themselves in front of their daughter, as if to protect her against a possible danger. I saw my mother-in-law sketch a furtive sign of the cross.

"It's Roger!" cried Jane, the first to recognize me.

My presence reassured everyone. I explained briefly how I had encountered Onésime Cynécarmieux.

"Monsieur is an astronomer?" asked Monsieur Sterneballe.

"At the Observatory of Floirac...three white domes...mushrooms in a clump of grass..."

"The comparison is striking," said Monsieur Sterneballe. "I'm in a somewhat similar line..."

"Aha! A professor of sciences?"

"I'm an optician—Rue Sainte-Catherine."

"Delighted," said Monsieur Cynécarmieux. "Aiee! Permit me to sit down. I have bloody feet...I've come from Bordeaux by road..."

"That's a record!"

"A Marathonian record...I'd make a communication to the Académie des Science is it weren't the end...but no, no! I promised your son-in-law. Evohé! We're going to eat!"

I unwrapped my riches, as the conquerors of old unwrapped their booty on returning from a victorious expedition, in the midst of the most exuberant enthusiasm. The blind horse stamped its hooves in order to join in.

Monsieur Cynécarmieux abridged the inventory; he had already nibbled through a few biscuits, but that only served to exasperate his hunger. He demanded a full dinner.

The meal was substantial, but without a satisfactory complement, because we had to eat without bread.

"Reason is ordering me to stop," said Monsieur Cynécarmieux. "I'd gladly swallow that ham, but indigestion would be bound to follow. Now, I don't want to suffer during the few hours that...that...separate us from further events."

Monsieur Sterneballe was listening attentively.

"Why is it so hot outside?" he demanded.

Monsieur Cynécarmieux became agitated. "What? You don't know the causes? May I speak, Monsieur Dantenot? It's so interesting!"

He was begging me, with his ten fingers in his beard. I sensed that what he was about to say would deliver a rude blow to Jane's tranquility and her mother's, but I was so eager to be better informed myself that I acquiesced.

We were grouped round the candle, our eyes fixed on the hirsute little man. His nasal voice rose up.

"Where should I begin? You're not unaware of the movements of the heavenly bodies?"

"Gravitation…gyration…," said Monsieur Sterneballe, with a knowing expression.

"Nothing is motionless in the celestial desert…the stars, the planets, the satellites of every dimension, bolides, comets…everything is in motion at vertiginous speeds. The parabolas overlap, the curves intersect, the ellipses are intertwined…there are thousands, hundreds of thousands of movements in the ether."

"All of that must be admirably regulated!" Monsieur Sterneballe ecstasized.

"No need! Millions of leagues separate the stars. It takes them hundreds of centuries to get significantly closer to one another. The small ones gravitate round the medium-sized ones, the medium-sized around the large, and the large around incandescent monsters. Why that intersidereal restlessness? Gyration and gravitation, as you said just now, Monsieur…yes, that's it, that appears to be it…until an individual cleverer than Newton has built a more ingenious theory and is lucky enough to find practical confirmations in nature. One can find all that one wants in nature, and even what one doesn't want, with patience and a little luck…"

He reflected momentarily on what he had just said.

"I could have written that," he said, "but my future has been so rudely broken…"

He was going astray, and I brought him back to his subject. "Tell us about the heat, Monsieur Cynécarmieux."

"I'm coming to that…but it exasperates me when people batter my ears with the same old stuff: perfect order, perfect movements, perfect trajectories…everything perfect, what! Except for what's happening to us… Order in the world? Then why is there radium in the sun, and uranium too, and oxygen here, nitrogen there, iron on the Earth, aluminum on some other planet? Disorder, muddle, strife!"

"You're troubling me," said Monsieur Sterneballe.

The little astronomer tugged at his beard as if to uproot it.

"I'm an anarchist of science, Monsieur! I claim that everything in the astral world is adrift! In a few million years, the pole star might indicate south. As for the moon, we'll long since have shed it along the way; it will be beautiful around some other sphere that we've grazed in passing."

"We won't be here to see that," said Monsieur Sterneballe.

"We won't be here to see the last quarter of the present moon..."

"Monsieur!" I said, angrily.

"Pardon me, Monsieur Dantenot...apologies..."

He continued, with a stunning volubility: "We Terrans, we depend on the sun. It makes the rain and the fair weather here. It hasn't always been tender in our regard. It made the Deluge, emptied the Aquitanian gulf... For a long time, though, it's been tender...a moderate and constant temperature. Perhaps its personal cuisine has sometimes not quite succeeded...chemical cataclysms have resulted on the subject of which the scientists trade insults, but they're no more than trivia. The gravest matter is the deviation of the entire system toward the constellation Lyra. It's in the course of that deviation that our sun has run into a dead star..."

"A dead star?"

"A black sun, if you prefer. Stars are born and die, only they live for millions of centuries. It appears that that's nothing by comparison with eternity. Then, when the stars are dead, they no longer shine, one can no longer distinguish them in the infinite obscurity. They circulate discreetly, and, in truth, without concern for accidents. On the twenty-fifth of December our shiny sun encountered a black sun. Telescopy should have spread the rumor, but we didn't hear anything. One of my colleagues simply saw a patch that was promptly erased...nothing broke, but the temperature has increased, for every impact engenders heat..."

Monsieur Cynécarmieux stood up in order to gesticulate more freely.

"It's the bankruptcy of physics and thermodynamics. There are laws concerning the velocity of the transmission of heat; they're false! Everything is false! Everything is false!"

We didn't know what to say. My mind was exceedingly troubled. More fortunate than us, Madame Sterneballe scarcely understood, for she had fallen asleep.

"The temperature's rising!" said Monsieur Cynécarmieux. "It will go one rising. It will rise until no one exists to observe that it's still rising! The solar clouds are eight thousand degrees. There are perhaps twenty or twenty-five thousand of them, or more. Must I insist of the consequences? You can foresee them as well as me, so there's no point in dissimulating them. We're all going to die together, on Venus, on Earth, on Mars. Civilization will be destroyed, along with human beings, but the elite will have the sole consolation of thinking that the planets will be rejuvenated, that the heat will invigorate them, that this catastrophe will double the duration of the existence of our group, which is nevertheless one of the paltriest in creation. Heatstrokes first, then conflagrations, then boiling, then evaporation…we'll witness the conflagrations…perhaps the boiling…but surely not the rest…"

"Will it take long?" asked Monsieur Sterneballe.

"Ask the physicists! They'll search their logarithmic tables, and by hurrying a little, perhaps they'll have time to publish new erroneous calculations… But the wisest course is not to worry about anything. Eat when one is hungry, drink when one is thirsty, and sleep while awaiting the final insensibility…"

Heads in our hands, we listened to him. When he shut up, the silence overwhelmed us.

9

Monsieur Cynécarmieux woke up agitated. He stretched himself, clucking like a mother hen. As soon as I heard him I lit the candle. At that moment, the blind horse demanded its pittance imperiously. It sniffed the hay, but only took a few wisps between its thick lips.

"It's thirsty," said Monsieur Cynécarmieux.

But what could I give it to drink? Of liquid, in fact, we only possessed three bottles of wine. The question of thirst would soon arise for us, as for the horse.

After our breakfast, we took stock of our provisions. Jane and I set about dividing the food into rations, while my father-in-law and Monsieur Cynécarmieux fraternized, lying in the hay. My fiancée was amused by the situation, but I felt invaded by pessimism. By eking out our provisions strictly, we had enough food for a week. But what would become of the world in seven days?

We organized ourselves, in order to avoid the afflictions of our implacable enemy, the heat. Gradually, it was infiltrating the quarry. The invasion was slow, but the number of calories was increasing sensibly by the hour. A hundred meters from the entrance it was no longer easy to breathe. It was important, however, in order to preserve our cool air, to seal the tunnel hermetically, as far as possible from the cul-de-sac we occupied.

After having removed the door of the redoubt where the horse was enclosed, we fixed it at the junction that the tunnel formed with the central gallery. It fitted perfectly. In order to render our artificial wall airtight, it was sufficient to fill the gaps and interstices with rags obtained by ripping up a sheet. Monsieur Cynécarmieux calculated that we were then assured of a reserve of about five hundred cubic meters of cool air.

That installation took up most of the day. Jane and her mother helped us in the measure of their strength. The astronomer had filled a role that was not without analogy to that of a circus ringmaster. He had not worked much and had talked non-stop. His nasal verbiage irritated me, but silence would have irritated us more.

When the door swung on its hinges, I experienced a proud satisfaction. We were now in a retrenchment where the defense would be dogged.

"Shall we dine?" said Monsieur Cynécarmieux. "To favor the digestion, we can then go to the threshold, in order to see what has become of nature. The birds will no longer be singing…they've stuck out their tongues…cooee…"

"You'll cut off our appetite," said Monsieur Sterneballe, half serious and half in jest.

"So much the better—the food will last longer."

Everyone wanted to economize on the food. In spite of those good intentions, the others agreed that the ration was insufficient. I flatly refused to increase it, and no one dared insist. It was thus that, without perceiving it myself, I became the chief of our little colony.

The candles were consumed with alarming rapidity. A time would come when we would be plunged irredeemably into darkness. It was hence necessary to restrict our light, mediocre as it was, and remain for hours in bleak obscurity. Jane's hands gripped mine nervously; my dear fiancée was placing all her hope and all her confidence in me. But what could I do to save us?

At about six o'clock, Monsieur Cynécarmieux and I set forth. Monsieur Sterneballe was not sorry to be the immovable guardian of his wife and daughter. He abandoned the glory of conquests to us, without jealousy. To give himself a little exercise, he came with us as far as the door of our subterrain. He tugged on my sleeve and whispered: "We only have one bottle of wine left."

"I know," I replied, in the same tone.

"Good," he said. "I was just discharging my responsibility."

The astronomer was the most curious among us. He had the vocation of an explorer.

"The left-hand corridor leads to the exit," he said. Not worth the trouble of going to overheat our blood. Suppose we follow the right-hand tunnel?"

I told him that my intention was to go to the village. He dissuaded me.

"The temperature has risen, Monsieur Dantenot. You'd fall on the road, and no one would come to our aid."

I let him know the situation: "We don't have any more to drink."

"Damn!" he said, perplexed. "Thirst is even more redoubtable than hunger. But there's always water underground! I'm certain that in excavating some gallery, the workers have broken into some seam. We'll find it!"

"And if we don't find it?"

"We'll find it!" he repeated, forcefully. There's water in all mines. While digging, one always finds pockets of it. What desolated the owner of this quarry will be our good fortune. Limpid fresh water will flow down our esophagus. We'll look for the spring tomorrow morning; that will extract us from our lugubrious idleness."

The tunnel we were exploring was rigorously horizontal. It permitted access to another gallery much wider than the one we knew. Monsieur Cynécarmieux stumbled upon the track of a narrow-gauge railway.

"This is the high road of our city," he said. "This gallery is parallel to the first, therefore, and a little to the left. Let's turn right again."

"We're risking getting lost, Monsieur Cynécarmieux," I said, hesitantly, intimidated by the dark mystery that surrounded us.

"Well," he said, "there is a lack of street signs. We can always baptize the galleries..."

We were intelligent men, serous functionaries; in spite of that, we started arguing like children. The first gallery obviously ought to have been called the Roger Gallery, but I ceded my rights to Madame Sterneballe, and in consequence, we called it the Amélie Gallery. The communicating tunnel was named the Onésime Passage, and the astronomer was prouder of that than if he's discovered a star telescopically. The central avenue, with the narrow-gauge railway, being the most beautiful, became the Jane Gallery.

A philosopher has said that man is a strange animal. We were in a frightful situation, the old world was in its death-throes above our heads, life was disappearing from the surface of the globe, and we were taking pleasure in ridiculously baptizing he excavations of our mole-maze.

Monsieur Cynécarmieux had found a little fossil incrusted in the stone. Everything was a matter of dissertation for him. He was so occupied in spouting banalities from the scholarly manual about ammonites and belemnites that I invited him to shut up twice, in vain. I put a hand over his mouth and blew out my candle.

He did not protest, because he quickly understood why I had submitted him to that rather cavalier treatment.

We were not alone in the Jane Gallery. In the direction of the exit, someone was walking with a light. A few seconds sufficed for me acquire the certainty that he was heading toward us.

"Let's move back," said Monsieur Cynécarmieux. "He hasn't seen us. He's a human being like us, but we don't need to make his acquaintance. If we make his acquaintance, we won't have the cruelty to abandon him to his misery. Now, we're vagabonds ourselves..."

I had not followed the same reasoning when I had und him, Cynécarmieux, suffering from hunger at the entrance to the quarry. However, I might have followed his advice if I had not heard the indefinable sound of scraping, of friction, that the intruder was making. I wanted to know the cause of that noise.

Lurking in the Onésime passage like bandits in ambush, we waited.

The light was that of a lantern whose ring the man was holding in his hand. He was pushing a barrel, a demi-hogshead.

It was my neighbor Fradinotte!

I was gripped by emotion. The old vine-grower, under the menace of an atrocious death, was saving himself, along with the wine of his vineyard. Nothing had been able to persuade him to abandon his full barrel. He might not have been able to bring his savings, but he had not been able to separate himself from his wine, a magical panacea.

Monsieur Cynécarmieux, who could not abide thirty seconds of immobility, caused a pebble to rattle. Ceasing to roll his barrel, Fradinotte raised his lantern at arm's length and scrutinized the shadows.

"Who goes there?" he shouted.

"Friends," the astronomer replied. "We're brothers before eternity..."

The vintner judged the muscular value of Cynécarmieux at a glance. "Be off," he said. "I don't know you."

"Me neither," said the scientist, tenaciously, "but we'll gladly enter into relations. Show yourself, Monsieur Dantenot, for the worthy fellow has no confidence in me."

At the sight of me, Fradinotte's cunning visage relaxed. We shook hands.

"Bonsoir, Monsieur Dantenot," he said, as if we were in the square of Roque de Thau. "You're alive?"

"My God, yes...and you too, Fradinotte?

"Not without difficulty. Since Christmas, it's been necessary to box clever for that. It's a memorable epoch."

He had a live chicken in his pocket. The terrified fowl stuck out its neck and contemplated us with its round eyes. Fradinotte sat down on his barrel.

"I don't know what's become of my wife," he said, without apparent emotion. "She wanted to go out and didn't come back. It's the story of all the victims. I went to ground in my cellar. I slept. On the second day I thought about the quarry. I didn't think I'd find you here..."

Monsieur Cynécarmieux tapped the barrel with his curved index finger. "Is it full?" he asked.

"Of the 1912," said Fradinotte. "It's the one I like best."

"Are you going to let us taste it?"

Fradinotte avoided the question. With a thrust of his thumb he indicated the route he had just traveled. "Don't go that way," he said. "There are some there squabbling."

"Who?"

"People from Berson and strangers. That's why I'm leaving those parts. The people from Berson claim that the quarry belongs to them. The strangers, who arrived in an automobile, want to stay. Every man for himself, you understand..."

"They're fighting?" said Monsieur Cynécarmieux.

"They're making their preparations for it. Don't get mixed up in it, Monsieur Dantenot. We'll doubtless see one another again. Bonsoir."

He left us in the shadows without asking us whether we had light. He shoved his barrel carefully, the chicken still sticking its head out of his pocket."

"Old miser!" said Monsieur Cynécarmieux.

But the sharp sound of a gunshot made us forget Fradinotte. A battle had started at the other end of the gallery.

The wisest thing would have been not to go any closer, but the demon of curiosity was needling us. Without consulting one another, we made our way up the slope. I must admit that Monsieur Cynécarmieux did not dispute the position of patrol leader.

We covered at least two hundred meters. Heat and bitter smoke caught us in the throat. There was a bend in the galley, and we didn't go round the corner. A violent, blinding light filled the subterrain. The strangers had aimed the headlight of their auto at the people from Berson. Five black silhouettes were gesticulating in the dazzling light.

Incontestably, the attackers had the advantage. They could see without being seen, because they remained behind the reflector. In both camps, people had revolvers, and were not neglecting to fire them.

The bullets ricocheted as far as us. If even half of them had struck home, the besiegers and the besieged would have been exterminated. But it is difficult to aim with Brownings, and the majority of the shots were too high.

Suddenly, darkness filled the quarry again. A bullet had smashed the searchlight. Then we heard furious cries and more gunshots.

The vanquished disbanded; they passed in front of us in the darkness. There were three or four. One of them brushed me.

Then the victors went past, three in number. They were shining an electric pocket torch intermittently, and talking breathlessly.

"Are you wounded, Pierre?"

"I've broken my radius. It doesn't hurt too much."

"The brutes! If we unearth them, we'll exterminate them without mercy."

"They fled like rabbits."

"All the same, it's good to breathe this cool air."

"My arm's swelling up. It's necessary to stop the bleeding."

"I've got a handkerchief; we'll make a bandage."

They were ten paces away from us. The electric torch illuminated them imperfectly. In the little cone of light, I saw a bloody arm, bare to the elbow, and the energetic face of a man in his prime. Then the light went out with an abrupt click, and the three men plunged on, with a vague hubbub of voices.

"We've had a narrow escape," said Monsieur Cynécarmieux. "If they'd discovered us they'd have killed us without giving us time to protest. The fabulist was right, Monsieur Dantenot: to live happily, live hidden..."

I was in a hurry to get back to our encampment, because I was fearful now for the security of Jane and her parents. We groped our way along Onésime Passage. We pricked up our ears frequently, but the silence of the quarry was now undisturbed.

Once we were back we consolidated our door by means of three beams whose extremities we succeeded in wedging in the stone.

Monsieur Sterneballe, his wife and his daughter were asleep. My future father-in-law interrogated us in a thick voice. I contented myself with telling him that all was well.

It took me a long time to go to sleep. Alongside me, Monsieur Cynécarmieux turned over and over on his bed of straw.

"Can't you sleep?" I asked him, discreetly.

"No," he replied, his voice hoarse. "I'm thirsty."

I was thirsty too. And the blind horse was thirsty. And we would all be thirsty soon, without being able to suffer it with as much resignation as the blind horse.

I had nightmares. It seemed to me that I was eating mouthfuls of salt, while Monsieur Cynécarmieux, having made a gash in his wrist, was drinking his own blood avidly, and that Monsieur Sterneballe was drinking a cup of molten lead...

10

Monsieur Cynécarmieux was sucking pebbles. A monotonous rattle was escaping from the throat of the blind horse. The shadow was heavy.

We had been thirsty for hours and hours. We could no longer eat. We were waiting for a miracle or the deliverance of death. We preferred to remain in the dark because our faces made us fearful.

Days had passed. I had been suffering for longer than the others because I had given my last drop of wine to my fiancée. Jane was not complaining, but her mother was whining for two. As for Monsieur Sterneballe, he sometimes said: "What can we do?"

In vain, I tried to forget our fate; I had only one thought, one desire: to drink.

To drink... To empty in a single draught a glass of crystalline water. To make the impetuous jet of a siphon spurt into a glass of vermouth. To drink... To pour old wine, Fradinotte's wine, the color of brick, as smooth as oil, into a glass in the form of a tulip. To drink… Glasses, bottles, babbling brooks...

I was becoming slightly delirious.

In the company of Monsieur Cynécarmieux I had explored the quarry from top to bottom within a radius of a kilometer. The galleries ramified infinitely, going upwards and downwards, and intersecting, but the walls were immutably dry; no trickle of water filtered through the white dust.

We had not encountered either Fradinotte or he strangers. There was nothing astonishing about that; the quarry extended a long way in the direction of Rigalet; it pierced the chain of hills like an immense ant-hill.

I had candles and matches in my pocket. I took four boxes and rolled them up in a strip of sheet, and I left. They heard me, but no one asked where I was going.

I only lit my candle when I reached the Jane Gallery. There was a heavy, overwhelming heat there. I was weak but resolute. I wanted to drink or die.

I went into a tortuous tunnel, so low that I was obliged to walk bent double. Rockfalls had occurred, and black soil had slid through the crevices in the saltpetrous stone. I picked up a handful of that earth. It was dry. No water; still no water!

The tunnel was long. It ended in another tunnel that descended at a forty-five degree angle, so I let myself slide down it, and I reached a high and broad excavation with an arched ceiling like the cupola of an oven.

I slipped through a fissure and found myself in a new gallery. It appeared to me that there was an odor of damp there. The soil was, in fact, damp, but so very little! That gave me a new burst of energy, however. But the galleries succeeded one another, changing direction every ten meters, with the result that it was difficult to get my bearings. My last candle was diminishing. When I perceived that, there were only a few centimeters left. It was impossible that it would last long enough to permit me to get back to our redoubt.

Darkness was certain death, but I wasn't afraid; I was suffering too much. I changed course as frequently as possible, rendering the maze inextricable. I no longer knew whether I was looking for a spring or a tomb.

That prolonged, desperate course exhausted my feeble strength. My candle fell to the ground and went out; the bottles slipped out of my hand and I heard the sound of breaking glass. I sank down, utterly resigned, and I lost consciousness...

It's probable that my faint was brief. On coming round, I reassembled my ideas painfully. I had the tranquil conviction that I was doomed. Only one thing rendered me desperate: expiring far away from my fiancée. I was no longer anything but a little child, humble before the definitive mystery.

Suddenly, it seemed to me that I felt something cool in my back, between the shoulder blades. The sensation was agreeable. The coolness increased, descending, bathing me delightfully...

I felt the wall. It was damp.

"Water!"

I recovered my strength with a surge. Feverishly, I searched for my matches. The light of the sizzling sulfur caused the stone to sparkle. The water was trickling drop by drop along the wall.

My candle had fallen a few paces away. I lit it, trembling, and placed it on a flat stone.

Water—I had water! It was filtering imperceptibly, not forming a stream or a pool, and was lost between the stones, but it was water,

I stuck my lips to the wall, and sucked in a mouthful of mud. I had water, but I could not drink.

To recover my calmness, I strode back and forth clasping my temples as if to extract an idea from my head. Then I planted myself in front of the semblance of a spring, hypnotized by that possibility of salvation.

An inspiration struck me. With my fingernails I hollowed out a little excavation in the rock that the damp had rendered spongy. Then, with a handful of earth, I fashioned a kind of beak. At the end of that beak a drop formed, than another, and another, and a fourth...

One bottle had broken but I still had three. I placed one of them under the falling drops. With incredible patience I waited, counting the drops savoring them with my gaze.

When there was a little water in the bottom of the bottle, I drank it. I recommenced twice, ten times, insatiably, and it was only after I had half-extinguished the furnace of my stomach that I thought about those who were dying elsewhere.

I would have experienced a veritable remorse had I drunk any more. I replaced the bottle; I extinguished the candle. I no longer had either the right or the desire to die.

How long did it take me to fill the three bottles? I don't know. When I had finished, I thought about going back. I no longer had any more than half an hour of candle-light. I expelled the doubt and apprehension from my mind, and I set out. At the end of the tunnel I made a cross on the wall to mark the place, and wondered whether I ought to turn left or right. I opted for left. I ran like a madman, calling out so loudly that my voice became hoarse, pivoting in all directions—and I suddenly found myself back at the spring, at which I had arrived from the other end of the corridor.

Then I collapsed and wept silently.

The candle flickered, flared up and went out. The darkness imprisoned me. Nevertheless, I set forth again. I still had thirty matches. I struck one at the intersection.

I soon had only three left.

I advanced with rage, but not so rapidly as to break my precious bottles. My wounded knee as still making me suffer; my leg was heavy and numb. I felt the walls with my free hand, and I walked, and walked, and walked...

Finally, my foot hit something hard that rendered a slight metallic sound. I bent down. I had tumbled over the rails of the central gallery.

Never had Providence been thanked with so much fervor.

Ten minutes later, I was in our cavern. The horse was snoring lugubriously in the darkness.

"Jane!" I called.

A feeble sigh was exhaled. An anguish gripped my heart. I struck a light. Madame Sterneballe was sitting down, supporting Jane's inert lead on her lap. Monsieur Sterneballe and Monsieur Cynécarmieux were lying face to face on the straw.

"I have water!" I cried, triumphantly.

That phrase suddenly rendered them life. I gave one bottle to Jane, another to her mother, the third to the men.

"After you," stammered Monsieur Cynécarmieux.

"No, Monsieur," said Monsieur Sterneballe. "You're the guest."

They drank religiously, with a kind of unction, and their features relaxed, the hallucination disappearing from their pupils. I begged them to be moderate, to slake their thirst prudently; they listened to me, regretfully.

Jane thought about the horse, which had not yet drunk anything. I agreed to return to the spring with the astronomer. We gathered our bottles, which we arranged in a large plasterer's bucket. On hearing the handle clink against the iron, the horse whinnied dully.

"You'll be able to drink soon," said Madame Sterneballe, amicably. "Be patient. These messieurs are going to the fount."

Monsieur Cynécarmieux, who had recovered his usual loquacity, told me how, during my absence, he had gone as far as the orifice of the quarry.

"I dragged myself to the top of the Amélie Gallery. What a steam-bath! I wanted to commit suicide, but I didn't have the strength. I crawled on to the ground, far enough from the hole. I was cooking, frying...it was dark outside, but the shadow was splashed with red reflections..."

"The trees were burning," said Monsieur Sterneballe.

"They had to burn, planted like torches in the middle of the roasted countryside. Solid and liquid matter were heated more than the air, which is easily traversed and only conserves a fraction of the heat. The water must have disengaged floods of vapor; it has been raining, or will rain boiling water! And yet, if anything can save the Earth, it's water. Perhaps the sun will grow weary before having emptied the oceans. Since we've been imprisoned, the temperature hasn't increased too rapidly, because of the intense evaporation. We're the impotent witnesses to a monstrous struggle between the elements."

His laughter resembled the grating pulley of a well.

"Are we leaving for the marvelous spring, Monsieur Dantenot?"

"Whenever you wish, Monsieur Cynécarmieux."

Suddenly I recoiled. The specter of Fradinotte was standing on the threshold of the cavern. He really was a specter, lived, fleshless, the skin plastered on the skeleton, the eyes flamboyant and terrible.

"Give me something to eat," said the specter, in a hoarse voice.

No one budged. Monsieur Sterneballe was sitting on the dismantled crate that enclosed our meager reserves.

"Give me something to eat," Fradinotte repeated.

Monsieur Cynécarmieux went to place himself in front of him.

"You're the man with the barrel?" he said. "We can't do anything for you. I can see that you're in a pitiful state, but we won't soften. We don't have a crumb to give you."

"You have food. Give me something to eat!"

The astronomer wagged his index finger in a sign of refusal. "Your insistence is misplaced," he said. "Monsieur Dantenot is as poor as you. He is good enough to tolerate me, and I'm only an intruder. I am, therefore, willing to be cut in two for him, and I intend him to know it."

"Give me something to eat!" said Fradinotte again.

"No," the astronomer replied, with implacable firmness.

"We might, perhaps...," I began.

"Oh, no, no!" said Monsieur Sterneballe and Monsieur Cynécarmieux, severely.

Fradinotte fell to his knees, his arms extended toward me. "Monsieur Dantenot, something to eat! Just a mouthful."

"Gives us something to drink!" replied Monsieur Cynécarmieux, suddenly.

The old vintner made a gesture of revolt. "Never!" And he added, dolorously. "The barrel is smashed, smashed..."

"You're lying," Monsieur Cynécarmieux said to him. "Give, give...you want to eat; we want to drink..."

"Give us wine and we'll give you herring..."

"Since I swear to you that the barrel is smashed..."

I no longer had any pity. The avarice of the wretch scandalized me. Madame Sterneballe proffered, harshly: "Two bottles of wine for one herring..."

"You're torturers" clamored Fradinotte. "God will avenge me, for you'll die sooner than me! You'll die of thirst! And I'll eat—I'll eat you! Ah, you refuse to give me something to eat! Torturers!"

"Go away!" intimated Monsieur Cynécarmieux."

"Not before spitting in your face!"

"Give us wine, or get out."

"Here! Here's wine for you!"

Monsieur Cynécamieux received a punch that instantly tumefied his right eye. He riposted as best he could, but he did not have the strength. Fradinotte, mad with rage, knocked him down, crushed him with his knees and took hold of his throat.

Stunned, we saw Monsieur Cynécarmieux agitating frenziedly, clawing at Fradinotte's face with his fingernails, but the latter squeezed with an incredible force.

Madame Sterneballe and her daughter screamed. Monsieur Sterneballe was still protecting the crate. I stepped forward swiftly in order to liberate Monsieur Cynécarmieux. As I leaned forward, the vintner butted me with his head and the blood sprang from my nose. Then I seized a bottle by the neck and I struck, once.

Fradinotte let go and gripped his head in both hands. He opened his mouth to shout an insult, and then fled at top speed.

11

Hunger, to begin with, is not very dolorous. It is irritating, but tolerable. It causes a sensation of emptiness in the body, with a few dizzy spells. Then there are torsions of the entrails, stabling pains, a finally an indescribable suffering, like a cruel bite that never ends.

Ten times, perhaps, I tried to go out. I ran into the heat as if it were a wall. Then, flanked by Monsieur Cynécarmieux, I traveled the quarry in every direction. We found several springs, but not the slightest nourishment. I strove to find subterranean mushrooms, because I knew they existed, but we never succeeded in finding a tunnel where they grew.

Our sleep had become very irregular, for our organisms were no longer obedient to the alternation of day and night. Monsieur Sterneballe and Monsieur Cynécarmieux distracted one another with interminable conversation.

For myself, I was no longer capable of taking an interest in anything. My strength gradually disappeared. My love for Jane, without having diminished, was no longer manifest in any but a vague fashion. For her part, my fiancée never addressed herself to me except to ask me for something. She only questioned me or commanded me.

Madame Sterneballe kept her gestures to a strict minimum. Her existence had become vegetative. She did not recriminate, did not speak, did not act. Her gaze fixed, she dreamed.

The blind horse still had a provision of hay and ate when it was hungry. Suddenly, the idea occurred to me of killing it and nourishing ourselves on its flesh. I ruminated the project for some time before communicating it to Monsieur Cynécarmieux. He qualified it as genius, and Monsieur Sterneballe accepted its realization with a blissful smile.

However, we could not bring ourselves to kill the animal. Our thinness became frightful. We went regularly to fetch water and experienced a sensible relief in swallowing the liquid. Monsieur Cynécarmieux almost always accompanied me.

The little man had an extraordinary energy. Like all braggarts, he was always talking about acing, and acted when it was possible. It was him who shook us up, who obliged us to take a little exercise, and who conserved within us, not the appetite for but the possibility of living.

Once, when we were coming back to our refuge laden with full bottles, we heard a voice. It repeated two almost-identical syllables, which we did not understand at first.

It was the cry of great distress; "Maman! Maman! Maman!"

We had suffered so much that we were inaccessible to pity. The man who is suffering no longer has any generosity, but he is curious. We hoped to see a being more unfortunate than us.

There was a man lying in the shadow. His eyes were so unaccustomed to any light that the flame of our candle forced him to turn his head way. He stopped crying out and waited.

Monsieur Cynécarmieux inspected him cautiously. The man was inoffensive. He gave him a drink. The unknown man emptied the bottle. He drank so avidly that the water spilled from the corners of his lips and over his beard.

"It's good," said the man, "but it's very late."

He looked at us. His eyebrows frowned and his eyes rolled.

"Thieves!" he said. "You've taken my package!"

He threw himself triumphantly on something lying by the wall.

"Aha! I've got it back. Ha ha ha!"

Terrified, we recoiled. The man was pressing to his breast a severed arm, an arm with livid flesh, the biceps of which had been lacerated, torn apart, as if gnawed...

"Human flesh!" said Monsieur Cynécarmieux.

With a cheerful expression, the man said: "I shall never again eat anything else..."

Indeed he did not, for he expired a minute later. We drew away silently from his cadaver and the half-devoured arm.

"We'll arrive at that!" said the astronomer, suddenly.

"Rather die!" I retorted, indignantly.

"One says that…and then…and then…do you believe, Dantenot, that we'll arrive at that?"

"Better to die immediately!"

"We have to kill the horse!" he said, authoritatively.

And when we went into the cavern, he said to Monsieur Sterneballe: "We have to kill the horse."

My future father-in-law stood up.

"Where are you going?" asked Monsieur Cynécarmieux.

"I'm going away with the ladies."

"We need you. Three won't be too many."

"I've never been able to kill a chicken," said the optician, piteously.

Monsieur Cynécarmieux lost his temper. "So you want to live? Do you want to enable your wife and daughter to live? Let's kill the horse. Mesdames, go out."

He had departed from his habitual politeness. The ladies went out, and the three of us remained.

"This is what we're going to do," said Monsieur Cynécarmieux, lowering his voice, as if the horse might have been able to understand. "We're going to tie its feet so that it can't kick."

"Yes," I acquiesced.

He pointed to a huge quarryman's sledgehammer.

"Then, we're going to hit it with that."

"Yes," I said, again.

"Who's going to hit it and bleed it?"

"Dantenot, of course."

"Pardon!" I exclaimed. "Why me, rather than you?"

He pulled a face, expressing weariness and scorn.

"This is ridiculous," he said. "Let's draw straws."

He picked up three pieces of straw and offered them to us. Monsieur Sterneballe drew first; suspiciously, I chose after him.

"You have the shortest one," said Monsieur Cynécarmieux.

I didn't protest.

The blind horse meekly allowed its hind feet to be tied, with pieces of string that we cut laboriously. It made a few difficulties when we tried to tie the front feet. Monsieur Cynécarmieux calmed it down.

"La…la…hold firm, Monsieur Sterneballe! La…la…"

But the horse remained upright. The astronomer braced himself, and pushed hard. The animal fell on to its flank.

"Over to you," said Monsieur Cynécarmieux to me. "Strike behind the ear. I'll hold the head."

I picked up the hammer. To grant myself a few seconds respite, I rolled up my sleeves to the elbow.

"Behind the ear," insisted Monsieur Cynécarmieux.

I struck weakly. It caused me a bizarre impression. The horse shuddered.

"Harder!" cried the astronomer.

I struck again, but weakly again.

"He said harder!" vociferated Monsieur Sterneballe.

But those memories are too atrocious…

The days continued to succeed one another. I believe that in order to cook the meat we built a fire in the feed-trough.

We argued. We wept. We recited prayers. Monsieur Cynécarmieux was hardly ever with us. He was afraid of being killed. However, no desire to murder him ever took hold of me. I had too many phantoms in my nightmares.

I don't remember anything more.

Everything was lost in darkness. Death was no longer a terrifying leap into the unknown, but a rational terminus…

"Come!"

The resumption of my human existence commenced with that word, uttered by Monsieur Cynécarmieux.

"Come!"

I was obliged to walk, to crawl. I don't know; I never will know…

"Come!"

Night. But cold night. A January night, with a serene moon in the middle of a pure sky, strewn with stars. The earth I trod was bare, but the atmosphere seemed normal.

It is necessary to have lived through that hour to comprehend...

The rest no longer belongs to a storyteller. Philosophers, statisticians and economists have, in any case, said enough. They have described the formation of the new society, composed of survivors issued from the mines and caverns where they had taken refuge. They have explained that enough engineers survived to have the tyranny of science recognized, enough advocates to constitute a truly political parliament, enough energetic men to take possession of the wealth of deserted Asia and Africa.

Change oscillates; the problem of Constantinople remains entire; the next election will determine the scrutiny of lists, with proportional representation of minorities.

The passions are the same in the embryonic new humankind. Humans are still human. I like them anyway, because they don't prevent me from being happy with Jane and the son that was born to us.

The appeased autumn sun is gilding my wife's forehead. She is rocking the sleeping infant. She has forgotten—I have forgotten myself—all our suffering. God is good, since he had permitted us to emerge unscathed and better from the terrible ordeal.

In the poultry-yard, Monsieur Sterneballe is repainting the henhouse. In the main courtyard, my mother-in-law and Monsieur Cynécarmieux are playing backgammon. We are all united in an indefectible manner, as if to affirm the verity of the Arab proverb:

Fear assembles individuals, and inspires a mutual love in them.

THE CHIMERICAL QUEST

I

Then the maid exclaimed: "It's someone for Monsieur!"

And she pulled the door shut forcefully, to hide the secret of the next room.

Silence filled the drawing room: a thick silence, so heavy that one had the impression that it was about to break the windows. It took a few minutes for Paul Duffaure to distinguish a noise in that silence. On the mantelpiece, between two candlesticks, a clock was alive, and its heart was swinging tranquilly to the rhythm of the seconds.

The furniture was Empire, excessively waxed. The rep of the chairs was showing its weft. A goat-skin, promoted to the rank of wolf-skin by the will of the dyer, covered a Récamier chair whose feet had lost their bronze claws.

In the center of the bouillotte table a white rose was shedding its petals. Its stem was short; attentive hands doubtless cut it every morning to prolong the flower's agony. The ceiling was eczematous, the carpet had leprosy. One sensed the humble poverty of apartments cleaned twice a month by an unenthusiastic housekeeper.

Mediocre engravings seemed to be hung at random, but that was only an appearance. *The Battle of Navarino* hid a stain and *Napoleon at Rivoli* masked a rip in the wallpaper.

Paul Duffaure approached several photographs grouped in a frame. One was of a soldier hunched in a trench-coat with stiff creases, who fixed you with a proud stare; another was of a young woman, perhaps pretty, who was brandishing a tennis racket; a third represented a chubby baby whose hair was ornamented by a ribbon tied with a butterfly knot.

Through the window, part of Bordeaux harbor was visible. The rising tide was bristling with little waves of yellow and viscous water. Opposite, a ship was being unloaded, and wheat was flowing in golden torrents. The gray mist was lowering the sky as far as the roofs.

The maid reappeared.

"Monsieur asks you to wait a moment..."

Short and stout, with eyes like a chicken, round and inexpressive, she shifted her weight from one hip to the other on the threshold. She did not hide her surprise that a stranger desired to see Monsieur Legrand, because the latter hardly ever received visits.

She was beating a retreat when the visitor slipped something into her hand.

"To thank you for being so obliging," he said.

It was a five-franc bill, which she turned over and over stupidly. The unexpected tip almost frightened her. "You're very kind," she stammered, eventually.

In order to interrogate her, Paul Duffaure adopted the falsely amicable tone of a minister visiting a hospital.

"Have you been in Monsieur Legrand's service for long?"

"Oh, yes, Monsieur," said the maid, with hypocritical modesty. "It will soon be twenty years."

"You knew him when was unimpaired, then?"

The maid's simian brow furrowed. "What, Monsieur?"

"When he had the use of his legs."

"Yes, Monsieur. He was as nimble as you or me. Unfortunately, the war took his legs."

"He's an amputee, then?" asked Paul Duffaure.

"Paralyzed by a bullet in the back."

To give more emphasis to her assertion, the maid bent over, dragging her slipper, feigning a sudden ataxia. Unimpressed by the mime, Paul Dufaure continued his interrogation.

84

"In spite of his infirmity, Monsieur Legrand works?"

The maid shook her head energetically. "No, Monsieur…he no longer works."

"Doesn't he occupy himself with scientific research?"

"Oh, if that's what you call work…" In a smile of commiseration, she showed her false teeth, as tightly-packed and regular as the seeds of a corncob. "He does, in fact, occupy himself with research. It distracts him, poor fellow…"

"Is his laboratory in the house?"

"The corner where he potters around? A shed at the back of the courtyard.. That's where he spends his days."

"Have you heard mention of his latest discovery?"

"Oh la la!" she exclaimed. "Have I heard mention of it? Every day, Monsieur…every day, for years."

"In what terms?"

She blinked slyly. "He'll tell you that himself. He has his ideas about that, you know…anyway, here he is…*au revoir*, Monsieur."

She swiftly beat a retreat. The castors of an armchair squeaked on the parquet, and Monsieur Legrand appeared.

He was a poor exsanguinated and emaciated individual, wrapped up warmly in faded plaid. The hair of a poet sprang up in a gray flame above his forehead. The thin lips were pursed in a bitter—or perhaps simply dolorous—crease. The square chin indicated a solid will. In the depths of the blue eyes, a kind of timid pride was distinguishable, with hints of suspicion and generosity. Suffering having ravaged his features, he was reminiscent of an aged child.

A tall swarthy fellow, his Arabic features emphasized by a meager goatee beard, was pushing the armchair.

Before the visitor had even bowed, the voice of the paralytic rose up, slightly hoarsely: "Monsieur Paul Duffaure?"

"Of the *Echo*," the young man specified.

"Ah! You're a journalist? What do you want, Monsieur?"

"To see you. I've come from Paris for that…"

"You have time to waste!" sniggered Legrand.

The journalist blushed imperceptibly, and continued without being disconcerted: "I'd like a chat with you..."

"I'm listening," riposted the invalid, pulling himself up in his armchair.

Paul Duffaure darted an indecisive glance at the Arab.

"Ali doesn't count," said Legrand. "He never leaves me. I can't do without him since a stupid steel slug made me the rag I am. But have no fear—he's discreet."

Legrand's gaze, keen and tranquil," made Paul Duffaure ill at ease. In the refallen silence, the noise of the little smithy of the pendulum was amplified.

The journalist suddenly made a decision. "Monsieur, I know that you possess the secret of gold."

The Arab's eyes were distant, pensive. Legrand passed a fleshless hand through is hair. "Really?" he said, unemotionally. "Who told you that?"

"It has been affirmed to me."

"And you believe it?"

Paul Duffaure hesitated. "Why should I doubt it, Monsieur? Science can render so many miracles possible."

"So you believe in the transmutation of metals?"

"Yes!" said the reporter. He did not have the slightest preconceived idea, because he was utterly ignorant of the problem.

Legrand stirred in his seat. "Who revealed the nature of my work to you?"

"I promised to keep the secret..."

The invalid was not content with that reply. "It's probably that idiot Beyerlein?"

Paul Duffaure judged it superfluous to deny it. "Yes, Monsieur, it was him."

"Well, he'd have done better to hold his tongue."

"He's so enthusiastic..."

"What do I care about his enthusiasm? Enthusiasm is often only a proof of impotence. If I've told him anything, it certainly isn't so that he can blab. For the moment, my affairs only interest initiates. It's true that I wrote to him, because I imagined that he was involved in the Great Work. As he flatters himself on making progress along the path traced by the ancient hunters of chimeras, I wanted to confide in him. I see that he's betrayed me. Yes, Monsieur, betrayed!" He struck the arm of his chair with the sudden anger of a sick man. "Beyerlein had no right to launch you on my heels! For years and years I've been seeking in silence. My task demands concentration, above all else."

The journalist attempted to get a word in: "Glory is the finest recompense..."

"I have a horror of glory!" exclaimed Legrand, his face crimson. "I only ask one thing: to live long enough to complete my work. I'm not a charlatan, Monsieur!"

The Arab, his eyelids half-lowered, studied the intruder ironically. But Paul Duffaure knew his métier. Frequently rebuked, he never quit his victims without having extracted sufficient information from them.

"Monsieur," he said, "I'm not entirely a profane, for I'm passionate about alchemy."

"You've studied the science, then?"

"My God, I...yes, a little..."

The invalid looked him straight in the eyes, with such acuity that he dared not persist in his lie.

"I'm quite ignorant; nevertheless, I divine marvels. Followers don't have to be as knowledgeable as apostles. I'm ready to transcribe, faithfully and scrupulously, what you reveal to me..."

"What I reveal to you?" snapped Legrand. "Nothing at all! I have no revelation to make, Monsieur."

"However, you have found...?"

"I've found nothing, and I won't find anything. Ali, show Monsieur out."

Without taking offense at the discourteous measure, Paul Duffaure persisted: "One moment more, Monsieur. Before throwing me out—which won't prevent me, I assure you, from making up an interview—listen to me for one moment. My director, Monsieur Gellé, willingly takes an interest in bold enterprises. If, by chance, his aid would be useful to you…he's extremely rich…"

"I'm not a beggar!" Legrand retorted.

The young man restated his idea in another form. "If his financial collaboration would be agreeable to you, I can do my best to obtain it."

Legrand passed his hand through his hair again. The gesture had to be habitual.

"Please excuse me," he murmured, after a few seconds of reflection. "I must seem boorish. I'm subject to fits of temper that have no other cause but my physical condition…"

"The journalist understood that he had almost won the game. Concealing a smile of triumph, he took pity on the fate of the sick man.

"Are you in a great deal of pain, Monsieur?"

"No, but the paralysis of the legs is complete. As soon as I try to stand up, I crumple up like a rag doll."

Paul Duffaure raised his eyes to the ceiling. "Oh, the war…!" he sighed.

"It was at Hartmannswillerkopf that I was left like this.[4] A banal story, in truth. After a patrol I was left between the lines…" He turned to the Arab still standing behind him. "My brave Ali came to find me. I owe him my life…"

"Three months before," the Arab put in, in correct but slightly guttural French, "Monsieur Legrand had saved me at Woëvre."[5]

---

[4] The Battle of Hartmannswillerkopf was a series of engagements fought during 1915 for the strategic possession of a pyramidal peak in the Vosges, which cost thirty thousand lives—mostly French—but ended in a stalemate, and both sides redirected their attention to more northerly points on the Western Front.

[5] The reference is presumably to the French Woëvre offensive launched in April 1915, although the Woëvre plain, between Luxemburg and Toul, was a constant arena of confrontation between French and German forces in the Great War.

"Well, we're quits," replied Legrand. "The government of the Republic pays me a nice pension..." He ruffled his hair again. "I don't have any reason to complain, because, fortunately, my daughter works. She's a dentist. Thanks to her, I don't want for anything. People have indulgence for my manias. They let me pursue my research, but they aren't far from treating me as a madman..."

"Oh...!" protested Duffaure, politely.

"Even my daughter!" the invalid insisted, without acrimony. "Fundamentally, she's not entirely wrong. It's disquieting, a fellow looking for the philosopher's stone. In the twentieth century, that takes on a slightly outdated appearance. And yet, my friend, my madness is an austere wisdom. There's not the slightest fantasy in that struggle of man against inert and mysterious matter. I've continued the prodigious work of Al Farady, whose manuscripts I once consulted in Leyden. I've tried to understand Paracelsus, and instituted myself as the heir of Nicolas Flamel. It required learning a great deal, and forgetting a great deal. Saint Thomas Aquinas, Arnault de Villeneuve and Roger Bacon furnished materials for the edifice that death prevented Raymond Lull from constructing entirely.[6] That edifice, I've finally concluded." His voice became almost strident. "I am the man who is no longer awaited; I shall become the master of things and men."

His eyes flamboyant, his diaphanous hand seemed to be holding the scepter of the world. A quasi-divine force emanated from that mutilated body. In the penumbra of the gently falling dusk, he was radiant with a supernatural light. And the tall Arab behind him appeared as straight and silent as an archangel.

---

[6] Most of the names on this list of famous supposed alchemists are familiar, the exception being "Al Farady," which might be a corruption of the name of the 10th century philosopher Al-Farabi, or Alpharabius, who is credited with one book an alchemy as well as numerous others.

Concerned with realities, Paul Duffaure said: "So you've made gold, then?"

With an emphatic solemnity, Legrand declared: "I have made gold."

"That's marvelous," said the journalist. But his wonderment remained artificial.

As for the Arab, he looked down at his master indulgently, as a mother contemplates her child when he declares, which brandishing a wooden sword: "I'm a generalissimo!"

Legrand's fever vanished abruptly. He seemed suddenly to shrink in his armchair. "Yes," he muttered. "You're like the others, you think I'm afflicted by mental alienation. I have all my common sense, though, Monsieur..."

"I don't doubt it," Duffaure affirmed.

"Yes you do, but it doesn't matter. I'm used to the incomprehension of others; it no longer amuses or exasperates me." He explained, more to himself than his interlocutor: "You can't imagine how that secret weighs upon me, and yet, I dare not reveal it. It's so formidable! But for the war, perhaps I'd never have found it. One works better when one can't live like everyone else. Asceticism has its merits. Immobile, I've traveled an immense road. You, Monsieur, who are scrutinizing my face with perplexity, don't know and can't know what I've done. It smacks of prodigy. I'm poor, and experimental chemistry is very expensive. I lack materials. My first decigram of gold cost me several thousand francs—all of my daughter's dowry!"

"You must already have recuperated that sum."

"I haven't produced any yet. I'd need radium."

The journalist made a note. "Ah! You employ radium?"

"It activates the transmutation."

Duffaure thought the moment favorable for obtaining precisions. "Could you give me a few details?" he asked, in his most honeyed tone.

"Oh, gladly!" said Legrand, ironically. "I apply the principle of my predecessors: splitting compounds in order to return to the component. The list of simple substances, which everyone knows to be arbitrary, is diminishing by the day. There are hardly any simple substances; there's doubtless only one of them, solid, liquid or gaseous..."

"Gold, perhaps..?" Duffaure suggested, timidly.

The invalid shook his head. "The gold state certainly isn't the primal state. It's rather the sidereal ether, a strange substance of fantastic density, which we call, ingenuously, the void, and imagine to be extraordinarily light. A void cannot exist in nature! We'd understand that if we had the notion of the fourth dimension...but I beg your pardon. I'm becoming tedious."

"On the contrary!" the journalist protested. And, returning his interlocutor to the subject that interested him: "With what substance do you begin?"

"With a metal whose specific weight is similar to that of gold: lead."

"Lead is considered to be a base metal..."

"That's a conventional idea! Lead is no more base than gold or platinum. That's what almost all my predecessors tried to transmute. More fortunate than them, I've succeeded."

"Astonishing!" exclaimed the journalist, in order to flatter Legrand.

"No more astonishing than the analysis of the air by Lavoisier, the synthesis of acetylene by Berthelot or the treatment of pitchblende by Curie..."

Paul Duffaure plunged resolutely into banality: "Science marches with giant strides!"

The invalid did not share that opinion. "It crawls, Monsieur, it crawls!"

"But the field of human knowledge is growing broader every day."

"We're still ignorant of the majority of fundamental principles; we're floundering in empiricism. Radium overturns the pretended laws of physics and chemistry, the theory of relativity demolishes the laws of gravitation. That doesn't prevent Einstein from being as far from the truth as Laplace or Copernicus. Nature doesn't yield her secrets kindly; it's neces-

sary to tear them away from her. Gold is everywhere…perhaps in the air, certainly in the water. The sea con-
tains a little more than six milligrams per ton..."

Paul Duffaure was not about to allow the illuminatus to
lose himself in generalities. "Do you have gold here that you
have manufactured? I'd be delighted to see it."

"Ali, the box!" Legrand ordered, laconically.

The Arab went out silently.

Satisfied, Duffaure cracked his knuckles. "Monsieur," he
declared, emphatically, "You're going to become the most
famous man in the world."

"And the most ashamed."

"Why?" asked the journalist, surprised. "Because of your
wealth?"

"Oh, I won't take any personal profit from my discovery.
Anyone will be able, like me, to make gold as he pleases."

"Everyone will be happy, then!"

Legrand laughed sardonically. "What an error! I have no
intention of making humankind happy. A misanthrope, I hate
humans as they are. It pleases me to do them harm."

"Do you think you're persecuting them by enriching
them?"

The invalid rummaged in his hair. "You're young, Monsieur. You don't reflect much. In a few months, like everyone
else, you'll execrate René Legrand, the wretch who will have
permitted all his fellows to become billionaires."

"On the contrary, we'll bless him."

"Surely not!"

Ali came back in, carrying a wooden box, which he set
down on the bouillotte table. The white rose abruptly shed the
rest of its petals, but neither Legrand nor Paul Duffaure inter-
preted that as an omen. Ali turned the commutator, and the
drawing room filled with light.

With his stiff fingers, the invalid tapped the box. "Gold!"
he announced.

The word resonated like the chime of a bell. All the joys
and dolors of the earth were in that syllable.

The Arab lifted the lid, and Duffaure, excited, looked inside.

At the bottom of the box he perceived blackish, spongy scoria, which seemed to him to be as devoid of value as iron slag.

"That's gold?" he said, disappointed.

The paralytic observed him ironically. "Yes, Monsieur, it is. It really is gold—my gold, as it emerges from the crucible after the formidable work of fire. Were you expecting to find twenty-franc coins in my box?"

"It's the color that surprises me," the young man admitted.

"Heat has naturally blackened the surface."

The journalist weighted one of the fragments in his hand. "Oh! How heavy it is..." He scratched it with his fingernail, without result. But someone had scratched the porous mass previously; Duffaure discovered a line of beautiful yellow gleams. From then on, he no longer doubted the nature of the metal.

"Keep it," said Legrand. "Pass it over a touchstone in order to convince yourself."

That demi-pauper was giving away gold, at least a hundred and fifty grams. It was so paradoxical that Duffaure wanted to refuse. He rummaged in the box.

"This one, then—it's not as big."

At the host's table, when the fruit-basket is passed, well brought up people always choose the smallest pear. They are, however, no better considered for that than those who take the largest.

"It's not a magnificent gift," said the invalid, with a disdain into which he put a certain affectation.

"A precious souvenir for me," protested Duffaure.

"You'll have difficulty selling that unstamped ingot..."

"I don't want to sell it, but to keep it."

"Political economists claim that wealth one keeps is worthless."

"I'll photograph it to illustrate my article," said Duffaure.

93

"Oh, that's true, you're going to publish an article," Legrand mocked. "Not too many scientific heresies, eh?"

"Have no fear," the other retorted. "True, good journalists almost all treat subjects about which they're ignorant, and make what they're saying comprehensible without understanding it themselves. Nevertheless, I need a few technical notes. Does the transmutation take a long time?"

"Only a few minutes—the time taken to bring the mass to the requisite temperature."

"And you obtain pure gold?"

"Yes…it only remains to melt it and strike coins."

"Thanks to you, then," Paul Duffaure joked, "France will perhaps be able to pay her debts."

"She won't have to pay them any longer, because they'll fall to zero. Creditors and debtors will be at the same point. That's my dream, Monsieur! Every louis in circulation is stained with blood. To obtain a few particles of precious metal, people are dying of cold and hunger; others have their throats cut. From now on, they'll have all the gold they want."

"It will be El Dorado."

The invalid's face took on a malevolent rictus. "Or Hell," he replied. "People will no longer kill one another in order to acquire wealth, but to be able to spend it usefully. That will be worse." Foraging in his hair, he changed his tone. "When will your article appear?"

"The day after tomorrow. I guarantee that it will be a success."

"As long as there isn't a crime of passion or a parliamentary scandal that day."

"That wouldn't be sufficient," Duffaure replied, cheerfully. "To push you into the background it would require a typhoon on the Basque coast, a volcanic eruption in the Auvergne or the assassination of the President of the Republic."

"Serous people will accuse you of lying…"

"I don't detest polemic."

"Are you ambitious, or paid by the line?"

The journalist opened and reclosed his mouth without breathing a word. Yes, he was ambitious, but he was still in the first manifestation of that virtue: vanity. His hair was wavy and styled; he ruined himself buying cravats and his shirt-front was false, but not very large; one might have thought that it was real, on condition of not biting it.

"After all, it's good to be ambitious," Legrand philosophized. "It permits one to remain young for longer than others. Unfortunately, my discovery will deal a rude blow to the greater number. Thanks to it, in fact, social inequalities will no longer exist. Everyone will be able to give his measure without being hindered by pecuniary cares. The deluded and the indecisive will suffer, but if you have the soul of a Caesar, I'm delivering Europe to you!"

That gift did not seem excessive to Paul Duffaure. He would have refused the direction of a modest factory, but would have willingly accepted a throne. Even kings think that, in order to lead people, it is useful not to know very much.

At that moment, a woman entered without knocking, with the bold step that one has in one's own home.

"My daughter," the invalid introduced her.

Mademoiselle Legrand murmured a "Pardon…," to which the journalist responded with an exceedingly worldly bow.

She was beautiful: brunette, with a mat complexion and immense eyes. A certain charm emanated from her person. She had a perfect mouth and an opulent bosom. Men are sensible to such adornments.

"Monsieur is a journalist," Legrand explained. "He's come from Paris to contemplate me at close range." He turned to the visitor. "I can't remember your name."

"Paul Duffaure," the other repeated, humiliated by that forgetfulness. He straightened his jacket with a swift gesture and stretched out his right leg, because he was rather proud of his socks. On principle, he always made the most of himself in the presence of woman. The tactic had already been worth a few benefits to him, but he was still waiting for a resounding victory, without knowing over what enemy.

Mademoiselle Legrand embraced her father placidly, picked up the rose petals, and did not cast the slightest glance at the irresistible sock.

"You know," the invalid continued, "I've let myself go...I'm divulging the secret of gold."

"Too bad," she said.

"Oh, Mademoiselle" protested Duffaure, with a sixteen-tooth smile. "Why too bad?"

"She's regretting her tranquility," sniggered Legrand.

"No, I'm regretting yours...."

There was an infinite tenderness in the young woman's voice. She raised her hand, full of petals, and breathed deeply of the perfume of the dead flower.

"Mademoiselle," commenced Paul Duffaure, with all the seduction of which he was capable, "don't exaggerate the annoyances of celebrity. I concede that it's sometimes aggravating, but it also reserves a few joys..."

"I have a horror of those joys," declared Mademoiselle Legrand.

"You'll see, Mademoiselle, you'll see...!

The young woman ceased sniffing the remains of the rose. "Papa," she said, "Rosita wants to know whether you want a steak or a cutlet."

The invalid laughed silently. "To be happy, it's necessary to restrict oneself to that preoccupation: steak or cutlet...what do you think, Ali?"

The Arab, still motionless behind the armchair, appeared to wake up from a dream, and replied gravely: "Cutlet."

"We demand cutlets!" cried Legrand. "Monsieur Duffaure, tell your readers, if they're anxious to know, that we adore mutton!"

II

Distractedly, Paul Duffaure allowed his gaze to wander. Everything was familiar to him: at his feet, the Rue Lafayette, which a whistling policeman was paralyzing continually; opposite, the fake mosque of Sacré-Coeur, springing like an enormous orange above the gray roofs; and in the foreground, an advertisement six stories high offering to the crowds an "exquisite complete aliment" with the sickening grimace of a wan infant. Nothing new. The only surprise might have been produced by the pedestrians, but seen from the rooftops, they resembled a family of black ants.

The journalist was content. In the article that he had just finished he believed that he had drawn an excellent portrait of the hunter of chimeras, the paralytic possessor of the greatest force in the world. The short piece, free of subjective considerations, did not contain Legrand's name; Duffaure preferred that a mystery should subsist, until further notice, around the identity of the alchemist.

"Not stupid enough to give his address to the mates!" he said, with satisfaction. "Every man for himself and the devil take the hindmost!"

His room was ripolined, like a clinic or a creamery. The bed was still unmade, and a pair of trousers lay on the mantelpiece. There was not a single trinket on the furniture, not a single engraving on the walls. Stuck in the frame of the mirror there was an envelope bearing the four words: *Last will and testament*—a simple desire to astonish visitors; the envelope only contained a blank sheet of paper.

Under the bedside table, two dumb-bells joined their cast-iron spheres, dusty enough to reveal that the reporter, committed to sportive doctrines, rarely put them into practice. On a neighboring bookshelf, the works of Paul Valéry were juxtaposed with those of Jack London and Ponson du Terrail.

Carefully, Paul Duffaure placed his interview in his pocket.

"This going to make an unholy row!" he said. And he went downstairs unhurriedly, ceasing to hum outside the concierge's lodge, because he had not paid his rent. Every time he crossed the threshold he bent his spine like a man crushed by destiny, going out in order to throw himself in the Seine.

But the concierge had eyes like a lynx. "Monsieur Duffaure" she shouted. "You need to think about me..."

The young man put on a taut and amiable smile. "Tomorrow, Madame Bouvet, tomorrow..."

"Without fail?" insisted the concierge.

"Without fail! I swear it!" And he murmured, vexed because there was a pretty chambermaid in the lodge: "Count on it, you old cow."

The *Echo*'s offices were near the Square Montholon, in a vast building with dirty windows. Pictures of current events retained idlers at the door. A short woman was insistently showing a photograph of Maisons-Lafitte to a debonair and myopic gentleman.

"Yes, dearie, there—the one whose mouth you can't see, that's me!"

Anselme Gellé, the founder of the *Echo*, had made a political newspaper of it at a time when it seemed to be in good taste to be a Republican, under the Second Empire. He had then edited a small paper in which advertisements of property for sale sat next to the leader attacking Badinguet.[7]

Eclipsed during the Terrible Year, it had reappeared in 1872, written, composed and printed by Anselme and his son Prosper. It was neither better or worse than the other dailies of the era, but, Gambetta having supported it, a few parliamentarians had involved themselves with it. Thanks to them, the

---

[7] Basinguet was an irreverent nickname bestowed on Napoléon III, allegedly because he had once escaped from prison, during the reign of Louis Philippe, with the aid of the identity papers of a painter of that name.

Gellés were soon doing good business—so good that by the time old Anselme was struck down in his office by a congestion, he had amassed a considerable fortune.

The role of the great press did not interest him. His newspaper did not reach the broad public; it was only addressed to slightly shady businessmen, always discreet and willing to pay to be talked about.

Prosper, succeeding his father, worked hard and played hard. He dealt in scandalous reportage and died suddenly, just when he was beginning to tint his moustache; an indigestion of truffles struck him down in his mistress' bedroom, from which he was mysteriously removed. He scarcely had time to stammer to his wife and son: "The banks and the oil companies...all the money comes from them..."

He had a magnificent funeral. Fortunately for the widow and little Jacques Gellé, the third in line, the *Echo* was now a solid paper. Its print-run and its influence scarcely buckled during the war. On his return from the front, Jacques put himself at the disposal of a few conquistadors, and served their interests as best he could. Without renouncing politics entirely, he reserved a large space for special information. He reduced the number of editors and increased that of reporters. He sent them to the Pole and the Equator, under water and into the air, to our allies and to Russia, among convicts and Academicians. Hot news became the sovereign in his house; he created prizes for anything and everything, opened competitions, spending considerable sums, sowing generously in order to reap abundantly.

The *Echo* proclaimed far and wide that it was the greatest French newspaper, and had almost become that. It was pleasant to read, and its feuilleton serials were good. Jacques had understood that honesty always ends up being more lucrative than dishonesty.

There are always idlers in the hall of a daily paper, especially in Paris, where half the population watches the other half work. The loafers were deciphering dispatches, or contemplating with an equal interest photographs of murderers and famous men.

Duffaure traversed the atrium rapidly, shouting "Bonjour, Celestin!" to the concierge clad in the uniform of a Balkan general. He did not hold the porter in particular esteem, but he thought he might impress two ladies who had paused near the threshold—who were so occupied with themselves that they did not turn their heads.

The editorial offices occupied three upper floors; the linotypes were on the ground floor and the rotary presses in the basement.

It was as busy as a beehive; in newspaper offices, everyone runs. The copy-sheets and proofs are transported at the gallop, although the saving of time is infinitesimal.

A stout bald man running toward an unknown destination bumped into Paul Duffaure.

"What! You!"

"Bonjour, Hiret."

They shook hands with a conventional cordiality that strangely resembled indifference.

"Where have you sprung from?" asked Hiret.

"The provinces."

"For the paper or personal?"

"Personal."

"I warn you as a friend, Peyrebrune's in a bad mood."

"He'll calm down."

The reporters of the *Echo* were dependent on Peyrebrune, the news editor, whom they feared while scorning his authority. Suffering from a stomach-ulcer, he had a difficult character and was not slow to sack those who did not please him.

Hiret offered his hand again. "I'm off to the Senate—see you."

Duffaure penetrated into the rotunda, where several people were smoking cigarettes. One of them exclaimed: "Finally, there you are!"

That was Peyrebrune: tall and thin, with a nose like a knife-blade.

"Here I am," Duffaure replied, phlegmatically.

"Come into my office. I need to talk to you."

The news editor's office was a lightless redoubt, scarcely lager than a telephone booth. Peyrebrune sat down, but left Duffaure standing. "Monsieur," he said, without preamble, "I'm not content."

Duffaure made a gesture indicating his total impotence to modify that unfortunate state of mind.

"You're taking things a little bit too easily. You left Paris without deigning to inform me."

"Only for forty-eight hours."

"Where were you?"

"Bordeaux."

"And what were you doing in Bordeaux?"

"Arranging some family matters."

"Serious matters, I suppose?"

Duffaure nodded his head. "Oh, very serious. An inheritance of which someone wanted to rob me. It's a matter of an old blind aunt who..."

"I beg you," Peyrebrune cut in, "not to tell me any absurd stories. I needed you, Monsieur, and you weren't there."

Duffaure's desolation attained the limits of despair. "I regret it infinitely."

"No, you don't regret it—but so much the worse for you, for it was a matter of an investigation in Poland. I've sent Maillet in your stead. He left yesterday."

Peyrebrune waited for a sign of regret, because such long-range assignments are fruitful. Duffaure, who knew better than anyone how to overestimate his traveling expenses, did not flinch.

"You don't have anything to say to me?" the editor demanded, with affected politeness.

"No, I won't keep you any longer."

Paul Duffaure returned to the rotunda, where the smokers were thickening the atmosphere. A short blond man who had

101

been trying for half an hour to balance on two legs of a chair, interrogated him laconically: "Reprimand?"

"Yes," said the reporter.

"Sacked?"

"No."

"I'll bet you were with a chick?"

"Can't hide anything from you," said Duffaure, sprawling on a divan. "Offer me a cigarette, then."

"Here, old chap."

Like the others, Duffaure breathed out torrents of smoke through his nostrils. He asked a question without addressing it to anyone in particular: "Is the Boss in Paris?"

No one replied immediately; then the short blond spoke: "The Boss doesn't exist. He's a myth. Anyway, the Boss has no defined role. The only interesting person is the cashier. Still, it's agreeable only to see him once a month..."

"Is Gellé here, yes or no?"

"No one knows."

Duffaure went away, little disposed to graze on syllogisms and paradoxes.

Intellectuals are the people most jealous of their prerogatives. At the *Echo*, hierarchical respect existed as in barracks. First the copy passed before the eyes of the sub-editors; they transmitted it to the deputy secretaries, who gave it to the secretary general. No one ever skipped any of the stages, on pain of seeing his article thrown pitilessly into the bin.

Now, Paul Duffaure wanted the Boss to be the first to read the Legrand interview. It was therefore necessary to go over Peyrebrune's head and those of the secretaries—and that was not easy.

Jacques Gellé seemed to be more difficult to reach than a minister. Three reception rooms full of solicitors flanked his office. If he did not have a fourth, for which there was no lack of demand, it was because the director of the *Echo* reserved himself the privilege of getting away when he was weary, or had somewhere else to be.

The clientele of a potentate of the press is varied. On the benches in the waiting-room, the influential politician rubs shoulders with the poor down-and-out. The latter often carries in his pocket a recommendation from the former. The cult of recommendations is still maintained, even though they hardly ever have any effect.

The unknown inventor, the man of letters, the presidents of ludicrous societies, strange courtiers and financiers suffering birth pangs watch one another and get impatient with one another, anxious to be received before a competitor who might perhaps make the same request. Their entrance is equally humble, their exit similarly triumphant. The punishment of liars is to believe the lies of others. They all go away with a blissful smile because they have been welcomed politely, listened to without flagrant irritation, and sent away with a kind word.

The sub-editors of the *Echo* went in through the fourth room, where the protocol was simplified. An usher transmitted the requests or an audience to a secretary charged with the supreme triage. That secretary, a little old man as jaundiced as a quince, had the skill of being deaf. As he knew all the questions interesting the paper from top to bottom, he only heard when he wanted to. He was the true master of the house; the general secretary and the editor-in-chief did not always succeed in vanquishing his Chinese impassivity.

"Thank you; I understand," he replied to them. "The Boss is sorry, but he can't spare you a single minute. I'll communicate his response...."

Sometimes, he unhooked a private telephone. "Hello! Monsieur Jacques, can you see Monsieur Someone-or-Other?"

The response was invariably favorable, because Gellé knew that his secretary would not disturb him for nothing.

The deaf man had just succeeded in solving a particularly difficult chess problem—his passion. He welcomed Paul Duffaure with an unusual affability and, five minutes later, Jacques Gellé's door opened before the reporter.

Jacques Gellé was one of those young men of whom it is said in France that they have "a British manner," and who do not exist on the other side of the Channel. Tall and thin, artificially stooped, he wore a sports-jacket—a ridiculous garment—admirably. There was no fault of taste in his attire. His trousers never had goiters at the knees, his shoes were never new and people resorted to base maneuvers to discover the address of his shirt-maker. He consecrated a great deal of time to his appearance, and almost too much money, but there was a reason for that. He estimated that dandyism without preciosity is a proof of intelligence and spiritual aristocracy.

An expert hairdresser curled his brown hair every morning. His face was prepared with care, close-shaven, massaged and powdered. His expression was immutably becoming, the gleam of his eyes—the brows cultivated with vaseline—was mild enough to permit him to wear a monocle. Jacques Gellé flattered himself on being a seducer, and did not disdain to go to some trouble for his humblest interlocutors.

"Bonjour, Plouvier," the Boss said, amiably. He claimed to know all his employees and invariably got their names wrong.

"I'm Duffaure," said the reporter.

"Oh, that's right! Plouvier's a big fellow with a full beard."

Plouvier was a short fat man, with no more hair than a billiard ball, but Duffaure acquiesced. "That's right, Boss."

"What do you desire, Duffaure?"

"To submit an article to you."

"I'll read it with pleasure..."

The Boss was about to bury the four sheets in a file; Duffaure stopped him.

"It's not a literary concern that motivates me. If I've come directly to you without informing my section chief, it's because my subject isn't banal."

"What is it about, then?"

"See for yourself—it isn't long."

Jacques Gellé scanned the article until the end, and then reread it slowly, in its entirety.

"Are you sure," he said, finally, "that your fellow isn't a con man?"

"Yes."

"Hmm. Your response is very clear."

"Because my conviction is firm."

The Boss wiped his monocle laboriously; that was the way in which he reflected.

"Has he shown you gold that he's made?"

Duffaure was only waiting for that question to place the scoria on the table. Jacques Gellé examined it curiously.

"Once, that was lead" said Duffaure. "Now it's gold."

The proprietor of the *Echo* smiled. "Perhaps it is, in fact, gold, but it's undoubtedly never been lead."

"Yes, Monsieur, it has. I haven't seen that gold emerge from the crucible, but I'm convinced that it really has been fabricated by my alchemist."

"You believe in miracles, then?"

"Like Saint Thomas."

Jacques Gellé meditated momentarily, his eyes glued to the piece of metal.

"If your story is true," he said, "it doesn't lack interest. What do you think we should do?"

"Whatever you wish."

The Boss stuck his thumbs in the armholes of his waist-coat, and beat an allegro march on his sternum.

"Do you have confidence in me?" he asked.

The reporter did not blink. "If I didn't have confidence, I wouldn't be here."

"Perfect," Jacques approved. "Is anyone else informed of the affair?"

"No one."

"What's the name of your extraordinary chemist?"

"René Legrand."

"Where does he live?"

"In Bordeaux."

"Can I see him?"

"I'm at your orders to take you to him."

"Well, we'll leave this evening."

"My valise is packed."

"I'll reserve two sleepers."

Duffaure was making as if to leave when Jacques called him back. "There's one thing I don't understand. You like wealth, don't you?"

"I think so," Duffaure replied.

"What do you mean, you think so?"

"I'm like the little woman who's never eaten truffles, and was asked whether she liked them."

Jacques deigned to smile, and said: "Legrand's discovery is equivalent to that of a gold deposit."

"A mine," Duffaure overbid.

"Then why not keep the secret to yourself?"

"Because Legrand, to begin with, needs a considerable investment of funds."

"Ah! Right...so my role will be that of a shareholder?"

"Probably." And Paul Duffaure went on, cynically: "A shareholder has a thousand legal—which is to say honest—ways of despoiling an inventor. If we steal Legrand's idea without having signed a contract in advance, we might not escape the criticism of fastidious individuals..."

"Well," said Gellé, "you don't lack judgment, my friend. But it's not necessary for my colleagues in the great press to hear about it. In order to exploit your gold mine, I'll constitute an anonymous company..."

"Of which you'll be the sole shareholder," Duffaure completed.

"Not at all. It'll bring a few friends into it, including a banker and a director of a telegraph agency."

"The three kings of France, eh?"

"Let's say the three consuls," said Gellé, modestly. "Until this evening, then."

"One more word. My Legrand is a visionary. He has no intention of enriching himself. He wants to divulge his secret so that everyone can profit from it."

The face of the *Echo*'s proprietor darkened. "Damn! We'll have to make him change his mind. Will we be able to do that?"

"I hope so."

"Then let's take our chances," Jacques concluded. "First, I want to submit this ingot to scientific examination."

"A goldsmith would suffice."

"No, no...a goldsmith would undoubtedly be intrigued by this bizarre mass of gold, while a scientist, from the Conservatoire des Arts et Métiers, for instance, will only have a purely scientific curiosity. We'll know the results of the scientific analysis when we get back."

"And if we've made the journey for nothing?"

"We'll still have had the pleasure of drinking a few bottles of Haut-Bailly or Evangile at the Chapon Fin."

Paul Duffaure withdrew, satisfied.

The deaf man observed as he passed by: "You seem content."

"I'm delighted."

"Has your salary been increased?"

"Better than that. I've been given a fine mission."

"What?"

"Exhuming the treasures of Golconda."

"Joker!" snickered the old secretary—and added, when he was alone: "Idiot!"

III

Armandine Villaret was no longer young, although she was obstinate in not wanting to be old. Her slimness had become thinness, two wrinkles issuing from her nose put her mouth in parentheses and her swan's neck was more like a chicken's. Perhaps she had once been charming, but she possessed none of what are conventionally called the remains of beauty.

When she lowered the hand mirror she was abusing, blue veins showed at her wrists: large veins that had surged forth like caterpillars. The hammer of maturity was striking her boldly-oxygenated temples. Since the fashion for short hair had come in she had shaved her nape, better to display the silk of her spine.

Armandine fabricated orthopedic girdles. She was good and sentimental, which do not always go together. She contemplated all men with affection; she was proud to be thought virtuous, and suffered obscurely therefrom.

In her spare time she knitted those frightful, humiliating sweaters in impossible colors in which little vagabonds are decked out and make them experience from infancy onwards a hatred of charitable people.

A friend of the late Madame Legrand, who had died in childbirth, she had served as a mother to Jeanne: an inexperienced, maladroit and lyrical mother, but affectionate and full of good will.

Every evening, the widower, then a teacher in a free school, found her singing a superfluous ballad to send the milk-gorged child to sleep. They were obliged to talk to one another about the deceased, and, while chanting the litany of regrets, they came to the natural conclusion. One rainy evening, they made love. Armandine succumbed, murmuring: "If poor Emilie can see us from on high, she knows that it's for her that I'm consenting. I don't want another woman coming in here..."

And the portrait of the deceased was ornamented with seasonal flowers.

Legrand did not experience a wild passion for Armandine, but she was pleasant and never left a hole in his socks undarned. Habit riveted them together. Wounded, he did not even think that she might abandon him. She did not think of it either, and passed from the rank of mistress to that of lady companion without the slightest sexual torment.

No one in the neighborhood was unaware of her former relations with Legrand, but it did not shock anyone. It is necessary that a woman should be someone's mistress; one always has time to reproach her in case of a rupture.

Armandine lived in the Rue Denise, an old artery bestrode by vaulted houses, and as black as a cannon-barrel. It was a few steps from the Legrand house, where she spent three-quarters of her days and her evenings. She had a key giving her free access to the apartment, and even if she had already come in ten times since the morning she always shouted: "Rosita, it's me!" from the antechamber.

Legrand, whose infirmity rendered him increasingly nervous, was often disagreeable. Armandine accepted his fits of anger with an indulgence that exasperated him. When the paralytic abused her too much, she went into the kitchen to weep, where the maid did her best to console her.

"You know that he's not wicked, poor thing. It's his bad legs that go to his head..."

Out of instinctive respect for Jeanne, they always called one another Madame Villaret and Monsieur Legrand. However, nothing in the young woman's attitude indicated that she was offended by her father's liaison. Everyone observed a tacit silence on the subject that had lasted for twenty years.

That Saturday, Madame Villaret, fully occupied with lunch, was presiding over the cooking of a guinea-fowl on a bed of potatoes. At every minute she scrutinized the bluish mystery of the gas oven. Rosita was patiently whipping the mayonnaise she was going to serve with a crab salad that was in the process of cooling in the sink.

"This morning," moaned Armandine, "he threatened me with going away. He'd be capable of doing it."

"He's been in a filthy mood for days," sighed the maid. "I don't know what's the matter with him..."

What had annoyed Legrand, only he knew. It was the unacknowledged irritation of never finding his interview in the *Echo*.

Madame Villaret raised her eyes to the heavens. "It's necessary to forgive him. It's not cheerful to spend one's life in an armchair and be a kind of living dead man."

"Bah!" said Rosita. "He's no more unfortunate for that. When I suffer from my varicose veins I'd be well content to sit down all the time..."

Madame Villaret uttered a cry; she had burned herself taking out the dripping-pan.

"He, who was so active, so restless once..."

"He'd have a better character without his tricks. It's not good to shut himself up like that in a hot wine-store. Oh, I wouldn't want to be in Ali's shoes."

"Ali's interested in his work..."

"Rosita corrected, in a low voice: "In his stupidities..."

Madame Villaret did not admit that term. "They're not stupidities, Rosita. Monsieur Legrand is a scientist—you can see that journalists are beginning to take an interest in him. It's a sign, that!"

The stout girl planted her fists on her hips. "Perhaps you believe that he really can make gold?"

"I won't go that for," Armandine replied, prudently, "but he's obtained curious results..."

Rosita plunged her spoon back in her bowl and whipped the mayonnaise with renewed energy. "Get away! Nonsense, nothing more! He could be happy in his misfortune. Eat, drink and sleep, that's all he needs to do..."

Madame Villaret's gaze as charged with scorn. "You only like the animal life..."

"And I'm right! Yes, eating, drinking and sleeping, there's nothing better."

"What about sentiment?"

"That doesn't exist," declared the maid, firmly.

"Speak for yourself," murmured Madame Villaret, suddenly feeling weary. "I'm afraid the guinea-fowl's going to be tough."

Rosita's spoon rapped the faience. "No, it doesn't exist," she repeated, with a muted fury. "I've never wanted to marry, me."

"You might have made a man happy, though."

"But the man might have made me despair. First, he would have cheated on me..."

"That's not certain," simpered Madame Villaret. "There are wives who've never been deceived..."

"Oh la la!" grunted Rosita. "I've been young and pretty like everyone else. I had a sergeant-major, a very distinguished fellow, who had magnificent handwriting. Not only did he eat me out of house and home but he took money from me. Well, he dumped me for a canteen slut..." She exhaled, in a tender sigh: "Oh, the swine..."

"All men don't have that mentality," said Madame Villaret.

"The best of them isn't worth the rope to hang him with."

"That's your opinion, but you're wrong to give it to Jeanne all the time."

"Why?"

"She doesn't idolize her fiancé already. She's marrying more for the sake of reason..."

The sergeant-major's victim decreed, solemnly: "To marry for the sake of reason is folly."

The doorbell rang. It was Raoul Gastal, Jeanne's fiancé. He was arriving, as usual, with a rum baba and two flowers in the bottom of an immense cornet.

A cashier in a large department store, Gastal, thanks to his talent, was assured of a brilliant future. One day, when he was about fifty, he would be the deputy, or even the chief, of the accounting department, with a listening post and lots of big red-bound ledgers.

"People don't realize," he said to Madame Villaret, "how arduous it is to hand out the money on pay day. The clients will have you sacked over ten sous in no time. It's necessary to have a very well-organized head."

He had met Jeanne at the dental clinic, one day when he had made the decision to have a premolar crowned in gold, simply to improve his smile—because, he affirmed, it didn't inconvenience him while eating.

From the start, he had found Jeanne beautiful in her while blouse. He liked women a lot, in the flesh, and abundant bosoms troubled him.

Head back and mouth open, he had contemplated her obliquely, with admiration.

"Am I hurting you?" she asked.

He always replied "Ho…! Ho…! Ho…!" That was practically all that he could say. His stoicism was a mark of love, but Jeanne remained impassive. The majority of her patients paid court to her, and those who had the worst dentition were the most audacious. Men could not imagine that they might disgust women.

After many smiles and a few timid pressures of the hand, Gastal dared to bring Jeanne a few carnations, which Jeanne accepted without apparent surprise.

"It's the last session," she said to him, one day.

"Oh, it's today that…?"

"Yes."

He would have liked to devastate his jaws and order a bridge. He preferred to wait for Jeanne on the sidewalk and request the honor of accompanying her. Having anticipated everything, he was holding an umbrella under his arm, to offer her in case of a downpour, but the weather was splendid.

Jeanne consented gravely—or perhaps coldly. During the journey, she remained so placid that her amorous swain could hardly pronounce ten words. He sought poetic phrases in anguish, and fell silent in bewilderment.

In the corner of the Cours de la Martinique, she smiled at him rather politely.

"See you," she said.

"When…? When…?" he stammered.

She looked at him tranquilly. "I don't know…whenever you wish."

His throat dry, he mumbled: "Tomorrow, all right? Tomorrow? Permit me to come back tomorrow!"

One might have thought that his life depended on that favor. A furtive blush covered the beautiful motionless face.

"If you like," she acquiesced. And, without leaving him time to express his gratitude, she went in.

"Thank you!" said Gastal.

That *thank you* was received with astonishment by an aged gentlemen of honorable appearance, who happened to be passing.

Gastal installed himself in his happiness like an Englishman in a train. And it was a strange engagement, that of two individuals who never mentioned love.

Until September, they limited themselves to exchanging reflections on the cost of living, the difficulty of renting an empty apartment and new books. Then, as the evenings were drawing in, the cashier thought to himself: *Next time, I'm going to kiss her*.

Before quitting one another, they remained face to face, close together, for several minutes. Jeanne waited; he did not make up his mind. Finally, he abstained from smoking for a whole afternoon, filled his mouth with mints, and their lips met…

"Tomorrow," she said, as she detached herself, "I'll introduce you to Papa."

"Certainly!" he exclaimed. And he gave her another kiss. His audacity was increasing in frightful proportions. He tried to take her hands with an awkward gesture.

"Shh!" she said. "Until tomorrow…"

Legrand welcomed his future son-in-law with curiosity, and then did not hide his disappointment. He had dreamed of something better. He did not understand why his daughter, intelligent and delicate, was linking herself with a young man who took pride in holding the record for the speed of addition.

"Why have you chosen him?" he asked. "He isn't handsome..."

"Or ugly," added Jeanne, without departing from her phlegm.

"He isn't rich..."

"He earns a comfortable living."

"Do you love him?"

"Don't worry about that."

"It's necessary to love one's spouse, damn it!"

"Well then, I'll love him."

She never revealed what she was thinking, even to her father. Legrand, weary of questioning her, contented himself with exercising his wit at Raoul Gastal's expense. The latter did not take offense at any mockery; he had been immutably blissful since the fixing of the marriage date. The "ceremony," as he put it, was to take place at the end of the year.

"One could perhaps have set it sooner," he declared, in confidence, to Madame Villaret, "but what's the point in hurrying? For the linen, we'll take advantage of the sales."

He lay in wait for "bargains" at his store, and heaped up, at the hazard of weekly discounts, a host of various articles.

"Isn't Jeanne here yet?" the young man asked, handing over his rum baba.

"She hasn't arrived," replied Madame Villaret.

Gastal seemed perplexed. "Well! That's odd..."

"Doubtless a client has delayed her."

"No, she's no longer at the clinic."

"She must have gone on an errand, then. What time is it?"

"Half past twelve."

"She won't be long. Excuse me, I have to turn my guinea-fowl over."

"Unwrap the baba, please. The rum will run..."

"Yes, I'll go unwrap it."

He remained alone in the drawing room, drumming on the window. Jeanne's absence disconcerted him; a confused jealousy was fermenting within him. He knew in advance that his fiancée would not give him any explanation.

"That will change!" he said to himself. "That will change."

The minutes went by. Gastal, unhappy, with nothing to do, stood in front of the mirror. Taking a small comb from his pocket, he disciplined the hair on top of his head, which was manifesting whims of independence. Then he pulled two or three faces and turned round swiftly, because he thought he had heard the door open.

The photographs retained him. Often, in the course of similar waits, he sought in the features of the chubby baby those of the present Jeanne.

Jeanne vaguely resembled her mother, the tennis player fixed by the snapshot in an abnormal leap. According to Armandine, Madame Legrand had been an impetuous and robust creature. She adored sports and had met her husband on a rugby field—for Legrand, now tragically inert, had appreciated the joy of Sundays squandered disputing an inflated bladder with lunatics.

Finally, Jeanne appeared, bare-headed.

"Bonjour," she said, simply.

"Bonjour, Jeanne..."

He examined her from head to toe without seeing anything suspicious.

"I went to look for you just now," he remarked.

"Oh?"

That was all. She bent down to caress a gray tomcat that was purring at her feet.

Gastal persisted: "You'd gone?"

"Yes."

She lay the cat's had in the crook of her arm and coddled it maternally.

"Where were you?" Gastal asked.

She observed, in a tone devoid of impatience, but in a one that brooked no reply: "I've never permitted you to subject me to such an interrogation."

Gastal did not persist. When he kissed her he thought he scented a slight odor of oriental tobacco, but he carefully refrained from saying so.

Jeanne headed for the kitchen, the door of which she opened slightly.

"I'm dying of hunger. When are we eating?"

"Right away!" replied Madame Villaret. "The guinea-fowl's done."

Jeanne addressed her fiancé. "Gastal, go tell Papa."

The young man went down, feeling melancholy. When she was in a good mood she called him Raoul; when he was in disgrace, she called him Gastal. He was very sensitive to that difference. On the stairs, he repeated, while clenching his inoffensive fists: "That will change! That will change!"

But he knew that nothing would change, because he felt incapable of imposing his authority.

At the end of a dark and oozing corridor a rather large courtyard extended, on to which opened the cooperage of a wine warehouse occupying the ground floor of the house. Staved-in casks were rotting there, and barrel-hoops were entangled. In one corner, a large 100 was ingenuously painted ornamented a sentry-box.[8] A white almost-new shed was backed up against the back wall. Four electric cables of unusual cross-section descended vertically there. Under the panel that supported them a spiked fame had been nailed, and an enameled plaque gearing the inscription: *Do not touch the wires. Mortal danger.*

Gastal knocked.

"What?" said the hoarse voice of the invalid.

---

[8] The number 100 was often employed in provincial France as an alternative label to W.C., probably not unconnected with the English usage of the term "loo."

"It's me," said the young man, stupidly.

Without amenity, Legrand retorted "Who's *me*?"

"Gastal, Lunch is ready."

"Just a minute!"

The minute lasted a long time. Gastal moped in the courtyard. On the third floor, two children were looking down at him, laughing, and that annoyed him. Finally, the taciturn Ali appeared.

The shed where René Legrand was working was only a laboratory by usage. It had no floor, just flattened earth. On the wall there was a marble slab with handles and latches. Scoria with bronze gleams crackled underfoot. The shelves were crammed with jars with numerous protrusions and pots marked with cabalistic formulae. A delicate precision balance sparkled under its glass dome. Formularies were scattered everywhere. But the principal fitment was an electric furnace in perfect condition, at the foot of which lay sticks of charcoal and magnesium crucibles.

The invalid, perched on a high chair made of broken rattan was rubbing out equations on a blackboard.

"How are you?" he said, without offering his hand to his future son-in-law.

"Very well," replied Gastal. "And you?"

"Much better. Let's go, Ali. It's necessary to feed the beast."

The Arab hoisted Legrand on to his back as he might have done a child.

"Let's go," said the paralytic.

His dead legs swung at every step the porter took. He spoke to Gastal over his shoulder. "And your figures? Still well-aligned? No insurrections in the columns of the Big Book?"

The young man was used to such mockery.

"My figures are behaving irreproachably."

"Big Book," Legrand went on. "You put a capital letter on each word, don't you?"

"That's the custom."

117

"Gently, Ali, you're hurting me old man..." He blasphemed into the Arab's neck. "Damnation! How stupid it is not to be able to walk like any imbecile!"

There was something grotesque and pitiful about that climb up the stairs. Ali bumped into the steps and began to pant. Gastal, who was coming up last, was thinking, with the obstinacy of weak minds: *Where had she come from? Oh, but that will change! Yes, that will change!*

Kitchen smells were floating in the dining room. Under the tablecloth, the table displayed legs like those of an excessively thin woman.

Madame Villaret had folded the napkins into bishop's miters, except for Legrand's, which spread out in a superb fan. Roundels of sausage and gray shrimp filled two dishes. The butter was too yellow.

"Sit down, quickly!" begged Madame Villaret. "My guinea-fowl's drying out..."

From the start of the meal, Legrand was peevish, in search of an argument. As his mistress was looking at him insistently, be snapped at her: "Would you like my photo?"

Ready to weep, she lowered her nose over her plate.

Then he turned against Ali, who was serving too slowly for his liking. "Hurry up, then! Do you think I'm going to stay at table until this evening? I'm not a glutton like..." He stopped, on the point of naming Gastal. "Like so many others!" he finished, instead. And without transition: "There's nothing in this morning's *Echo* again?"

"It's astonishing," murmured Madame Villaret.

The invalid foraged in his gray hair.

"Astonishing, astonishing...no, it's not astonishing. That good-for-noting couldn't take me seriously. Think about it! How could he believe in a poor wretch crouching in a hovel?"

"Thanks for the hovel!" protested Rosita, from the next room.

"All right, a pig-sty! The ceiling's falling in, the parquet's buckling, the plaster's blistering. Oh, if I had money...I fabricate gold and I don't have a sou. What a joke! At present, I lack lead, charcoal, crucibles..."

Until then, Jeanne had not said a word. She interjected, softly: "I'll buy them, Papa..."

He looked at her with a suddenly tender gaze.

"I know, I know...you'll deprive yourself again, for me. It's six months now that you've been wearing the same dress."

"It's still perfectly all right..."

"Certainly!" affirmed Gastal, with base complaisance. "Anyway, next Monday we have a kasha coupon sale.[9]"

But Legrand was pursuing his own agenda: "I need radium! Oh, poverty...!"

He thrust his fists forward. "Society will pay me back a hundredfold! I'll turn it upside-down and destroy it like an ant-colony!"

"Monsieur Legrand," said Madame Villaret, indulgently, "Leave society tranquil and eat your guinea-hen wing."

He muttered between his teeth: "Guinea-hen yourself!" And pushing away his late angrily: "I'll leave my share for the cat."

"No, it's me who'll eat it," said Rosita.

"Oh, you...eat, drink and sleep!"

The fat maid was in a combative mood that day. "For sure!" she said. "It's better than your silliness."

"My silliness?" exclaimed Legrand, suffocating. "I'll throw you out."

"I wouldn't expect anything else from you."

"Shut up! I order you to shut up!"

"If the good God gave me a tongue it's to make use of it..."

But the other protested. What as the point of getting upset? Why not have lunch tranquilly? Once again, Madame Villaret recommended the guinea-fowl.

---

[9] Kasha is a satiny fabric, nowadays used mostly for upholstery and lining garments, but used for a wider range of purposes in the 1930s.

"It's admirable," said Gastal, ever servile. Out of discretion, he had only served himself the head and neck, affirming that he adored those tidbits.

"That's all right," muttered Legrand. "Since you're all against me, I'll shut up."

No one was unduly troubled, because the invalid's commensals were accustomed to his violence. Nevertheless, it required a few minutes for the conversation to recover a normal tone. As usual, it was limited to a dialogue between Madame Villaret and Gastal. And they spoke, in accordance with the ritual, about the economic crisis and the latest railway accident—which is to say, that day's.

Suddenly, the doorbell rang. Everyone looked at one another in surprise.

Rosita slipped into the dining room. "Someone's ringing!" she whispered, mysteriously.

"Yes," said Madame Villaret, stifling her voice. "Someone's ringing!"

"Shall I open the door?" asked Rosita.

"Naturally, blockhead!"

Legrand's exclamation chased her away at a gallop. She reappeared a few seconds later.

"It's the reporter from the other day," she announced, almost scornfully.

Legrand ruffled his hair. "Paul Duffaure?"

"It seems to me that that's the one," the maid said, negligently. "He's in the drawing room with another gentleman."

"What other gentleman?"

"I don't know. What should I say to them?"

"Nothing—I'm coming. Ali, push me."

"What about the baba?" asked Gastal.

"And the coffee?" groaned Madame Villaret.

Legrand withered them with his gaze. "Peace, eh?"

The armchair rolled over the parquet.

Paul Duffaure's companion was Jacques Gellé, who bowed graciously to the invalid. "Monsieur," he said, with exquisite urbanity, "may I introduce myself? Jacques Gellé, director and proprietor of the *Echo*. Forgive my intrusion, but what my collaborator has revealed to me impassioned me so much that I wanted to see you as soon as possible."

That preamble flattered Legrand. "Well, Monsieur, you see me. I'm not, alas, a specimen of euthanasia..."

Gellé made a gesture devoid of meaning. He appreciated that theatrical entrance esthetically: the tall Arab impassive behind the paralytic with the unruly hair.

Duffaure extended his hand to Legrand. "What did you think when you didn't see my article?"

"Nothing," the invalid lied. "I never read the newspapers." And he bit his lip, because a copy of the *Echo* was sticking out of his pocket.

"The article will appear," Gellé said, "but before publishing it, I wanted to confer with you..."

"Oh!" said Legrand, simply. He frowned, and Gellé already felt that he was on the defensive. Suspicion is always exacerbated among the sick; it is as if they possess a sixth sense to put them to guard against those who wish to dupe them.

The director of the *Echo* was untroubled. "I confess," he said, "that at first I doubted your discovery."

"That doesn't astonish me," replied the invalid, pulling up his plaid to keep him warm. "Once, they nearly burned Galileo, and Le Bon could never make France understand the utility of gas lighting."

Jacques Gellé wiped his lips with a dainty silk handkerchief that he took from his pocket. "Now, I no longer doubt. I know that you can fabricate pure gold. Monsieur, you're going to turn the world upside down."

"I only live for that," replied Legrand, with a smile of satisfaction.

Gellé took note of that relaxation and continued: "If I've understood what Duffaure has reported to me, you don't want to obtain any personal profit from this affair?"

"None!" proclaimed Legrand.

"You're right," Gellé approved.

Duffaure looked at his Boss with astonishment, but the young man seemed sincerely in agreement with the alchemist's idea.

"Pasteur didn't exploit the anti-rabies serum commercially," he said. "His glory is no less great for that."

Glad of that kind of approval, René Legrand became excited. "True seekers are disinterested. Didn't Sauvage, the inventor of the helical propeller, die in poverty?[10] What was the fortune of Ader, the first man to fly?[11] What was that of Branly, Curie and so many others? Personally, I want to give away my formula gratuitously. It will be the most formidable joke of all the centuries. Everyone will know how to get rich..."

"And that way," Gellé completed, "everyone will become poor."

"Exactly!" cried the invalid, stirred by a malevolent joy. "The consequences of the transmutation of lead are incalculable. It's the collapse of our hideous financial systems, the tragic denouement of the comedy of exchanges, the collapse of all bankers' fortunes..." He shook his hair like a mane. "I'm suppressing the old society, Monsieur! I'm overturning the whole present regime. A regression will result that it's impossible for me to measure exactly, and a great deal of suffering..."

"Unmerited, for the most part," Gellé noted, in passing.

"Agreed," conceded the invalid, after a brief silence, "but they won't be more iniquitous than those we've always endured."

---

[10] Frédéric Sauvage (1786-1857) demonstrated the helical propeller in 1832 but failed to interest the Navy in it and went bankrupt trying to develop it on his own, ending up in debtor's prison.

[11] Clément Ader (1841-1925), who made a short flight in 1890, did persuade the French army to fund his research for a while, but they withdrew funding after the failure of the first test-flight of his *Avion III* in 1897, perhaps too soon.

"The value of monetary units falling to zero, we'll return to barter," said Gellé.

"Undoubtedly. It won't be comfortable, but very amusing. An entire education to undergo! Once again, peoples will stutter, but I hope that, armed by the deplorable experience of the squandered centuries, they'll be able to construct a solid social edifice. Good architects will surely be found!"

Paul Duffaure wanted to put in a word: "You think that will be easy?"

"I don't care about that!" riposted the invalid. "My fellows need to be shaken out of their torpor. I'll take charge of giving them a few worries! It's high time to react! Guglielmo Ferrero has summarized in his discourse on the deaf the history of the civilized world..."[12]

And he quoted from memory:

"'Humans have two means of enjoying abundance, either being content with less than they have or procuring more than they desire; either by reducing their needs or augmenting their wealth. All civilizations anterior to the French Revolution employed the first means; for a century, occidental civilization has employed the second...'"

He meditated momentarily on that prodigiously simple analysis.

"I'm sure," Legrand went on, "that I shall teach all the street-urchins who believe themselves to be men to be content with less than they have. I shall rid them of the preoccupation that they wrongly qualify as imperious: class struggle. It's time to get back to a sane comprehension of communal life.

---

[12] The Italian liberal historian Guglielmo Ferrero (1871-1942) is best-known for his five-volume history of Rome, but the present reference is to the "epistle to the Americans" he produced following the end of the Great War, translated into English as *Problems of Peace, from the Holy Alliance to the League of Nations* (1919). When Pujol wrote the present novel Ferrero had recently accepted exile after four years of house arrest by the Fascist regime in Italy.

Messieurs, repeat to all the echoes the prophetic phrases that I am about to read to you, and which ought to be posted everywhere instead of the imbecile speeches of our parliamentarians."

He took from his pocket a piece of paper in a poor state and declaimed pompously:

"The people of today accuse the rich of being insatiable. That is true. But if the rich were not prey to the desire to augment their fortune indefinitely, would they spare a part of their income every year to manufacture and activate new machines?

"The rich accuse the people of never being content, of wanting more the more they have, of aspiring to all the ease and luxury of the rich. But if the masses were to content themselves with living as of old, poorly and simply, where would the clientele be that enables industry and commerce to prosper?

"It is in vain that the rich and poor accuse one another reciprocally of being tyrants. There is at present in occidental civilization only one tyrant, but it is pitiless. It is the innumerable population of giants of iron and steel, moved by fire, that force us all to work and feast without respite, whether we like it or not, because, if the rich, the middle class and the masses wanted to live more simply, the great world machine would stop. All of us suffer from that tyranny; no one can deliver himself from it. That is why everyone is angry with his neighbor."

Jacques Gellé listened, slightly gripped and slightly mocking. Behind Legrand, the impassive Arab, perhaps not understanding, maintained his hieratic immobility. As for Paul Duffaure, he wondered what his Boss was trying to achieve.

"People are demanding reforms?" Legrand added. "The opportunity is favorable to make them!"

"If I'm not mistaken," said the director of the *Echo*, "you hope for the extinction of poverty?"

Legrand plunged his fingers into his hair yet again.

"I'm not a demagogue! I'm attempting a terrible experiment, whose result I can't predict in any precise fashion. Society is badly made, it is going the wrong way; I am casting it down. What will become of it after the fall? We'll be in the front row to see. After all, the spectacle will be as good as any other..."

"The peasants," said Paul Duffaure, "will doubtless be the masters of the situation. It will be the reign of the producers..."

Legrand did not let him continue. "Not for long, for the intellectuals will be the first to preach the abolition of property rights."

"That will be frightful," sighed Jacques Gellé, tranquilly, adjusting his monocle. "But, collectivist or not, people will still be obliged to constitute a monetary medium of exchange."

"Work orders, perhaps. Or perhaps something new will be found. Are you an anglophile, Monsieur?"

"Not excessively," Gellé confessed. "But the English dress irreproachably; that's why I don't detest them too much."

"Well, I'm far from working for the prosperity of England. The countries that live on trade will fall to the lowest rank. And why? Because a little man broken by the war had realized the dream of Nicolas Flamel."

Someone knocked discreetly.

"Come in!" shouted the invalid.

Madame Villaret appeared, with a humble smile on her face and a cup in her hand.

"The coffee is going cold," she murmured, to justify her intrusion. And she bowed ceremoniously to the visitors. "Excuse me, Messieurs…it's because of the coffee…"

"I see," said Legrand, without getting carried away. "All three of you are dying of curiosity. Jeanne! Gastal! Come in, my children. Monsieur Gellé, you're disturbing the whole family. Mine are astonished and alarmed, because for them, I'm not so much a prophet as a wretch who plays at alchemy as children play skittles…"

And he made the introductions. Madame Villaret brought in a tantalus whose pretentious goblets resembled the cartridges of 37mm shells, and offered curaçao. Jacques Gellé found Jeanne very beautiful and Gastal insignificant.

"Now shut up," said the invalid, to cut short Madame Villaret's compliments. "Where were we, Monsieur?"

"I was listening to you with interest," said Gellé, without ceasing to look at Jeanne with a calm effrontery. "You were talking about the imminent suppression of currencies..."

"Oh yes...for too long, currencies have been circulating. Holy Writ already mentions the number of shekels that Jacob paid for his field. The first coins doubtless originated in Asia before the *gerahs* ornamented with *gomor* that were the first measure of cereals..."[13]

"Monsieur Legrand knows a great many things," Madame Villaret whispered confidentially to Paul Duffaure.

"Enough!" Legrand cut in. "I know what I need to know."

"You're erudite," declared Gastal, his hand on his heart.

The invalid struck the arm of his chair. "You too, enough! An hour of reading would have taught you, as it did me, that although the Greek Amyntas struck money officially and circulated coins on which the head of an ox recalled the unit of barter, the first serious, scientific striking only goes back 289 years before Christ, and that it was a century later that gold coins were born."

"That's not yesterday," murmured Gastal.

"Enough!" retorted Legrand again, raising his voice. "If you interrupt me again I'll send you back to the dining room!"

The accountant sighed, humbly and resignedly, and shut up.

---

[13] The *gerah* and the *gomor* are among the early coins cited in the 1774 *Encyclopédie*'s article on "*Monnaie*" [Money]. The *gerah*, or obol, is there alleged to be the value of sixteen grains of barley. Legrand appears to be taking all his information about the history of money from that article, or a later derivative thereof.

Legrand gave a ten minute lecture on money, listening to himself talk complaisantly.

"Now," said Jacques Gellé, without giving the slightest sign of impatience, "it's my turn to specify the object of my visit. Duffaure has told me that you're a trifle embarrassed in the continuation of your work?"

"There's nothing paradoxical about that. I'm so poorly equipped that my production costs are considerable. With improved equipment, the ratio of cost to return could be reduced in a proportion of ten to one."

"Do you think that your invention could be industrialized?" asked the director of the *Echo*.

"Certainly. In any case, fundamentally, I haven't invented anything. All the modern alchemists know my method. They know that orpiment favors the transmutation of silver in the electric furnace. There's no sorcery in that..."

"But they've only ever obtained infinitesimal quantities of gold," Gellé observed. "There's only ever been mention of traces of precious metal."

"Agreed, but the principle is sound. I've simply worked on the dosimetry. With the tenacity of a Benedictine, I've calculated the proportions. I've carried out thousands of experiments without discouragement. I've replaced silver with more fusible lead, modified the Clerc-Minet furnace, and finally, involved radium in certain conditions."

"You have radium, then?" asked Gellé.

"The director of the Hôpital Saint-André confided a milligram to me. I wasn't able to keep it for long, because the cancerous are legion..."

"How much money do you need?" asked Gellé, bluntly.

Legrand's eyes sparkled with naïve covetousness. His fleshless index finger pointed toward his interlocutor. "You?" he stammered. "You'll furnish me the funds?"

"I'm at your disposal," said Gellé. "Like you, but for other motives, I hate society..."

"Impossible!" exclaimed Madame Villaret, putting her hands together. "Monsieur doesn't have the appearance of a revolutionary..."

The invalid was so emotional that he did not rebuke his old friend. She was surprised by that.

"Then...? Really...? You'll give me...?"

"All that you wish. Open cash-box."

The invalid scratched his head. "And if I accepted...what would become of my liberty?"

"It would remain entire. I'm not an exploiter. I'll commence by giving you a small provision...a check made out to the bearer..."

He opened his check-cook, slowly uncapped his fountain-pen, and began to write. The silence was so complete that the scratch of the pen was audible. Only Ali was disinterested in the events that were unfolding around him. Gellé shook the check to dry the ink.

"Please accept this..."

Legrand seized the piece of paper, which trembled between his bony fingers.

"Fifty thousand francs!" he exclaimed.

"Oh Lord!" exhaled Madame Villaret.

Two tears ran down the invalid's pale cheeks. In spite of her calmness, Jeanne had gone pale.

"Above all," Gellé said, "don't economize. You'll have as much money as you need."

"Monsieur," said Legrand, mopping his brow, moist with sweat, "what are you asking from me in exchange for this sum?"

"Nothing," said Gellé.

"But...?"

"Spend without remorse. I repeat to you that this is only an initial payment. To facilitate your work, I'll send you radium myself, and I'll have a factory built on the plans that you furnish."

"A factory!" repeated Legrand, amazed. "I'll have a factory?"

128

"In a few weeks," Gellé specified.

The director of the *Echo* had a sense of theatrical effect. He had nothing more to add, and stood up immediately. "Now, I've importuned you sufficiently. *Au revoir*."

The invalid did not sketch a gesture to retain him.

"Already?" deplored Gastal, his hand on the doorknob.

"I shall see Monsieur Legrand again tomorrow."

"You'll surely take another drop of curaçao?" offered the flustered Madame Villaret, shifting bottles and glasses.

"No thank you, Madame…I never drink alcohol."

"Me neither," added Paul Duffaure.

Rapidly, Gellé bowed and left, with the reporter, before the others had recovered from their bewilderment.

"Excellent sortie!" he joked, on the somber stairway. "Good theater!"

"Indeed," agreed Duffaure. "You've certainly put yourself in view."

They found themselves back on the quay in the disorder of the end of the day. The laborers were sauntering away in dense groups, along with the warehousemen with their bags, in which their meal-tins were rattling, the powerful and weary shipwrights, the blackened faces escaped from coal-boats, and the shady crowd of gleaners, the workless and hooligans. Trucks and carts were fleeing at a rapid trot toward the stables, and heavy tractors were clanking over the disjointed cobble-stones.

The two young men went back on foot toward the Place des Quinconces.

"Did I deceive you?" asked Paul Duffaure.

"You were right, his daughter is splendid."

"And Legrand?"

"He's an apostle. What a beautiful girl!"

"There's nothing to be done with that fellow," estimated the reporter.

"Do you think so? One can obtain anything from visionaries; it's sufficient to know how to handle them."

Duffaure looked at his employer. "I confess that I don't understand your strategy."

"It's elementary, however. You don't suppose, I hope, that I share Legrand's ideas?"

"No," said Duffaure.

"Thank you for that mark of esteem, my dear friend. I'm neither a philanthropist nor a misanthrope; I'm an egotist."

"Like everyone..."

"It's the sole fashion of serving Society well. Thus, I consider that it's necessary to profit from that tormented gnome's extraordinary discovery. It's necessary to force him to profit from it himself, for I don't want either to deprive him or to rob him. Can you see how we have to proceed?"

"In truth, no..."

"Then you're not a psychologist..."

Serenely, Jacques Gellé lit a cigarette. "Your fortune will be made, my dear Duffaure, and mine will be multiplied a hundredfold, on the day when Legrand will find himself happy. It's necessary to render him happy; it's necessary for him to love life. It's necessary, therefore, that he be cured and his legs recover their vigor. By caring for his body, we'll cure the ulcers of his soul. Remember this: when Legrand stands upright, like you or me, he'll no longer think about anything but his family and himself. He'll become terribly conservative. The fate of Society will no longer preoccupy him. He'll laugh at poverty, and he won't say anything more about divulging the secret of gold. He'll guard it jealously, and will even lament having communicated it to us..."

"Admirable!" said Duffaure, by way of flattery, by no means fully convinced.

"Properly reasoned, no more. By accepting my check, that honest man has accepted his future subjection. He belongs to me. In any case, we're all honest, aren't we?"

Duffaure nodded his head energetically.

"It's agreeable to be so profitably," Gellé went on. "So, we're going to utter the tragic and poignant cry of Lourdes: 'Heal our sick!' The greatest physicians and the most celebrated surgeons are going to file past Legrand's bed. One day, he'll walk. And on that day, my lad, his friends will be content."

"He has none more faithful than us," said Duffaure, half-serious and half-mocking.

"You've understood me now?" said Gellé, smiling and honoring him with a clap on the shoulder. "But enough about that. I imagine that it's possible to amuse ourselves in this Louis XVI city...take me dancing, or something...I'm hungry for a pretty girl."

IV

Jacques Gellé sought allies. Jeanne received a bunch of roses, Gastal a box of cigars and Madame Villaret a bag of bonbons. So, on their return to the Legrand house, the director of the *Echo* and Paul Duffaure were welcomed with a warm sympathy by the woman with the yellow hair.

"Oh, Monsieur…how grateful…"

The invalid had been dressed in his best clothes, and Ali had donned one of the dark blue gandouras beloved by the Touaregs.

"Monsieur," said Legrand, after the welcoming compliments, "I haven't yet cashed your check…" He took the precious piece of paper from under his plaid. "I prefer to return it to you…"

Jacques Gellé was cordial, and not at all anxious. "Why don't you want the money?"

"Perhaps I haven't insisted enough on my conception. I repeat to you that you'll never obtain any profit from the affair."

"On the contrary," Jacques replied. "I know that I'll lose a great deal…my entire fortune. No surprise in that direction." He smiled at Jeanne in a familiar fashion.

The invalid then put the check away in the folds of his blanket. He searched his mind for the reasons for Gellé's abnormal generosity.

"However," he said, "you're rich, happy…"

"Perhaps," said Gellé, suddenly very romantic.

"You'll be ruined, like all capitalists."

"Bah! That will be moral."

"I have reasons for being bitter, but you have none."

"I adore perilous adventures," Jacques explained. "Let's only talk about the imminent future, and let me explain my plans to you. First of all, I'll take you to Paris—with your family, of course."

"To Paris!" murmured Madame Villaret. "The dream of my life!"

"But my daughter has a dental office…?" Legrand objected.

"She'll close it."

"Her fiancé has a job as an accountant."

"He'll abandon it. You'll all come. I'll supply your future son-law with work. To succeed, it's necessary to be physically strong, and you're weak. I want you to be cured, to be able to walk…"

The invalid struck his dead legs. "For that, it would need a miracle!"

"It will be accomplished," said Paul Duffaure, confidently.

"May God hear you!" said Madame Villaret, stupidly.

"Afterwards, we'll have the factory constructed, without anyone knowing its destination. It's necessary that no one knows in advance what purpose the establishment will serve."

"It will take a long time," said Legrand, "because the construction of the furnaces is delicate work. Every modification of the capacity determines extraordinary variations in temperature. One can only proceed hesitantly."

"Time is not an issue," Jacques went on. "Don't hurry, and when we're ready to manufacture large amounts of gold, the role of my newspaper will commence."

"Yes!" enthused the invalid, riffling his gray hair. "Then we'll throw the secret to all the echoes. We'll distribute the ardent metal in profusion, while everyone, including the poorest, will attempt the transmutation of lead. Let's go downstairs, Messieurs. I want to show you that I'm not a joker. You're going to witness the most prodigious experiment of all time!"

Ali having picked him up bodily, they went downstairs. Madame Villaret and Jeanne did not follow them.

"You're not coming, Mademoiselle?" Jacques Gellé asked the latter.

"No…I'm expecting someone…"

133

"But I shall see you again…?"

"Oh, certainly..."

And they exchanged a smile.

Hat in hand, almost devotedly, Jacques Gellé and Paul Duffaure went into the laboratory. They were disappointed by its wretched appearance. The director of the *Echo* allowed a disdainful gaze to wander over the furnace and the shelves, and then removed his monocle.

The Arab sat Legrand down on a high chair, to the feet of which four castors had been fitted.

"It is here," said the invalid, bombastically, "that the fate of the world is in play. Everything is simple: a little Clerc-Minet furnace…forty amperes under sixty volts. It's a modest apparatus, the electrodes of which I've modified in order that the charcoal rods can be drawn apart without decreasing the temperature of the arc..."

Leaning over, Jacques Gellé examined the interior of the furnace.

"Nothing extraordinary," said the invalid. "It's there, however, that the mystery is accomplished. Once again, I deny having invented anything. I've only continued the work of my glorious predecessors, Langevin, Becquerel, Ramsay, Thomson, Bourciez, Jollivet-Castelot…they put me on the track, but I've marched more rapidly than them. According to the gripping expression of a scientist, I have dissected the atom..."

Paul Duffaure could not resist the temptation to display some newly-acquired knowledge. "Atoms…electrons…," he said, with a false assurance.

"Don't interrupt!" said Legrand, who detested chatter-boxes. "Do you even know what an atom is? It's a world, Monsieur! Around a minuscule central star those electrons gravitate that you mention at hazard. They're like planets around a sun. All of that is so tiny that twenty million atoms scarcely make a millimeter! Are those figures not frightening?"

Gradually, Legrand's face became radiant.

"It's a matter of disemboweling atoms," he said, and attaining the nucleus through the saraband of electrons. Bohr has demonstrated that they protect the corpuscle whose artificial disintegration is sought marvelously. Ernest Rutherford, the genius of Cambridge, estimates that the atomic nuclei of all substances are uniformly composed of electrons, helium atoms, and almost all of hydrogen atoms. Admitting that, you'll understand how it's necessary to proceed theoretically in order to transmute metals?"

"I'm not following you," Jacques confessed. "Excuse me, I'm so ignorant..."

"But yes!" the invalid said, impatiently. "It's theoretically simple. It's sufficient to modify the number of electrons to obtain different substances! In any case, without human intervention, Nature effects transmutations herself. In a few million centuries, uranium becomes thorium, then radium, and finally lead!"

The two auditors opened their eyes wide, for their imagination was being subjected to a rude proof. The infinitely small and millions of centuries were not familiar to them.

"Now that I've explained the mechanism of the operation to you," said Legrand, "I'll go more quickly. Already, in many circumstances, it has been observed that a projection of pulverized arsenic trisulfide and kermes on to molten silver permits the production of gold, in the proportion of one per cent.[14] That has been denied, but nothing is more certain. In

---

[14] This method of "producing" gold by means of treating silver with arsenic trisulfide, in the mineral form of orpiment, was promoted by François Jollivet-Castellot (1874-1937), the most recent of the predecessors cited by Legrand and the founder of the Societé alchimique de France [Alchemical Society of France] and several periodicals, including *L'Hyperchimie* [Hyperchemistry]. He claimed to have made gold by that method in 1925; he was an enthusiastic communist and a spiritualist, but his attempt to fuse those ideas into a common creed led to his virtual ostracism by communists and spiritualists

addition to the coloration of the mass, the reactions of stannous ferrocyanide or chloride are always conclusive. In any case, that's as old as the world. All the operations to be accomplished are listed in the *Chrysopée de Cléopâtre*, written several hundred centuries ago and discovered a few years ago by Berthelot[15]..."

Legrand picked up a gilded scoria

"It's not sufficient, to obtain interesting results, to submit atoms to the heat of an electric furnace. We bombard them with the alpha and beta rays of radioactive substances, whose respective velocities are 15,000 and 200,000 kilometers per second. That's why I need radium. In addition, I had to find a catalyst. A catalyst is a substance that, by virtue of its presence alone, without anyone being able to understand how it intervenes, favors a reaction. My catalyst, for which I search for a long time, is none other than radium..."

He dropped the scoria, which rolled at the Arab's feet.

"The rest was child's play. Precautions, and that was all. I worked with a milligram. Finally, I was able to establish the immutable proportions. Everything happens automatically, as you'll see..."

With a spatula, he placed lead shot on a pan of the precision balance. Attentively watching the needle of the beam, he continued: "You're the first profane individuals to whom I've spoken about my work with any precision. The members of my family scarcely take any interest in my work and make fun

---

alike. Skeptics opined that his process merely tinted the silver yellow.

[15] A translation of the document known as the *Chrysopée de Cléopâtre* [approximately, The Gold-Book of Cleopatra] is included in Marcellin Berthelot's *Collection des anciens alchimistes Grecs* [Collection of Ancient Greek Alchemical Texts] (1887). Its antiquity is dubious and its authenticity even more so, but Jollivet-Castelot, who was acquainted with Berthelot, probably took his inspiration therefrom.

of atomic dissociation. It's better to eat, drink and sleep, my cook says. Fundamentally, perhaps she's right...."

The lead shot filled a small crucible. The invalid weighed out the orpiment just as meticulously, and then the kermes. The two Parisians contemplated him in silence.

"We're ready..."

Legrand tipped back the lid of a heavy metal box and took out a tube a few centimeters long.

"This is the radium," he said. "It's been confided to me again for one day only. This tube encloses an almost imperceptible amount, which emits a formidable artificial fire of rays, indefatigably. I place it in another crucible—for, in spite of the precautions, the protective tube is volatilized every time..."

The furnace open, Legrand introduced the crucible, adjusted the carbon rods producing the arc, and, with his eyes riveted to a large watch, lowered a handle.

The spark fulgurated inside the furnace. The invalid waited for a few minutes, without anyone daring to budge. Pressing a bulb fitted to the end of a pipe, he suddenly projected the orpiment and the kermes. Then he raised the handle again and vigorously blew air into the furnace.

Finally, he armed himself with a long forceps and precipitated the crucible and its contents into a bowl, in which the water instantly boiled.

"It's finished," he said.

At the bottom of the bowl lay a black, spongy scoria similar to the one that Paul Duffaure had given to Jacques Gellé. The invalid held it out to them, still fuming.

"Here's a hundred grams of gold, Messieurs..."

Jacques Gellé turned the hot scoria over and over. It was porous and blistered, reminiscent of the foamy head of a glass of beer solidified. The primitive base metal, submitted to a titanic effort, had changed into gold.

"Do you still have doubts?" said the invalid, proudly.

Jacques Gellé did not reply. Beyond the walls, he seemed to see millions and millions of avid hands extended toward the paltry gnome whose science had something demonic about it.

V

Aaron Schmitt was a type specimen of the operetta financier: a swollen face framed with Louis-Philippe side-whiskers, hair straightened very morning, a fleshy nose overhanging a moist lip, and a capacious abdomen striped by the classic chain from which trinkets dangled.

Schmitt had understood from the outset of his career his interest in exaggerating his physical vulgarity. The naïve—which is to say, almost all the players of the stock market—did not suspect the finesse of that entirely round man. He cheated them with a charming bonhomie, and even when ruined they remained convinced of his inferiority.

Jacques Gellé was not duped by that reputation, because he considered Schmitt to be the boldest financier in Paris. He had, therefore, chosen him to set the Legrand affair in motion.

Schmitt had listened carefully to the story told by the director of the *Echo* without interrupting him once. His little eyes always remained inexpressive, but his attention was keen.

"In sum," he said, when his young interlocutor had finished speaking, "what are you proposing to me?"

Jacques sighed impatiently. The fat Schmitt was truly too slow in comprehension.

"It's a matter of two things," he said. "Firstly, of taking possession of our alchemist's production..."

"But will he give it to you?"

"Yes, if I'm able to bind him by a contract..."

"What contract?"

"A contract of partnership, of course..."

"Ah! Good," said Schmitt, innocently. "And the second thing?"

Gellé stated, cynically: "It the profits don't roll in from Legrand and his invention is a con, it's necessary that the shareholders console us for our disappointment."

"How's that?"

"By subscribing."

"And we pocket their money?"

"Coldly."

Aaron Schmitt assumed an artful expression. "It's not a bad plan," he admitted,, "but if it fails, what a scandal!"

"What does it matter, since it will be an anonymous association?"

"The master blackmailers will discover us."

"We'll pay them off and, if necessary, prosecute them. Legally, we'll be unassailable."

"Oh, I know that kind of honesty well," said Schmitt. "I render myself culpable of it every day. One last question: why do you want to bring Guichard into the affair?"

"Because Guichard is the master of a French telegraphic agency, my dear chap. He opens and closes the tap of news at will. He'll talk or keep quiet, when necessary."

His collaboration is always onerous," deplored Schmitt, with a grimace. "Humanity reserves too large a place among the merchants of lies."

Gellé was not there to criticize the social system. "Let's sum up," he said. "If Legrand really can manufacture gold, we'll keep the shares for ourselves; if he doesn't, well sell them on to middle classes, so fond of reliable investments."

"That's right!" Schmitt acquiesced, with a broad laugh. And, contemplating his sausage-like fingers with an artistic delectation: "What will our initial capital be?"

"Three million?" Gellé proposed.

"That's stingy."

"Suggest a figure."

"I don't know…nine million?"

"All right. You put in three, Guichard three and I'll supply the other three. How many initial shares?"

"Let's say five million. And what rogation will you throw into your Legrand's plate?"

"A million in shares."

"Do you think he'll accept that? It's not much."

"He'll think it's too much."

"Good, good," said Schmitt. "That's not my concern. You take care of that side of things. I'll occupy myself with the subscription. We'll issue the shares at a thousand and I'll blow them up to two thousand. That way, the placement will assure us, to begin with, a profit of a hundred per cent, by way of pin money. It remains to regulate the quota of the founder's shares."

"That's not urgent," Gellé replied.

"When shall we see our phenomenon?"

"Legrand? Next week—I'm bringing him to Paris."

"We'd better have him close at hand."

"Not you, me," Gellé specified.

"Isn't it the same thing?"

"Not entirely. *Au revoir*, my dear associate."

"*À bientôt*, my dear friend."

VI

Jacques had installed Legrand and his family at the Parisis-Palace. Rosita had stayed in Bordeaux, firstly because her presence in Paris had been deemed unnecessary, and secondly because Madame Villaret would never have consented to abandon her furniture and that of her friend completely. The stout maid was big enough to struggle victoriously in both lodgings against the sly invasion of dust and the eczema of mildew.

"Come back cured," she had said to Legrand, amid the tears of their adieux. "But above all, don't let them operate on you—that never solves anything. I knew a lady who had a whitlow...they grilled the thumb and would have had to cut off the far-lanx without me, who cured it be wrapping the finger in spider-webs. Don't let them put you to sleep either, you swallow your tongue and can die of it. Don't worry—everything will be neat and tidy when you get back. Don't trust the journalists. It's not natural that anyone would give so much money to a man like you, who's never done anything with his ten fingers. There's surely some shady maneuvers underneath it all."

Three bedrooms, a drawing room and a dining room formed the Legrands' apartment, on the first floor overlooking the Boulevard des Italiens. Gastal was higher up, expedited to the sixth floor by an elevator that he never entered without anxiety.

"When was the last accident?" he had asked, in a detached manner.

The lift attendant had had the question repeated before replying: "There's never been an accident, Monsieur."

"That's what they all say!" Gastal had sniggered. And he always went down by the stairs, because he abhorred the sensation of falling into an abyss.

Madame Villaret, whose hair was getting increasingly yellow, was happy. She chatted in a familiar fashion with the chambermaids she encountered in the immense corridors, and admired unreservedly the *maîtres-d'hôtel* who transported plates balanced on their upturned hand at shoulder height.

The journey had fatigued Legrand, rendering him even more irritable and unjust than usual. To Jeanne, who exhorted him tenderly to patience, he replied: "I hate my body. It's because of it that I'm in pain and I'm humiliated."

"But you're not humiliated..."

"Yes! I'm being given charity. I know that they're spending money on me." He had not overcome his anger since seeing the price of the apartment posted behind the door.

"We're costing you a thousand francs a day, and that annoys me," he said, peevishly to Jacques.

The latter had affected disdain. "What does money matter to us? I'll never succeed in spending my fortune before it's no longer worth anything." And he changed the subject.

At his request, several agencies were looking for a plot of land on which to build the factory. The factory had to be as far as possible from large cities, preferably in the South-West."

"What about the article in the *Echo*?" Legrand asked, one day.

"You'll have the proofs tomorrow, but as we've decided, it won't appear until you're under way...yes, when you're standing upright on your legs."

The invalid's expression darkened.

"Will I ever walk?"

"Don't doubt it. Even against physical illness, we can do as we wish. Have faith."

"I've had enough of that," said Legrand, his teeth clenched.

The visit of the physicians was announced. Three celebrities: Pioc, Lesistaz and Professor Camelère-Daguercy."

"I've also mounted a search for the major who treated you during the war," Gellé announced. "He's been here since yesterday evening."

The major in question was a campaign doctor named Peyrasson, originally from the mountains of Auvergne. He was the last to arrive at the consultation, harassed and sweating, stammering that he was late because he had feared being early. He had a fine peasant's face and thick hands with rounded thumbs.

The three experts examined Legrand like a rare animal. Lesistaz, red-haired with slow eyes behind round lenses, seemed determined to understand what had been said to him the day before. Pioc affected an artistic elegance and gave off an odor of iodoform. As for Camelère-Daguercy, small and ferrety, he was poisoning himself with his relentlessly bitten fingernails.

Jeanne and the woman with the lemon-tinted hair were not present at the consultation. Legrand, as pale as usual, looked in turn at Jacques, impassive in his corner, the three masters of science, and Peyrasson, standing in front of them, as anxious as if he were in the dock at a court-martial.

"We have summoned you," Lesistaz began, with a nasal solemnity, "so that you can give us precise details of Monsieur Legrand's wound and what you have done. Where was your hospital?"

"Bar-le-Duc, Monsieur le Professeur."

"Speak—we're listening."

Peyrasson swallowed his saliva awkwardly. "Here goes…the wounded man, if I remember correctly, was treated as soon as he arrived…"

"That's not true," said Legrand. "I was left for twenty-four hours abandoned on a straw mattress."

"That's possible," conceded Peyrasson. "We were overflowing…we didn't know where to start."

"That's not an excuse," snapped Camelère-Daguercy. "The operation should have been attempted immediately."

"My dear master, I didn't have a quarter of the necessary staff..."

"Me neither," said Pioc, "but I put in demands until they sent me the personnel."

Peyrasson confessed, pitiably: "Me too, I put in demands...and they sent me to Salonika... The wounded man was very dirty. He was cleaned..."

"Very badly," Legrand interjected. "You didn't take any antiseptic precautions."

"I apologize for that," said Peyrasson, nonplussed. "I had no more phenol, no more Dakin, no more anything! I recognized that it was a matter of a wound in the lumbar region..."

"It was necessary to be a sorcerer to divine that," murmured Camelère-Daguercy, sarcastically, to his two illustrious colleagues.

"The projectile had entered immediately beneath the first lumbar vertebra. It was so close to the surface that I was able to extract it with forceps. I iodized the wound, and cared out an antitetanic injection."

"After twenty-four hours, it was high time," muttered the ferrety individual, again.

"Where did you put the wounded man?" Pioc suddenly demanded.

"But...in a bed," replied the Auvergnat, timidly.

Pioc smiled scornfully. "Inconceivable! You should have kept him extended on horizontal planks. He needed a very hard bed." And, addressing Jacques Gellé: These are culpable negligences. I remember a very similar story at the Val-de-Grâce. Can you imagine that..."

Lesistaz interrupted him. "Pardon me, my dear colleague, but I'm pressed for time..."

Pioc bit his lip.

The embarrassed Peyrasson coughed, and continued: "The wounded man showed signs of paraplegic motor-sensitivity..."

"Of course!" said Lesistaz. "Vertebral trauma had occasioned a medullary compression..."

Camelère-Daguercy ceased biting his nails. "Was there any urinary retention?"

"Yes, Master," said Peyrasson. "and…incontinence of fecal matter."

"The treatment?"

"The wounded man was in a coma," said Peyrasson. "I gave him the injection…"

"And then?"

"I monitored the wound, the scarring of which was rapid."

"And the lumbar picture?"

Peyrasson blushed ashamedly. "I didn't attempt one. The man was so weak…"

"You were wrong," said Pioc. "You might perhaps have evacuated a part of the sanguo-rachidian blockage."

Lesistaz elongated his lips. "Not sure!"

"I said *perhaps*," Pioc riposted, dryly. "Continue, Doctor."

"The patient recovered his strength. He accepted the Hayem serum without any reaction, and the biodynamine as well…"

"I can foresee the consequences," Lesistaz cut in. "The paraplegic signs are attenuated; the flaccidity gives way to a spasmodic state, and the reservoirs are repaired, proof of a certain obedience."

"Yes, Master. Then the patient was sent to the rear. And I never saw him again. I'm glad to find him in good health…"

He was glad above all to have reached the end of the interrogation, judging that he had not come out of it too badly. He had told his little story without jabbering too much, but in truth, his memory was confused. He had received so many of them, those inert, bloody, muddy, lousy vagabonds who died without a complaint, as if to flee the pain. He only remembered one, a little Breton, who had agonized for an hour before his eyes, incessantly calling out: "Papa! Papa!" in a heart-rending voice.

Legrand undressed—or, rather, allowed himself to be undressed. In the hands of the three men of science, he had the manner of a patient being put to the question. Finally, as naked as a worm, he was on the bed.

His body was frightfully thin. The ribs circled the narrow thorax, and the dorsal spine told its chaplet in such a way that every vertebra was threatening to break through the skin.

The practitioners palpated, tapped and tested the articulations.

"It's at the beginning of convalescence that it's necessary to combat the muscular retraction," muttered Lesistaz.

"We'll succeed at length, by massage and electrification," said Camelère-Daguercy. "There's something more serious…the patient has suffered a kind of localized osteomolacia."

Pioc tapped the sacrum with his index finger and observed: "The column has collapsed, as in Pott's disease…"

"The trophic troubles still persist," concluded Camelère-Daguercy, "but I believe that Monsieur Legrand will be able to walk…"

The invalid uttered a kind of sob. "I'll be able to walk? I'll be able to walk?"

"Laboriously," added Lesistaz. "But you'll progress with sticks, on condition that you submit rigorously to the treatment we indicate."

"I consent to anything!" Legrand cried. "Torture me, tear me apart, but cure me! I want to cease to be a living dead man who's carted around with a weary pity!"

The three masters, indifferent to that joy, went into the drawing room next door to confer. Madame Villaret was summoned to dress Legrand again. She lowered her eyes modestly on perceiving him naked beneath the sheets, but he hugged her impetuously.

"Armandine! I'm going to be cured! To walk!"

"You're joking!" she exclaimed, without reflecting on her lack of diplomacy.

"The physicians have promised. They're scientists, aren't they, Monsieur Gellé?"

"Celebrities," Jacques overbid.

Legrand's emaciated face took on a new expression. The invalid was agitated; he buttoned his waistcoat wrongly, and was unable to find the armholes of his jacket. He finally perceived Peyrasson, whom the others had not invited him to go with them into the next room.

"Oh, they're a fine lot, the war doctors! They let people croak out of incompetence or negligence!" He suddenly calmed down, understanding that he was causing the worthy man a superfluous chagrin. "You did what you could...I hold you in esteem and I'm grateful to you...the responsible ones are those who directed the health service..."

"We all did our duty," replied Peyrasson. "We only had five minutes to devote to each wounded man, and we would have needed hours. And then, we lacked everything..."

"Who was culpable, then?" asked Jacques.

The Auvergnat extended his robust arms. "Death," he said.

The secret conference only last a few minutes. The three augurs emerged, in accord with regard to the treatment and in haste to get away. A rendezvous was arranged for the following day at the Pioc clinic, and they went out with Peyrasson, who jabbered guttural *master*s as if he would never finish.

Jeanne, who had been forgotten, came in. Her happiness was no less sincere for being sober when she learned that her father was curable.

Legrand grew increasingly excited. "When I have strength, they'll see! They'll see!" They were those he hated, the white-haired professors, the official scientists, whose hostility he anticipated. "They're results, not formulae, that I'll wave under their noses. After that, we'll talk a little, for a laugh, about Proust...the hypothesis of quanta...and all their nonsense! I'll make them look ridiculous." He rambled, prolix and confused, citing Boscovich and Clémence Royer,[16] dragging them into a hermetic jungle. Then, fatigued, he went to sleep like a baby.

Madame Villaret picked up her knitting, and the young people remained face to face.

"Do you think you'll succeed?" Jeanne asked, after a rather long silence.

"Yes," said Jacques. "I always succeed."

"Then...all your desires are realized?"

"All of them," he affirmed.

They observed one another covertly, with a slight gleam in their eyes.

"I'll be very happy," Jeanne confessed, "when my father is cured."

"Me too," said Jacques. "When he's on his feet, all will be well. He'll be able to work at his ease."

"And you'll be able to collaborate?" said the young woman.

"My collaboration, I hope, will not be useless..."

"I want that with all my heart..."

He leaned forward slightly, in order not to be heard by Madame Villaret. "You'll help me?"

"I'll help you," she promised, in the same tone.

"The two of us," he continued, emphasizing the words, "might overcome many difficulties."

They did not have time to say any more, because Gastal came in. The honest fellow was satisfied. He had taken out an

_____

[16] Roger Boscovich (1711-1787) developed an early version of modern atomic theory, which he attempted to integrate into a broader philosophical context. Clémence Royer (1830-1902) was a feminist theorist whose translation of Charles Darwin's *Origin of Species* proved highly controversial because of her extensive annotations, some of them challenging. The Proust previously cited is not the novelist Marcel but the chemist Joseph Proust (1754-1826).

option on a plot of land at the mouth of the Gironde, between Soulac and Le Verdon.

"It's called Le Grapon," he said. "Twenty hectares bordered by the railway...we'll have everything for a loaf of bread..."

Legrand, woken up, was brought up to date with the affair.

"Leave this evening!" he ordered.

"I don't like to leave you," sighed the accountant.

"You ought, on the contrary, to be glad," said Madame Villaret.

"It's because of Jeanne..."

"Don't worry, no one will abduct me," replied the young woman, tranquilly.

It had been agreed for a long time that Gastal would aid in the construction of the factory from beginning to end, in order to supervise the expenditure and hasten the work. The technical direction would be ensured by an engineer named Duret, for whom Jacques answered. The plans for the furnaces had already been checked and approved by Legrand.

"Above all," the latter recommended, "activate! Activate!"

"I'll activate," Gastal promised. "You know full well that I never waste a minute. You'll write to me, Jeanne?"

"Yes, my love," she promised, with a perfect serenity.

"Regularly?"

"Yes, since you value regularity more than anything else."

"It's just that my affection for you..."

The invalid became impatient. "Don't get soppy, Gastal. You can bill and coo later, at your leisure."

Madame Villaret exhaled languorously. "One has all of life to love one another..."

"And to understand one another," murmured Jeanne, so quietly that only Jacques Gellé heard her.

VII

After Gastal's departure, Jacques Gellé often came to the Parisis-Palace. Now known to the personnel of the immense caravanserai, he no longer waited in the reception room or the winter garden until he was authorized to go up; he went directly to Legrand's apartment.

The invalid always received him with pleasure, even at the height of his neurasthenic crises—which, in any case, were more widely spaced. Jacques brought him the comfort of his speech, and he was persuasive. He preached confidence in the physicians and affirmed that they would succeed in regenerating the invalid if he had the necessary patience. It was necessary to nourish the atrophied muscles to give them strength, and to extract the nervous system from its lethargy.

Legrand listened avidly. He asked questions, provoked lies, and declared, to finish, with increasing conviction, that he felt much stronger than at the beginning of the treatment.

Madame Villaret doted on him, maternal and irritating. He scolded her, as usual, without regard to her dog-like devotion, but waited for her impatiently whenever she went out.

"What's got into you, then?" he grumbled, when she returned. "You're always out!"

At first, the yellow-haired woman had manifested the intention of visiting the museums, but the Louvre had frightened her. She had fallen back on the great department stores, which, she said, were also museums of a sort. It was not a dangerous mania, because, in spite of the temptations, she never bought anything.

Outside of the hours of treatment, Legrand fretted. The agitation of the streets made him uncomfortable; he scarcely consented to make the occasional excursion to the Bois de Boulogne, in one of Jacques Gellé's automobiles, in the company of Jeanne and the faithful Ali, on whom the change of residence did not seem to have made any impression.

151

By contrast, Jeanne Legrand adored Paris. She understood the character of the enormous city. She had immediately discerned that, in spite of the resident aliens and their excesses, Paris remained the capital of taste and measure. And very rapidly, unconsciously, she had refined herself, so thoroughly that no man encountered her without admiring her. But did she perceive it? One could doubt it, for she always conserved her immutable placidity.

Everything interested her. At her request, Jacques Gellé had taken her with Madame Villaret to Notre-Dame, to Sacré-Coeur, to the Invalides—everywhere that the guide-books one can purchase on the boulevards advised people to go. By the same token, the director of the *Echo* learned his Paris, of which he was ignorant, as incurious as the montagnards who climb mountains without ever experiencing the curiosity to turn round and admire the view.

Every day, during the siesta that Legrand took, exhausted by massages, she spent an hour or two at the Tuileries, on her own. She loved the irreproachable garden, and the perspective of the Champs-Élysées, at the end of which the Arc de Triomphe mounted guard over the poor remains of the unknown soldier.

"Mademoiselle Legrand! Oh, what luck!"

Jacque Gellé bowed ceremoniously, molded in a suit of extreme audacity, bright blue and bordered with black silk braid.

The young woman offered him her hand. "Indeed, it is lucky…"

"I was passing," he said. "It seemed to me that I recognized you, and I made a little detour."

He was lying, the hypocrite. He had come to the Tuileries for her.

They were good comrades—to the extent that one could believe oneself the comrade of that frigid and distant virgin. She pleased him infinitely, but he dared not admit it to himself. Nevertheless, the elimination of the fiancé had liberated him from a paralyzing hindrance. And he remained standing, bare headed, waiting for an invitation that finally came.

"Sit down, then, Monsieur."

"Thank you."

He freed his gaze from the glass of the monocle. Jeanne looked him straight in the eyes. He found a pretext to turn his head away.

"What are you reading?"

He lifted up the closed book and deciphered the golden letters on the spine.

"Chamisso…the man who lost his shadow. Oh, very good…very amusing."

"I like the story very much," Jeanne admitted.

"What! Are you an imaginative person?"

"Why not?"

He hesitated slightly. "You don't give that impression. Your gravity…your conversation…I don't know…"

She laughed, in a very youthful fashion, but immediately became serious again. "You imagine that you know what I'm thinking, then?"

"No, for you hide it with such jealous care."

"You're mistaken. I don't hide my thoughts systematically, but I don't experience the need to divulge them."

"To anyone?"

"To anyone…at least for the moment…"

With the tip of his cane, Jacques Gellé made a few small pebbles jump. "And," he went searching for his words, "you're not bored?"

"I'm never bored anywhere."

"In any case, Paris is an agreeable city."

"I suspect so."

"What, you only suspect it?"

"But yes…in sum, I'm ignorant of the delights of Paris."

"Oh! You know…it's better be reduced to conjectures…"

"What egotistical reasoning! You're the millionaire who complains to vagabonds about the inconveniences of wealth."

"You'd like to go to the dance-halls? The theaters?"

Jeanne Legrand made no reply.

"Frankly, is that what tempts you?"

"I adore dancing, and I have a passion for good plays."

Then why confine yourself to the hotel?"

"My God...perhaps out of timidity...anti-social tendencies..."

"Why do you always refuse my invitations?"

Jeanne's eyelids fluttered. "For personal reasons," she said.

"Your fiancé has forbidden you to go out with me?"

"I beg you...," she interrupted. "I don't exercise any constraint over others, but I never permit them any control over my actions. Certainly, I'd like dinner in a luxury restaurant, to attend a gala, to drink a glass of champagne afterwards...but it isn't possible."

"It only depends on you..."

She smiled in a melancholy fashion. "No...I'm only a poor girl, Monsieur Gellé...I don't want to acquire tastes and needs that will make me suffer later."

"What! You'll soon be the richest woman in the world."

"The future isn't the present. I don't even have a silk dress."

"And that's why you claustrate yourself?"

"Of course," she said. "I'd be ridiculous among the other women."

"You'll always be the most beautiful," declared Jacque Gellé, gallantly.

"It's not a matter of beauty but of adornment," Jeanne relied. "I've observed that in Paris, people scarcely pay attention to people's clothes; nevertheless, it would be uncomfortable to feel inferior. So I stay at the hotel."

"There is a means," suggested Jacques Gellé.

"What?"

"With the assent of your father...and Gastal...I could open a line of credit for you in the Rue de la Paix.

"Oh, thank you," said Jeanne. "You're very kind, but..."

"Why refuse?"

154

There was a short interval, and then she continued, in her tranquil voice. "I accept…what point is there in making a lot of fuss? You're offering generously, I accept with pleasure."

The young man was surprised by that abrupt acceptance. Truly, the strange young woman had sang-froid, or cynicism. Moreover, she did not exteriorize her joy; she limited herself to seeming slightly satisfied, not excessively.

"I hope," Jacques Gellé continued, "that Monsieur Legrand won't oppose it?"

"Don't worry," she said, with a hint of irony. "My father is sure to return to you a hundredfold the money that you're advancing us so generously. So he'll accept…"

"He's right," replied the young man.

"Since we're talking about that," said Jeanne, changing her tone, "I'd like to ask you something."

"I'm at your orders."

"What is the exact motive for your conduct in father's regard?"

That brutal thrust disconcerted Jacques.

"The motive? But you're not unaware of it."

"Yes I am," she said.

"I share Monsieur Legrand's ideas…"

With a gesture of her slender hand she cut him off. "Not for me, that story! Be frank, Monsieur Jacques, and don't treat me as an enemy or someone indifferent. I want to be your ally…your accomplice, if you prefer."

The word made him shiver. "Accomplice?"

"Like Paul Duffaure," she went on, in the same soft voice. "I think that it would be a pity if my father's discovery didn't profit anyone, not even us. I'll help you with all my heart to recuperate the million that you're in the process of spending. But I won't hide it from you that, even with my help, it will be difficult."

"Now that there are two of us, I'm confident," said Gellé. "Let's let the architects work first…"

"And the physicians," Jeanne completed. "In the meantime, in order to while away the time, we'll dance…"

"Frantically!" finished the young man, joyfully.

Their plan could be put into execution without delay. Legrand refused, at first, any supplementary liberality on Jacques' part, but Madame Villaret, in order to have a lovely dress herself, pleaded Jeanne's cause and won it.

It was a great day when they went to Chez Maquin. In spite of their modest attire, they were received in the porphyry store like princesses by an elegant and distinguished saleswoman. Had not many young women as modest as Jeanne, and not as pretty, become queens of fashion by virtue of a simply caprice of fortune?

"We'd each like a day dress and an evening dress," simpered Madame Villaret. "The same model for both of us, of course."

The saleswoman did not blink. "Very good, Madame. If you'd like to follow me, I'll show you our models of low-cut dresses...we'll choose the fabrics later."

The room into which they were introduced was luxurious and dull, of a gray tone designed to make the originality of the costumes stand out more. The mannequins filed past on a little stage, skillfully lit, hung with pearl velvet.

"Evening Delight," announced the saleswoman, indifferently. "Caprice... Oriental Night... Graziella... Orchid Queen..."

And the beautiful girls advanced one by one, twirled around, nonchalantly manipulating a fan made of a single plume. They were distant and hieratic, like the priestesses of some bizarre cult.

Jeanne felt embarrassed, incapable of deciding. She dared not look. Fortunately, Jacque Gellé came in. He must have been known in the house, for the obsequious director accompanied him, with urgent courtesies that were obviously artificial.

The file recommenced. The third mannequin, a slim blonde, slightly affected, smiled at the young man imperceptibly. One of his mistresses, no doubt. With a glance, Jeanne made Gellé understand that she had glimpsed the maneuver.

"This one is delightful," said the director. "It's my most original creation…it's entirely suited to a young woman…the neckline isn't excessively low…the tunic is sober, with two panels of Chantilly and a slender girdle of marcassite with a jade clasp. Jenny, show the dress…"

A nothing, that dress: scarcely a handful of satin and lace. In Madame Villaret's hands, it was suddenly no more than a formless rag devoid of chic.

"There's not much furniture," sighed the old lady, "And it's so dear!"

Leaving her companion to simper at the mannequins, Jeanne chose an afternoon dress, and then had a cup of tea with Jacques in the greenhouse of Chez Maquin.

"Content?" asked the young man.

"Yes. When will it be delivered?"

"Tomorrow," replied the owner. "We have orders to go quickly."

"Don't fail," Jacques instructed. "I have a box for the Russian gala at the Opéra."

"But will Father consent?" said the young women, in a slightly anxious voice, which proved that beneath her somewhat cold exterior, she was a coquette.

"That depends on you," Jacques insinuated.

"And…"

She was about to add: *and my fiancé, how would he react if he knew?* But she bit her lip, and did not finish.

"I'm listening?" said Jacques, divining the objection.

"Nothing," she murmured. "This tea is excellent."

A new life commenced. Without Legrand, who was preoccupied with himself, raising any objection, Jeanne frequented establishments where people enjoy themselves. She learned to eat in luxury restaurants, where the napkins are so stiff that they bruise the lips, where the meat dishes arrive on rolling tables, where *maîtres-d'hôtel* dressed like diplomats carved birds with so much skill that a fair-sized pheasant is mysteriously resolved into four or five thin slices of white meat. She drank venerable wines and smoked blond cigarettes under the tender gaze of Madame Villaret.

In brief, she blossomed, in a world previously unknown.

"Go on, my girl, instruct yourself," Legrand said, naïvely. "That imbecile Gastal probably wouldn't be delighted with what you're doing, because he's a timorous bourgeois, but as yet, you don't depend on anyone but me, and I'm glad that you're getting to know all these stuffed shirts and marionettes. Observe them—they're stupid, but interesting. They're evil, vicious and useless. It's shameful that society is at their service. You dominate them all with your purity, and it's moral that you witness their death-throes. For they're going to die, all of them. They're incapable of adapting to the new conditions..."

He became animated, his hands in the gray hair that the hairdresser tried in vain every day to put in order.

"Their existence is just one bad deed. One doesn't have the right to live when one doesn't know how to live."

"You're right, Papa," Jeanne replied, indifferently.

Madame Villaret thought that she knew how to live. Slowly but irresistibly, her hair turned jonquil. She decked herself out in costumes of a dangerous audacity, corsages outrageously open over her deep cleavage. Even by day, she gladly denuded arms with veins like pipe-cleaners. It did not alarm anyone. In Paris, one needs so much indulgence for oneself that one tacitly accords it to others. Madame Villaret was able to believe that she was beautiful, since no one made her understand that she was ridiculous.

Gastal's letters, calligraphic, dated with an oblique stroke between the day and the month, arrived every day. A simple delay of twenty-four hours would have revealed a catastrophe. Those missives indicated, in a commercial style, that the formalities for the purchase of the terrain of Le Grapon were concluded. The notaries were redrafting the deeds, the materials were accumulating and the earth-movers were invading the domain.

"He'll see you again before long?" asked Jacques Gellé.

"Why not?" replied Jeanne, ambiguously.

"Let's take advantage of the last days of the vacation."

"The last days?" she said, with a mocking glance. "We won't go out any more when Gastal's here?"

Jacques Gellé played with his monocle. "Less..."

"My fiancé can come with us...."

"That wouldn't be amusing."

"On the contrary! Papa will be on his crutches, for he's making astonishing progress. He'll soon be walking. It'll be necessary to distract him..."

"Well then, we'll distract him," accepted Jacques Gellé.

"It won't be difficult...he has the mentality of a child."

"In the meantime, don't forget that we're going to the dress rehearsal at the Gymnase this evening."

"We'll be ready at eight. I don't like to arrive late at the theater.

"You're not Parisian yet...until this evening."

Jacques Gellé was furious with himself. The evolution of his own sentiments disconcerted him. He was almost never seen at the *Echo* any more, where he only went to sign his correspondence, He had abruptly abandoned his club, his friends and his mistress. He spent his time at the Parisis-Palace with Legrand, or out with Jeanne and the woman he nick-named irreverently "the old image."

He often interrogated himself as to what he thought of Jeanne. Did he love her, yes or no? He replied no. She attracted him, he judged her desirable, he coveted her, but he did not love her. He paraded her around as much for others as for himself.

That evening, she was very beautiful, very Junoesque in her cerise plush dress, under the helmet of her blue-tinted hair. At the theater, she caused a sensation. The gentlemen's opera-glasses were focused on her, and the women's tongues wagged.

Jacques knew a great many people. He responded to greetings, made amicable little signs and affected at every opportunity to lean familiarly toward Jeanne. He was flattered that she was assumed to be his mistress, and exerted himself to compromise her gracefully.

All Paris was there. The sharks of finance, the most decorated, those who were thought to be in prison, whores aping honest women, honest women—a matter of chance—aping whores, and inverts with the allures of esthetes, the true "having the right" to share, as usual, to share the tip-up seats.

A play by Ranstein, *Les Fauves*, was being performed. In response to a question from Jeanne, Jacques pointed out the author, alone in an avant-scène. He did his best to huddle there, but as the first act went on he moved gradually forward, as if attracted by the actors defending his work. He showed his livid, anxious and tormented face to everyone. When the curtain went down and the bravos rang out in salvoes, he threw himself backwards.

His works, of which he was not prodigal, were criticisms of mores. Ranstein fustigated his contemporaries pitilessly, ferociously displaying their debauchery, to the great admiration of audiences who always recognized their neighbors in the characters, and never saw themselves.

"You father is right," Jacques Gellé philosophized. "Our society is rotten. It would be an easy game to point out the lovers of those women, the mistresses of those men. Prostitutes, embezzlers, thieves…evidently, one can desire without remorse the destruction of that band, to facilitate the advent of new beings…"

"It's better to take advantage of life as it is," Jeanne replied, a joyful gleam in her eyes.

The second act was triumphant. Clamors of admiration sprang forth; the curtain went up and down ten times. Ranstein, demanded with loud cries, was obliged to bow from his box.

"Let's go and congratulate him," Jacques proposed.

The orders appeared to be strict: no one was admitted to the wings—but the card of the director of the *Echo* was an open sesame that no bolt resisted. Ranstein, surrounded by a few intimates, was standing in the foyer. He had a frightfully weary expression. He straightened up when he saw Gellé.

"How kind it is of you to have come…"

The man, at the summit of his glory, had need of publicity. He, who scorned the majority of his contemporaries, acted as a humble subject of the press magnate.

"Mademoiselle Legrand," Jacques introduced.

Ranstein bowed; all the others did likewise. Jacques Gellé went on: "Legrand! Remember that name, dear master. In a few weeks, it will be as famous as yours."

The author in fashion was politely astonished.

"Oh?"

"René Legrand," Jacques explained, "Is an inventor."

"Of what?" queried an old fox, the director of the *Soleil Levant*.

"You'll see, my dear Charet. But until further notice, permit me to keep the secret."

And he withdrew without further ado, cutting short the reverences of Madame Villaret, who would not have been reluctant to be interviewed. One remark, however, reached them.

"René Legrand probably won't be as famous as predicted, but his daughter is damnably beautiful."

"Did you hear that?" said Jacques, smiling.

"No…what?"

"Those gentlemen find you beautiful."

"I beg you…," she murmured, with the air of an offended queen. And she turned round to look at those who were admiring her.

Until the end of the performance Jacques observed her. Twice, he was tempted to draw closer to her, to brush her knee, but she seemed so surprised that he drew back, apologizing.

"If you wish," he offered, throwing her cape over her shoulders, "I'll offer you a bottle."

"It's very late," she said, tempted.

161

"Bah! Madame Villaret isn't sleepy. I'll take you some-where you've never been.

"Where's that?"

"To Montmartre."

"Oh yes!" exclaimed the romantic Madame Villaret. "We'll see the Bohemians!"

"Your conception of the Butte is a trifle outdated," Jacques replied, smiling. "You'll see more foreigners and prostitutes."

In fact, the clientele of the Imperial consisted of little else. At the back, a negro jazz band was thundering. In the middle, in a rectangle that was gradually shrinking as more tables were added, couples were bobbing up and down on the spot.

Little balls of hardened cotton wool were being thrown, mirlitons were being blown, rattles were being twirled. A fat sweaty monsieur was coiffed in a Pierrot hat. All of it was noisy, cordial and ridiculous.

The three of them sat down and were briskly served a bottle of champagne. Nothing was being drunk but champagne at two hundred francs a bottle, and the price did not seem ex-cessive to anyone.

Stunned, Jeanne examined the atria. She felt that she was incapable of shouting like those people, of laughing with her bosom deployed, like that tall blonde who was staring at her insolently.

She agreed to dance a blues with Jacques, but found her-self horribly embarrassed in the midst of couples who were embracing one another, indecently and cynically, mouth to mouth.

"We're not going to stay for long," said Jacques, when the dance was over.

He suddenly seemed preoccupied, troubled.

"Oh, we still have a minute!" exclaimed Madame Villaret, who hoped to find a dancing-partner.

"I assure you…it's better to go…."

Already, he had called the waiter—but the tall blonde who had been staring at Jeanne a little while before advanced, and leaned her hands, laden with rings, on the table in a familiar manner.

"Bonsoir, Jack," she said.

The young man, very pale, rose to his feet. "I beg you, Mademoiselle…"

"Am I upsetting you?" sniggered the prostitute.

"Go away!"

"You're annoyed? Why? You don't give any sign of life, so I'm taking advantage of the opportunity to enquire about your health. Are you well?"

Jeanne looked at her intently, much less emotional than Madame Villaret, who was trembling like a leaf.

"Go away!" Jacques repeated, his teeth clenched. "No scandal, eh?"

"I'm too well brought-up for that," the prostitute mocked. "You see, I'm not talking loudly. Everyone believes that we're still friends, that we're exchanging compliments..."

Her smile uncovered superb teeth. "So this is my replacement?" she asked, advancing her chin toward Jeanne. "Not bad, not bad…when you're tired of her, pass her on to me..."

"If you continue, I'll call a policeman," Jacques threatened.

"Don't do that! A policeman? Oh, you can boast about knowing how to live!" She addressed Jeanne: "A man I was with for two years. He'll abandon you as he abandoned me, with a check he'll send you via an office boy. Peasant!"

"Mademoiselle," commenced Madame Villaret, in a dignified fashion, "We are not Monsieur's mistress..."

But the prostitute stopped her without ceasing to smile: "Shut up, you old bawd."

Jacques had seized her by the wrist. "Are you going to go away?"

"You're hurting me," she said, without budging. "Your nails are digging into my skin. I adore that! I wanted to open my heart, my dear Jack. Now I'll leave you, and I bless you. Mademoiselle, I live at 14A Rue de la Pompe…Edith Gravière. Come and see me…no one regrets it. Let me go, Jack, and until the next time…"

She turned round to blow them a kiss and rejoined the people with whom she was having supper.

Jacques and his two companions did not exchange a word. The bill settled, they left. In the shadow of the auto, Jacques finally dared to speak.

"I'm very sorry about that altercation…very sorry!"

"She called me a bawd!" moaned Madame Villaret.

"If I'd been able to warn you…but I didn't think..."

Words failed him. Jeanne came to his aid.

"All is forgotten," she said.

"I swear to you...it's not my fault..."

"All is forgotten," the young woman repeated.

He was sitting facing her, and tried in vain to distinguish her features.

At the door of the Parisis-Palace, he got out first in order to help them down to the sidewalk.

"Goodnight, Monsieur Gellé," said Madame Villaret, in a lamentable voice.

"My respects, Madame. And forgive me for that unfortunate incident.…"

"Yes, of course…I don't blame you..."

Jeanne offered him her hand. He pressed it, but she raised it gently to his lips. For the first time, he kissed her wrist.

"Thank you for the excellent evening..."

"You're not angry with me?"

"Not at all."

"Truly?" he insisted.

"I never lie."

He remained on the asphalt, pensive, until the moment when he realized that his immobility must be astonishing the chauffeur.

VIII

Jacques Gellé was riffling through an art catalogue while a cup of coffee as big as a thimble fumed on a low table.

The room was excessively modernist. A great deal of wood had been employed, of the rarest species, in order to fabricate very small items of furniture. Everything was square and unusual in appearance. There were large cushions everywhere, obese and crooked, in heaps in corners or abandoned on the carpet. Enormous gold pochoirs maculated the overly violet drapes.

Jacques' town house was one of the largest and oldest in the Rue de Presbourg. It contained splendid antiques and the follies of hallucinated artists, marvelous classical canvases, paintings by Picabia and fantasies by Dufy, humorously incoherent.

Every corner of the building had its own character. One drawing room was Persian, another Louis XV, another Brandt, and one passed without transition from the Dutch dining room to the Chinese smoking room.

So, Jacques Gellé was riffling through his catalogue. He had never been more admirably dressed. Three different specialists had signed his arched jacket, his embroidered waistcoat and his trousers. The stripes of his shirt were both extravagant and discreet, and his cravat had reflections of moonstone.

A ceremonious valet appeared: one of those domestics so stylish that one never knows when they are mocking people.

"Does Monsieur wish to receive?"

Immediately feigning a futile ennui, the young man fixed his monocle. "Receive whom? Where's the card?"

The valet seemed embarrassed, but the embarrassment was conventional. "The Monsieur did not want to give his name."

"Then I won't see him," Jacques concluded, accentuating his affected lassitude.

"I believe, however, that Monsieur would be content...," the valet insisted.

Jacques had a desire to question him, but judged it ill-fitting to be so ostensibly curious. With a gesture devoid of meaning he said: "Show the fellow in."

The man who came in was René Legrand, unsteady but upright, suspended on two crutches, which he was holding too tightly, and launching his poor weak legs in a disorderly fashion.

"What a marvelous surprise!"

"Eh! This delights you?"

Behind the invalid came Jeanne and Madame Villaret, whose hair became curiously green under the effect of the drapes.

Legrand unhooked himself and collapsed in an armchair, like a heavy cloak falling on to a coat-peg. "I'm tired," he said. "It's terribly difficult to walk. I'm beginning to think that it's better to live sitting down..."

"It's only the first time that costs," said Madame Villaret, sententiously.

"For several days I've been storing up this surprise for you," Legrand continued. "Those worthy doctors have succeeded in getting me back on my feet, after a fashion. I now make a human figure, although a flick would knock me down. My first visit is for you. I've simply come to thank you."

Tears were pearling in his eyelashes.

Jacques turned his head in order that it might be thought that he was emotional. In reality, the logical sequence of events only made him feel proud of having foreseen them. "I'm very glad," he murmured.

"I can climb stairs!" the invalid added, triumphantly. "Nothing stops me! I'm beginning to live again. I already see things from a different angle..."

"Really?" said Jacques, satisfied, with a glance at Jeanne.

René Legrand sniggered. "It seems to me that I'm the king of the world!"

"It only depends on you to become so," said the director of the *Echo*. "You have in your hands everything necessary for that."

Monsieur Legrand sniffed scornfully. "Pooh! King of imbeciles and rogues—that's not an enviable title. I'd rather tip the cooking-pot over. That won't be long delayed, now I'm on my feet, and we're going to take action."

"Of course," Jacques acquiesced, without conviction.

The invalid's tenacious rancor against society disconcerted him—but Jeanne repressed a smile, and the young man understood that she had not despaired of the future.

"It's today," proclaimed Legrand, "that it's necessary to publish the article."

That haste seemed untimely to Jacques. "Today?"

"Yes, of course—this evening, as agreed."

Jacques Gellé consulted Jeanne with his gaze. She nodded her head imperceptibly as a sign of acceptance.

"Perfect!" said the young man, with his usual phlegm. "The article will appear on the first page."

"What an upset!" crowed the invalid, rubbing his hands together. "What a pebble in the frog-pond!"

"Tomorrow, we'll be famous!" ecstasized Madame Villaret.

"And the day after, we'll be cursed!" Legrand completed.

"They'll certainly see!" riposted the woman with the green-tinted hair, boldly. She was in the state of mind in which one accepts anything to satisfy one's pride.

Coffee was served, and liqueurs. To give satisfaction to Legrand, who could not keep still, it was necessary to drink quickly and leave for the Square Montholon.

As always, there was a crowd in the *Echo*'s waiting rooms, but the faithful secretary was on watch, and no intruder succeeded in crossing the threshold of the patronal office.

Jacques asked for Paul Duffaure; it was the lanky Peyrebrune who appeared.

"Duffaure isn't here," he revealed, in a lugubrious voice.

"Where have you sent him?"

"Nowhere, Monsieur. I haven't seen him for forty-eight hours. I'm taking advantage of the opportunity to let you know that he's been irregular for some time. I can scarcely count on him any longer..." Suddenly softly-spoken, he continued: "You know that when I complain about one of my collaborators, it's because there's no longer anything much to be obtained from him..."

"That's annoying," said Jacques.

"I have someone very good to replace him," the section-head hastened to declare.

"Introduce that someone to me," Jacques Gellé ratified, coldly. "Duffaure's leaving you, transferred to my particular service."

Peyrebrune's elongated nose became even sharper. The director's remarks were nuanced with irony.

"That...irregular fellow...has found Monsieur René Legrand in Bordeaux, whom I have the honor of introducing to you, on whom we're publishing a major article this evening..."

Peyrebrune examined the paltry cripple to whom the Boss was giving the honors of the first page.

"Monsieur Legrand," Jacques explained, "manufactures gold from lead."

"Gold?" repeated Peyrebrune, stunned.

"It's extraordinary, isn't it?"

"Oh! Yes, Monsieur..."

"Send me Clavier."

Peyrebrune folded his thin body respectfully and went out backwards. Shortly afterwards, Clavier, the general secretary of the editorial section, as obese as his predecessor was skeletal, appeared. He was already up to date, because his first glance was for Legrand.

"I called you," Jacques Gellé explained, because I want a particularly careful presentation of Duffaure's article, which you have on the slab.

"We already have the Nancy catastrophe with seventeen dead, one of them an artillery colonel," the secretary objected, "and a speech by the President of the Republic."

"Relegate the President to page two. I want a three-column headline: *The upheaval of the world. The most sensational discovery of all time.* You'll find in photography a portrait engraved and set up a few weeks ago: Monsieur René Legrand. Here's the article, tell me frankly what you think of it..."

And Jacques Gellé read Paul Duffaure's prose aloud, with a certain emphasis.

It was the first interview with the invalid, completed, more direct and more vigorous. Not a single word about Legrand's subversive intentions. Nothing but the skillfully told story of the experiment that the journalist had witnessed. The article gave an impression of gripping verity, which the public would surely share."

While listening to his own panegyric, Legrand trembled with emotion. Madame Villaret blew her nose too frequently, with a noise like a blind man's clarinet. The most tranquil and most lucid were Jeanne and Jacques.

"Well?" interrogated the latter, when he had finished. "What do you think?"

"Formidable!" replied Clavier. It was evident that the former colonel of artillery no longer existed for him.

"Have you any objection, Monsieur Legrand?"

Too troubled to speak, the invalid shook his head negatively.

"Then the die is cast. Go, Clavier."

Clavier went out, and silence reigned. With all the discretion of which she was capable, Madame Villaret wept.

"Would you like to see the newspaper born?" Jacques proposed.

The offer was accepted enthusiastically, and they went down to the workshops.

The linotypes were clicking. The overseer had divided Duffaure's article into three equal columns.

"I've had it set in nine-point elzévir," he said, as if he were announcing something perfectly intelligible."

Jacques explained that the size of characters is measured in points. Three points are approximately a millimeter. Nine-point letters are easy to read, especially in the elzévir font, both elegant and stout.

Sitting before a keyboard similar to that of a typewriter, the operator scarcely brushed the keys. At each touch, a copper matrix fell with a click. When the line was full of those matrices, it slid automatically on to a vertical disk. Various mysterious movements were accomplished in the machine; a piston pushed back the hot metal, and then a lead sheet came down—the line already set—a lever took possession of the matrices with a quasi-human gesture, and presented them at the extremity of an endless screw. The matrices filed along the screw, each one coming to rest above its case, and was spirited away as if by magic.

Sometimes, there was a cry of: "Stop!"

Immediately, a mechanic surged forth. In a matter of seconds, he located the breakdown, repaired it, and the linotype recommenced clicking.

As soon as the "quota" was finished, a worker in a black smock carried it away. He was the compositor. He tied the packet of lead lines with a cord, inked it with a turn of a gelatin roller, blackened in advance on a stone plate where the ink was spread out, covered it with damp paper, passed a few strokes of a brush over it, and obtained a proof, immediately transmitted to the corrector.

The latter, ignorant of the general meaning but attentive to the letters, the punctuation and the grammar, covered the margins with cabalistic symbols. Poor lines were reset, extracted from the grip and replaced by good ones with a remarkable dexterity. All those tasks were rapid and intelligent.

The definitive proof was sent to the secretary, who re-read it for the "secondary" corrections; then the packets of composition were arranged in zinc boxes known as galleys, in proximity to the marble of the page-setting.

The newspaper was elaborated in a solid steel frame. The secretary indicated the placement of the articles, which the setter filled with the columns after seeing them measured by a thread. Here, ten lines were added, there, three were removed. Headlines made by the compositor or the machine were modified and characters changed on brief instructions.

"Cheltenham type... Egyptian... Roman... Robur... Astrées."

The page was made up in a matter of minutes. Another proof, brushed, the final proof, examined rapidly and minutely by two secretaries, then the tightening by means of a special key. The form of the first page was ready.

"Take it away!"

They followed. An oven-like heat reigned in the print-room populated by bare-chested men—the laborers of the house. At the back a furnace reddened, under a vast cauldron in which several tons of an alloy of lead and antinomy were boiling.

The printers accomplished their work with precise gestures. One washed the form with turpentine. One passed a block of wood—the plane—from one and of the frame to the other, striking it with a few blows of a hammer, because it was necessary that no character surpassed the others. After that, a special cardboard was laid out, and then felt, and the whole was slid on to the plate of a hydraulic press with enormous uprights.

The dull thrusts of the piston shook the mass and the needle of the manometer oscillated, advancing notch by notch until it marked a hundred and twenty kilograms per square centimeter.

"Halt!"

The plate was slowly lowered. Under the frightful pressure, the characters were driven several millimeters into the cardboard. The "flong" was ready for delivery; it only remained to trim it to the exact dimensions and sprinkle it with talc. Skillfully, the printers adapted sheets of paper of varying thickness in the hollows, according to the size of the blanks to be reserved.

A mold in the form of a semi-cylinder was brought down, in which the flong was plunged, and, cotter-pins tightened with the twist of a lever, the molten lead was allowed to flow.

"Doesn't the cardboard burn?" Legrand asked.

The head printer shook his head. He was counting the seconds.

"Go ahead," he said, suddenly

Again the mold opened, uncovering the fuming stereotype, which was rapidly removed from the cavity. While a second was being run, the first was sealed at the extremities, smoothed at the edges, shaped with a graver and carried out of the room.

In the hall, eight two-story rotary presses loomed up. They were both delicate and robust, and their innumerable cogwheels were entangled in a manner inextricable to the profane. Rolls of paper of the width of the newspaper were brought forward on compact cylinders stouter than hogsheads, each made of a single sheet several kilometers long. The rotary press unwound, printed, cut, collated folded, counted and packaged thirty thousand copies an hour.

The stereotype was solidly fitted to a cylinder, and the press slowly began to roll. The spidery feet of the folder delivered a gray sheet, on which Legrand confusedly distinguished his photograph.

The stereotype was withdrawn, cellulose cuttings were stuck underneath it in various places. That was the "warm up," to make sure that the impression was regular. After that operation, the stereotype was put back in place, and the following ones were awaited. The machine was "dressed" with a dozen prints.

"In ten minutes," Jacques Gellé announced, "the paper will emerge. In a quarter of an hour, the first copies will be on sale in the boulevards. In an hour, you'll be famous—all Paris will be talking about René Legrand.

"What will tomorrow bring?" said the invalid. "At the moment of reaching my life's goal, I'm wondering whether..." But he chased away his pessimistic thoughts with his hand. "Let's wait! It's too late to turn back......"

The last stereotype was already screwed on to its cylinder. The rotary press was ready to roll. The chief mechanic, making sure with a glance that everything was ready, launched the traditional cry of: "Watch your hands!"

The wheels turned; the paper slid, irresistibly caught.

"Roll!"

The prodigious mechanism was animated. With a thunderous din, the rollers began to gyrate, so rapidly that their gear-wheels no longer seemed to be anything but shiny rim. The white bobbins spun at top speed, and at the other end, mouths spat out, relentlessly, a flood of papers that men carried away in hundreds toward the dispatch gates.

Workmen were busy on the iron walkways, lubricating the cushions, nourishing the monster with an ink as thick as wax.

One by one, the other presses shook. The racket increased immeasurably; the papers fell in an avalanche.

Legrand watched, clinging to his crutches. That mad haste, that satanic precipitation to inform humankind, caused him to marvel, and frightened him. What was about to become of him?

Already, outside, the vendors were running at top speed and their cries rose up: "Read the *Echo!* The upheaval of worlds! The *Echo!* The most sensational discovery of all time! Read *the Echo!*"

IX

Forty-eight hours later, Legrand was famous. Celebrity is quickly acquired in Paris, where the idle always need an idol or a victim. René Legrand become the man about whom everyone was talking, the Medieval sorcerer abruptly resuscitated in the twentieth century. Singers were writing stanzas about him, caricaturists were making burlesque sketches of him. Since all the dailies were publishing drawings, there was such profusion that no one bothered to choose, as of old, characteristic faces. But Legrand was a cripple, huddled in his armchair or perched on two crutches; he was not a man at whose expense one could amuse oneself with the ingenuous malevolence that one delights in thinking ferocious.

Those who had approached him and those who thought they had seen him having found him rather sympathetic, it was decreed that it was necessary to like him. Paris adopted him with the bulimia of an infatuated girl. In a matter of days, his photograph ornamented all the shop windows, and his biography was familiar to everyone—which is to say that his life was rendered practically impossible. He was assailed from dawn to dusk. Reporters wanted to question him on the most baroque subjects, tailors wanted to dress him, and in a single morning he received four orthopedic armchairs, one of which had a small internal combustion engine.

Cursing, but fundamentally delighted—for popularity is a poison agreeable to drink at first—Legrand jealously barred his door. The curiosity of people became importunate; solicitors were already flocking, and he could no longer go out of the hotel without dragging a hundred idlers in his wake.

He rarely took Ali with him any longer, because the Arab gave him away, involuntarily denouncing by this costume and tall stature the presence of his master in a crowd. He was reduced once more to furtive excursions in Jacques Gellé's auto.

He perceived that what is known as glory is often no more than the adulation of a host of imbeciles.

The print run of the *Echo* was increasing day by day. The whole of France, from the cities to the most remote villages, was avidly following the series of articles by Paul Duffaure on the secret of gold.

The journalist stretched his copy. Receiving hundreds of letters every day, he had every opportunity to respond to them in a prolix fashion. After a week of ratiocination, he described the factory at Le Grapon, whose imminent inauguration he announced, without revealing its geographical situation. Finally, he exposed René Legrand's ideas, in dribs and drabs, in a fashion all the more simplistic because he did not really understand them and thought them absurd.

It was thus learned that the alchemist did not want to enrich himself, and did not want to obtain any personal profit from his discovery. That disinterest was commented on in all the papers in the world, with enthusiasm or irony, according to the state of mind of the editor or the political coloration of the director.

But there was a great tumult when it became known that Legrand, as soon as he was certain that the production of gold could be industrialized economically, would deliver his secret to all nations and all individuals.

"Everyone will be rich!" the newspaper proclaimed. And in the following editions, on the contrary, one read: "Everyone will be poor!"

Political economy, the most false of the exact sciences, established its imperceptible right. One of the qualities of the election of precious metals is their necessary rarity. That had been forgotten. Eyes were suddenly descaled, and the immense majority of those who possessed something understood that the value of that seething was about to fall to zero.

It only took a few hours for the formation and almost perfect organization of two enemy clans: on one side, the rich; on the other, the poor—the fatal struggle between those who entitled themselves as defenders of order and those whom they qualified as revolutionaries. It was not a matter of the masses themselves, of course, but of the ambitious leaders who guided them.

The British were under no illusion regarding the consequences of the transmutation of lead. The London Stock Exchange was the first to panic. Gold stocks and South African diamond stocks fell with disastrous rapidity. In vain the mine-owners tried to hold back the drop. They were ruined in a single session, without reversing the trend by a single point. It was then easy to foresee a banking crisis unprecedented in the history of finance.

That first result amazed the French, because the panic was far less intense on the Paris Bourse, where the franc rose, in spite of the efforts of the Americans. A well-informed quasi-official newspaper published an editorial in which it was said in three columns that René Legrand, whose patriotic sentiments could not be put in doubt, desired to collaborate with all his might in the prosperity of his country, and that it was for that reason that he was undermining foreign fortunes.

Words—but those words sufficed to lower the value of sterling to sixty francs, and then to fifty, at which it was judged prudent to maintain it.

Then a campaign commenced, very skillful and treacherous. The *Soleil*, without accusing Legrand of fraud, demanded palpable proofs. Its article was signed by a member of the Institut, a redoubtable polemicist and ever-incredulous scientist.

He did not deny the possibility of transformations of chemical elements, which are accomplished in nature in the course of thousands of centuries, irresistibly and in an inexplicable manner, but he declared forcefully that no radioactive treatment could change lead abruptly into gold and reduce its atomic weight from 206 to 196.

Furthermore, he added, the price of the gold being tiny compared to that of the radioactive substances whose intervention was necessary, René Legrand's discovery could only have a purely scientific interest. It had, in any case, been known for a long time in laboratories.

In spite of his fury, the invalid did not yield to the temptation to respond. He bided his time.

"A day will come, and soon," he said to Jacques, "when gold will be so abundant that it will no longer be possible to use it as a monetary standard. I shall not respond with words but with deeds. As Edmond Théry[17] puts it: 'the civilized nations, having lost any common notion of the value of things, will be obliged to return to the politics of barter.' Now, they lost that habit back in the distant times when Solomon lived. This is going to be fun!"

"In the meantime," Jacques observed, "it's a catastrophe for the Bourse."

"What can I do about it?" sniggered Legrand. "It's not me who advises people to speculate."

"You're ruining quantities of large and small shareholders."

"I regret it, but I don't have the impression of being an Arton.[18] There's not the slightest dishonesty in my affair."

"The American MacLing committed suicide yesterday."

"I mourn him less than the prospectors washing the icy sands of the Yukon. They, who are not yet informed of my projects, don't merit the annihilation of their hopes. But one can't make an omelet without breaking eggs. Are you already regretting what you've done? I thought you had a better-tempered character. These are, however, only skirmishes before the battle."

---

[17] The political economist Edmond Théry (1854-1925) was a prolific commentator on the economic fortunes of France and those of other nations.

[18] "Émile Arton" was the pseudonym of Léopold Aron (1849-1905), a crooked financier who became notorious for his role in the Panama scandal and various other scams, which eventually resulted in his prosecution and incarceration.

"I don't regret anything," Jacques protested, readjusting his eternal monocle, "but people will soon be killing one another in the streets..."

"No, no!"

"You'll see—it won't be long..."

That prophecy darkened the expression of the invalid, who reacted after a brief interval.

"Take me to the Bourse," he said. "You promised to show me how the speculators devour one another."

That was one of the bees in the invalid's bonnet: he wanted to see the Bourse. It was an easy desire to satisfy. In order to pass unperceived, they decided not to take Ali.

As soon as the extremity of the Rue Vivienne, they heard the indistinct cries, always surprising, escaping from the temple of shares. From afar, it represented a bewildering concert of braying, yapping, and brief interjections as stinging as oaths. At close range, it was nothing but an exchange of offers and requests.

From one end of the peristyle to the other, and in the hall, a thousand men were agitating. None of them was shouting at the top of his voice, but as they were all talking in a high register, hurling titles and figures without any discontinuity, a deafening cacophony resulted.

Legrand, marveling at that swarming activity, applied all his faculties of comprehension to what he could see.

Around the basket, groups confronted one another as if ready to come to blows. It was impossible to grasp the meaning of what they were saying. Suddenly, a crier scribbled something. A deal had just been concluded, while the brokers continued to vociferate relentlessly.

Young men brandishing slips of paper were galloping back and forth, shoving people out of the way indiscriminately. In the corners and at the feet of the columns men were sitting down, as reserved as the others were feverish. It must, however, have been them who were giving the orders and modifying the prices on account of mysterious financiers. The Bourse had the appearance of a great mysterious fair in which nothing was being sold. Thus, children play at commercial transactions in which merchandise is lacking.

Legrand was soon disappointed. No one paid the slightest attention to his presence. The fall of mining stocks doubtless accentuated during the session, but he was reduced to suppositions in that regard because the official price was being established in that hubbub, and, in the wake of a few operations, the newspapers would be able to publish exact figures in a matter of hours.

It had seemed to him before going in that his entry into the Bourse would have something theatrical about it, that his incognito would soon be penetrated, that fingers would be pointed at him, and that people would say: "He's the one who fabricates gold! He's the gnome who's ruining the civilized world."

But nothing of the sort happened. The runners and the brokers had enough to do in their work, which required all their attention. None of them thought of differentiating Legrand from the curiosity-seekers and parasites that encumber the Bourse every day, in spite of the surveillance of the ushers.

"Are we staying any longer?" asked Jacques, shouting into his companion's ear in order to make himself heard.

The invalid wheeled on his crutched. "Oh, no... I've had enough. Let's leave these hyenas to yap."

But someone blocked their path.

"I'm not mistaken...it's really Monsieur Gellé to whom I have the honor...?"

Jacques stared without amenity at the polite individual with dead eyes, whose irreproachable politeness skirted insolence.

"Yes, Monsieur, it's me."

"Excuse me for introducing myself," the other went on, "but I've been seeking an opportunity for a long time... Lévy-Durand..."

"Delighted, Monsieur..."

It was a mere formula, for Jacques Gellé knew Lévy-Durand, who had been calling the tune at the *Soleil* for years.

The banker smiled in spite of his dull gaze. He suddenly became too unctuous, too much the merchant of fake Oriental carpets.

"When can you grant me an interview? I know you're very busy, but it's a matter of a considerable affair." He indicated Legrand courteously. "In addition, it also concerns Monsieur, to whom I have the honor of bowing down, with the respect that is owed to genius..."

"Thank you, Monsieur, but I'm scarcely sensible to flattery," muttered the invalid, never amiable at first.

All of that was shouted very loudly, in the exasperating hubbub that sometimes swelled up in gusts.

Lévy-Durand was not put off. "With your permission, I'll go with you if you're returning to your office."

"No, not today," Jacques replied.

"I beg you," said the financier, "in memory of my amicable relations with your poor father..."

He was making cynical allusion to monetary loans once granted to Prosper Gellé, for which he had always refused interest. Jacques therefore accepted, with an ill grace. Not having any contract or engagement as yet signed by René Legrand, he did not like anyone to approach the holder of the secret of gold."

They returned directly to the *Echo*. During the journey, Lévy-Durand was charming. He talked about the theater and racing, with a lightness of tone that contrasted with the solemnity of his person. Scarcely had he sat down in Jacques' office, however, than he changed his tone to broach his subject, like a man who knows the value of time.

"Without flattering myself," he declared, "I'm strong. I have money and influence. I work with a group who can do anything. Our legs have been pulled for too long; I've come to propose an alliance...an association..."

"To me?" Jacques said, astonished, to give himself time to prepare his response.

"To you and Monsieur Legrand."

"To do what?" asked the latter, swiftly.

"To exploit your discovery."

The invalid ruffled his silvery hair. "Well, well! Do you think I need associates?"

"Yes, since you've chosen Monsieur Gellé."

"Monsieur Gellé is not my associate, but my friend," said Legrand.

Lévy-Durand darted an ironic glance at Jacques, and became unctuous again. "Well, then, I shall also be your friend..."

René Legrand replied, in a surly tone: "That's flattering for me, but I don't feel any need to increase the number of my intimates."

"Oh, one more or less...." Lévy-Durand smiled. "You already have more than you even know..."

"Who are you talking about?" demanded Legrand.

Lévy-Durand appeared to search his memory. "I don't know...Schmitt, a slightly suspect banker...Guichard, director of a specialized telegraph agency..."

"I don't know those people," the invalid protested.

Lévy-Durand turned to Jacques. "And you..?"

The young man did not blink on receiving the direct thrust, and replied without hesitation: "I know them, but they're neither my friends not Monsieur Legrand's."

"Oh!" exclaimed Lévy-Durand, innocently. "I thought they were interested in the affair."

"Not at all," Jacques replied, without apparent indignation.

He knew that he was strictly covered. In spite of all his precautions, it was known that he had met with Aron Schmitt, but no one had proof of any conspiracy with Guichard. The three men carefully avoided being seen together. They were ready to launch the anonymous company. That was sufficient for the moment. The best affairs are not those that require daily conferences.

Lévy-Durand understood that his disguised threat had fallen short, and did not insist.

"My greatest desire," he said, "is to collaborate actively in the creation of the new work."

"I don't want to create, but to destroy," said Legrand, harshly.

"I only want to believe you," said the financier, whose gaze had become bleaker, "but I don't understand you very well. You're building a factory. Is that in order to destroy it?"

"It's to test myself in the practical domain, Monsieur. In the beginning, we'll certainly have miscalculations in the manufacture..."

"And when you've corrected those miscalculations?"

"I shall surrender my secret."

"You're not going to permit any small businessman to manufacture gold?" exclaimed Lévy-Durand, scandalized.

"Yes, Monsieur," Legrand replied. "Does that inconvenience you?"

"Personally, no, but it would be a crime. *Margaritas ante porcos*,[19] isn't it, Monsieur Gellé?"

The latter refrained from any response. The invalid, however, became angry.

"Why are you sticking your oar is? It's none of your concern."

Lévy-Durand lost none of his composure. "You're upsetting everything, Monsieur. You're creating chaos in the market. Since there's been talk about you in the press, the price of lead has shot up. And radium!"

"I'll find something else," Legrand retorted. "I don't stop at details. What I've done with lead I can do with another metal. You're proposing an association to me? What would your contribution be? Money? You're joking! It's me who could offer it to you."

"There are other things," retorted Lévy-Durand. "Money isn't everything. You'd gain from being well surrounded. *Vae*

---

[19] Pearls before swine.

soli! the ancients wrote.[20] In addition, if you like honors, one could facilitate..."

"He's going to offer me a decoration!" the invalid interrupted, with indescribable disdain. "Let's leave it there, Monsieur, without delay."

Lévy-Durand rose to his feet, meekly. "Don't get carried away, Monsieur. I have the impression that my visit hasn't been completely futile. You'll reflect, and we'll see one another again..."

"Should I take that as a threat?" said Legrand, immediately aggressive.

"As a confession of spontaneous amity," replied the financier. "*Au revoir*, Monsieur Gellé...until we meet again...very soon...."

And he went out at a tranquil pace, without looking back.

"That's violent!" said the invalid, indignantly. "There's a man who has no suspicion! I'm not for sale, me! What do you think about all that?"

"I'm already no longer thinking about it."

"Personally, it revolts me."

His ill humor only increased, because he found a packet of newspaper clippings at the hotel, which exasperated him. The *Soleil*'s campaign was making noise. Other newspapers were beginning to take sides against the alchemist. Legrand was accused of fraud, compared to Lemoine[21] under the pretext that both of them used electric furnaces, and a hundred other stupidities.

---

[20] The quotation is from *Ecclesiastes* 4:10: "Woe to him that is alone [when he falleth; for he hath not another to help him up.]"

[21] Henri Lemoine was a fraudster who claimed, in the first decade of the 20th century, to be able to produce synthetic diamonds, tricking the English banker Sir Julius Wernher out of tens of thousands of pounds, ostensibly to build a factory. Marcel Proust used the affair as the basis for one of his literary pastiches, having apparently lost money in the scam himself.

By the end of the day, the invalid had obtained results with his commensals. Jeanne had shut herself in her room in order to obtain a little respite, and Madame Villaret was once again weeping, according to her own expression, "all the tears in her body."

To provide a digression, Jacques took them all to a music hall. They were lucky enough to applaud a good program, but Legrand was still ruminating his ire. He charged Gastal with negligence because the factory at Le Grapon was not being built quickly enough. He claimed that Paul Duffaure wrote nonsense. The only one he did not dare accuse to his face was Jacques Gellé, but the director of the *Echo* sensed that he was suspect henceforth, carefully watched.

"Your Paris irritates me," Legrand said. "I want to go away. You're all running around perpetually in this frightful city. I'll give you back the notion of time! Look at those imbeciles, fleeing their pleasure like the plague!"

Without waiting for the end of the performance, people were indeed hastening toward the exit. They got up, summoning the usherettes, getting in one another's way, while two acrobats in clown costumes were exerting themselves on the stage.

"If they're in such a hurry to sleep, why are they here?"

"They're not going to sleep," Jacques said. "They're going to supper, dancing, gambling…"

"That's even more stupid!"

"That stupidity is contagious and not unpleasant," Jacques replied. "One doesn't always get bored in the nightspots…"

"People drink champagne there with prostitutes," Legrand continued. "It's a noble enough occupation."

"People amuse themselves greatly," simpered Madame Villaret. "On Jeanne's behalf and mine, I'll ask Monsieur Gellé to take us wherever he wishes…to hear a good jazz band…"

"I want to go to bed," the invalid complained.

Jacques interceded. "Grant these ladies an hour…"

"These ladies annoy me," said Legrand, stubbornly sulky. But he did not put up any more resistance, and agreed to go up to Montmartre.

La Sauterelle was the cabaret in fashion. Paris is capricious; without any decree, publicity or prior agreement, partygoers always have a place of predilection, where they believe themselves dishonored if they do not meet up there. The vogue might last a month or a year. Then it moves to another establishment, without any valid reason for abandoning the first.

The sign bearing the name of La Sauterelle was rutilant in the Place Pigalle. Luxury automobiles took many jewels and a great deal of money there after the theaters emptied. The familiar and respectful porters had plenty to do opening carriage doors and filing the elevator.

Upstairs there was the chaos of country fairs. Two negro orchestras dressed in red were working in shifts without interruption. The dances succeeded one another incessantly, trepidant and frenetic, destined above all to work the clientele up into a sweat. The waiters kept watch on the tables, authoritatively emptying any bottle open for too long, and signaling to the sommelier to bring another, which no one dared refuse,

A scornful smile was fixed on Legrand's lips. Ignorant of the intoxication of the senses, he did not understand how intelligent men could desire those beautiful but vulgar women, who offered themselves with an unaffected indifference.

The establishment's dancer, a seductively handsome young man, was inviting the dowagers to dance. By virtue of his bows one could evaluate the size of his tips at a distance. He came to invite Madame Villaret, to the confused delight of the yellow-haired woman, who nevertheless did not dare to accept.

"Oh," she sighed to Legrand, "if only I could dance with you."

"In a few months, you'll be dancing to the sound of a singular music. No, but take a look at humankind!"

No one found grace in his eyes. That prostrate woman with the vague eyes who must be using narcotics…that other one, thin and dark, monocled like a man, making eyes at a bewildered blonde…and that one, overripe, with red arms, was creating a jealous scene over a weary adolescent…all of them were worthless.

Playthings were distributed. The grating of rattles beat the measure. The dancers passed paper brushes under one another's noses. Old gentlemen decked themselves out in a fringed fez and continued drinking as gravely as before.

A group irrupted, dragged along by a quadragenarian fake adolescent. "Bonsoir, Gellé!" he shouted, and came to tell his little story.

"We're burying Dufflot's bachelor life. We've drunk I don't know how many martinis…we're as drunk as all Poland!" And with two taps on the thighs: "But it's Legrand! You've brought the phenomenon! It's Legrand!"

It was impossible to shut him up. He bounded on to a chair, and in a stentorian voice shouted: "Mesdames, Messieurs! We have the honor of having among us René Legrand, the man who makes gold!"

Those who were far away applauded without knowing why. Others repeated: "The man who makes gold! The man who makes gold!"

Everyone got up, and examined him curiously.

"It's him!"

"It's really him!"

A woman ran up, drink in hand. "I want to clink glasses!" In front of the table she sang the opening of the quintette from *Phi-Phi*:[22] "What does he need to be happy? A little gold…"

The invalid smiled complaisantly. He no longer had complete control over himself. Obedient to a sudden inspiration, he threw an ingot at random.

---

[22] The quintette is the penultimate number of Henri Christiné's highly successful operetta, immediately preceding the finale. The play opened at the Bouffes-Parisiens on Armistice day in November 1918 and ran for three years,

"Don't do that!" said Jacques, alarmed.

But the damage was irreparable. All the drinkers, all the dancers, all the waiters and all the musicians rushed forward. There were cries of distress.

"Encore! Encore! What are you waiting for?"

The invalid hesitated. The people who were looking at him had frightfully cruel eyes. But Jacques Gellé had not lost his presence of mind. Deliberately plunging his hand into the invalid's pocket, he brought out several scoria, which he threw across the room as hard as he could.

The battle became fierce. Bottles were smashed. A negro from the jazz band was wielding a chair like a sledgehammer. One man was supporting his howling companion, his nose bloody, repeating to her: "Don't cry, darling...don't cry...I've picked one up!"

Jacques seized the invalid around the waist and carried him away like a child. The women followed at a gallop, without collecting their coats from the cloakroom. Madame Villaret ran downstairs, saying: "I'm going to fall...I can't feel my legs any more..."

They piled into the limousine.

"Quickly, Gustave! Go! Go!"

The chauffeur pulled away. They were breathless, devoid of strength, half-unconscious.

The invalid mopped his moist brow, "Oh, the swine!" he exhaled.

X

The scandal at La Sauterelle made an enormous noise, and everyone was indignant against Legrand, accused of only taking pleasure in disorder.

Madame Villaret, consternated, was now demanding to leave Paris as soon as possible. The departure would have taken place soon in any case, because Gastal had announced the imminent inauguration of the factory at Le Grapon.

Legrand's life became increasingly tedious. He no longer went out except for his treatment. He dared not show himself any longer, because as soon as he was recognized, he was met with gibes and sarcasms everywhere. The experiment had, therefore, produced results opposite to those for which Jacques Gellé had hoped.

Paul Duffaure spaced out his articles. He had been seen several times going to see financiers, most notably Lévy-Durand. Was he going over to the enemy camp?

In collapsing, the mining companies of the Transvaal and Mexico had claimed victims. Especially abroad, numerous banks had set down their balance-sheets, and the Banque de France was supporting with millions several large establishments of credit whose honesty, in spite of the disillusionment, remain certain.

It was increasingly difficult to know what Legrand was thinking. An evolution was perhaps taking place in him, because he consented to receive the delegates of the Action Démocratique Française, officially mandated by that important political association.

There were three, all members of parliament, serious representatives of the sovereign people, but only one had the right to speak: Monsieur Rouby, a former minister, the president of the group.

The invalid received them wrapped in his checkered plaid, in the presence of the impassive Arab. In spite of his affirmed scorn for glory, he never renounced his little stage-setting.

"Monsieur," Rouby began, "we are not presenting ourselves to you as skeptics. We really believe that you can manufacture gold…"

"I thank you for that confidence," said Legrand, "but even if it were lacking, it wouldn't change anything."

"We are your friends," the former minister continued, slightly confused. "You know us by reputation, don't you?"

"Not at all," replied Legrand

Monsieur Rouby, frankly offended, declaimed as if at the tribune: "Since the foundation of the Third Republic, our party has been working for the prosperity of France and the wellbeing of the people. We invoke Gambetta and Waldeck-Rousseau. In the difficult moments that all democracies go through, we have often served the fatherland, and…"

Legrand interrupted peevishly: "Monsieur, politics will always remain Hebrew to me. If you have often saved the fatherland, I congratulate you, but I don't suppose that it's to list your services to the state that you're here, so speak briefly; I'm listening."

Rouby, increasingly disconcerted, continued: "We have come to make you a proposal…an offer…a request…"

"The three things do not resemble one another," observed the invalid.

The former minister suddenly extended his hands: "Will you join us?"

"With pleasure," Legrand accepted, "but to do what?"

The three men looked at one another with the indulgent surprise of apostles.

"To collaborate in our work," Rouby finally explained.

"With Gambetta and Waldeck-Rousseau?" said Legrand. "That's too much honor you're doing me. I imagined, in any case, that those Messieurs were deceased."

"Monsieur," said Rouby. "France needs money."

"That's incontestable," replied the invalid, "but don't count on me to give it to her."

"But Monsieur..."

"I shall give it to all nations, not to her especially."

"You're forgetting that you're French?"

"Indeed, I'm trying to forget it. It's rather difficult, but I hope that I might succeed."

Rouby had difficulty mastering his indignation. "I'm sure that's not your final word, Monsieur Legrand?"

"You're mistaken," said Legrand. "It's the whole of my final word."

With that, someone knocked. The *maître-d'hôtel* brought a visiting card. Legrand scarcely glanced at the Bristol card before bursting out laughing.

"Send him in. It's too comical! Do you know who's here, Messieurs? Randal, the Undersecretary of State. I'm confused by so much glory. Come in, Monsieur, you're truly not too many."

Randal recoiled slightly on recognizing Rouby, but the invalid continued, in his ringing voice: "It's complete! You've been given the word? The democrats, the Government, the whole forum! Tomorrow I'll receive the socialists, the day after, the communists and secret agents for foreign powers. Everything's for sale, isn't it? Everything except René Legrand, mutilated in the war, victim of Society, who only lives to bring down that society, his evil stepmother! Go, Messieurs, I won't keep you. Having come separately, go together. You can exchange comments about that on the stairs. You can exchange your paltry ideas. I'm convinced that you won't boast outside about the affront I've given you. I'm expelling the merchants from the temple! Go on, get out!"

"Monsieur," said Rouby, with compunction, "our politeness prevents us from responding to you."

They withdrew in a dignified manner, and went downstairs with their tails between their legs.

"We've had a sharp lesson," admitted Rouby, on the sidewalk.

"He's a visionary," added Randal, officially casual. "He's less dangerous than is believed. I feared a strategist,

I've found an apostle. He won't go through with it—he'll commit suicide."

And Rouby, his rancor overflowing, declared in his turn: "If necessary, if he doesn't die quickly enough, we'll suicide him ourselves. That's more reliable."

XI

From the mouth of the Gironde to the Spanish frontier, the Atlantic struggles against a land as fluid and mobile as itself, with no advantage on either side: no bays and no promontories. A straight shore, extending to infinity, guarded by the innumerable army of Le Pignadar, which pushes pines, isolated like sentinels, all the way to the tide-line. It is the delightful and nostalgic land that Maurice Martin[23] has baptized the Côte d'Argent, where roads and towns are rare, where wild cattle prick their muzzles on gorse whose flowers are drops of gold, where heather blurs the sand with the mauve cloud of its delicate florets: a land of peace and silence, where trees slowly bleed resin, and die standing up, like soldiers.

For centuries, the tide has been undermining the point of Verdon, bristling with dykes in the form of groynes. Gradually, the sea is eating the land, but long years will go by before the pointed cape sinks beneath the waves.

Le Grapon was a domain of dream. Trees everywhere— oaks and pines. On the edge of the road, turning its back on it in order to face the Atlantic, a modest bright villa, where it must be good to live. And on the other side, on the edge of the railway, the new factory, with its white stones and red tiles. It comprised six independent buildings, separated by broad pathways. The electricity generator was relegated to the forest, and its tall chimney seemed as high as the lighthouse of Cordouan, which could be glimpsed, all white, in the middle of the estuary.

The workers were lodged in comfortable barracks, which it had been necessary to build, for the village was a long way off and the staff had been recruited from all over.

---

[23] The journalist Maurice Martin (1861-1941)—a native of Bordeaux, like René Pujol—created the appellation in question in 1905.

As it was, the factory did not have a forbidding appearance. When Legrand arrived, it was immediately seductive. He did not take long to visit everything, to check everything and to begin the great experiments in transmutation.

The engineer Duret had a face like a retired warrant-officer. Beneath his eyebrows, as bushy as moustaches, his eyes were mobile and hard. He spoke bluntly and his gestures were curt.

"Monsieur," he said to Legrand, "You are a genius. I'm glad to work under your orders.

The invalid, paltry before that solid man, responded by holding out a bony hand. "We understand one another marvelously, and we'll soon obtain magnificent results. It's you who have chosen the workers?"

"One by one…I'll answer for them as far myself."

"And from the moral viewpoint?"

"I make no pronouncement. Its habit one sees there. They go to work, eat and sleep together. What will come out of that promiscuity? I don't know. The manual workers are mostly Spanish. They don't speak French—that's a guarantee."

"Do you have any fears with regard to discipline?"

"In principle, I'm always suspicious. Collectivity and discipline are two words that express antagonistic ideas. But if we organize the work in a suitable fashion, if the work demanded of each man is in accord with his productive captivity, all will be well, and our men will manufacture gold without having time to reflect. What makes the superiority of industrialists is that they don't give their workers time to think."

Gastal irrupted into the room. The worthy fellow was glad and proud, convinced that the factory was his work, and that without him, it would never have existed.

His meeting with his fiancée had taken place in front of Jacques Gellé and Paul Duffaure, who had naturally made the voyage. Jeanne had offered her cheek to Gastal without enthusiasm and without a smile.

"Did you have a good journey?" he asked, with a disproportionate anxiety.

"Excellent, thank you," she said, without returning his kiss.

Gastal remained utterly awkward before the beautiful girl. "I've been longing to see you," he finally stammered.

"Me too."

And the expansions stopped there: timidity and dullness on the one side, indifference and hostility on the other.

So, Gastal irrupted into the room where Legrand was talking to Duret. He came to tell them that the workers, assembled in the entrance courtyard, were awaiting the alchemist.

Legrand had himself rolled to the factory gate by the Arab. Then he took hold of his crutches and progressed in graceless hops.

In front of the concierge's lodge, a man with one leg amputated was making a net while smoking a pipe.

"May I introduce Minois, our concierge," said Duret.

Minois suspended the movement of his shuttle.

"Salut, Messieurs!" he exclaimed, jovially. "I'll wager that this is the Boss..."

"In person," replied Legrand, amused.

Minois stood up and offered his hand, familiarly. "How are you?" he asked. "Looking well, so far as I can see. Don't wait on my account—we'll have time to chat again."

"We'll never make a head of protocol of him," said the engineer, smiling. "He's rough-hewn, but one could chop him into pieces rather than make him fail in his duty."

"Ah! There are my lascars," murmured Legrand

The workers formed a compact crowd. There was a movement of amazement when they saw that gnome dragging himself toward them. They softened, for they had not imagined Legrand so weak, so infirm.

He stopped some distance from the group in order better to embrace them with his gaze.

"Bonjour, my friends!" he cried, in his hoarse voice, always impressive when one was not used to hearing it

A respectful murmur replied to him; with a common gesture the workers doffed their caps.

"I hope," Legrand continued, "that we shall be able to congratulate ourselves for having come together at Le Grapon. You have arrived confident and poor; you will leave satisfied and rich. You will go to work for yourselves. I make you the categorical promise now that everything you produce will one day belong to you."

"Long live the Boss!"

A seagull was soaring over the factory; it plunged like an arrow.

"Do you believe in omens?" Duffaure asked Jacques.

"No, do you?"

"Me neither. That one would have constrained a Roman..."

The workers went back to their posts, while Legrand and Duret headed for the electricity generator.

Duffaure said to his employer: "Since the day when I talked to you about René Legrand, there's never been a question of interest between us."

Gellé screwed in his monocle nonchalantly. "I was waiting for you; I'm at your disposal."

"First of all, are you satisfied with my services?"

"Yes," Jacques replied.

"So much the better," Duffaure joked. "You'll pay more dearly."

"Why are you talking to me about payment today?"

"Because I consider my task to be concluded," the journalist admitted, "and I want to leave you without further delay."

"What?" said Gellé, surprised. "You want to leave me?"

"Oh, perhaps not definitively," Duffaure protested. "Perhaps I'll come back, but at least I'd like to take a long vacation."

Silently, Jacques Gellé waited for the explanation.

"We're sliding down a slope," said Dufaure then. "We believed that Legrand would be easy to convince and to bring back to reason. We were grossly mistaken, for he's as stubborn as he was on the first day."

"Wrong!" Jacques rectified. "There's no abysm at the bottom of our slope. Legrand is evolving from day to day without being aware of it..."

"In any case, I want to enjoy life. If we're heading for catastrophe, I'd rather divert myself now. It will be as much gained. If nothing bad happens, so much the better for everyone. That's why I'm asking you now for the viaticum that will enable me to profit from some fine days."

"Your philosophy is rudimentary," said Jacques.

"I'm a simple man," Duffaure philosophized. "What has decided me is the retreat of Schmitt and Guichard, who were marching with you."

The director of the *Echo* opened his check-book, inscribed figures and signed.

"With my thanks," he concluded.

Paul Duffaure read it and murmured: "This is an advance?"

"You're greedy," Jacques reproached.

"No, I'm just. I know what things are worth."

"Here's the balance, then." Jacques held out a second check.

"*Au revoir*, Boss," said the journalist, then, satisfied. "I wish you a perfect success. Who knows? Perhaps you'll have lots of gold and...the rest."

"What rest?"

"Oh, we understand one another."

He drew away with the secret of his mocking smile.

Jacques took out his monocle.

"The rest," he said, in a low voice, "is harder to obtain."

XII

In September, dusk comes rapidly. The immense cupola of the sky darkens, while the sun gives the ocean the reflections of molten metal. The ebb tide untiringly casts up sheets of lace on the beach, and the mystery of twilight is born in the green shade of Le Pignadar.

Jeanne closed her book. She liked that moment when the day leaves regrets behind, while awaiting the seductions of the night.

The immaculate sand of the dunes had the aspect of a rough sea suddenly frozen by a prodigious spell. In the foliage of needles, the chatter of the cicadas had fallen silent.

"You're dreaming, Mademoiselle?"

It was Jacques Gellé, very "worldly acrobat" in his impeccable white flannel suit.

Jeanne raised her velvety eyes to look at him, without emotion. "I am, in fact, dreaming..."

"About whom?" he asked, sitting down on the sand.

"Oh, no one," she replied. "It's only a subjective dream. The hour is mild...I was floating at hazard..." And her cheeks reddened slightly.

Jacques allowed sand, of which he had picked up a handful, to trickle through his fingers.

"I'm bored," he sighed.

"You're bored with me? That's gracious!" Jeanne said, with a burst of laughter.

"Would you like me to correct you? It's superfluous, because you understood me. I'm bored when I'm not with you. And if I suffer even more ennui when I'm by your side, it's because I think inexorably about things...things...what a pity I can't explain my entire thought!"

The young woman's lips trembled, but she made no reply. Then Jacques went on: "You've surely perceived...something?"

He stopped. She did not question him.

"This evening, I'm at your feet," he said, in a lower voice. "I can no longer keep quiet. Often, already, I've tried to speak...now, my secret is springing irresistibly from my heart... I think I love you."

The first star lit up in the depths, its drop of gold changing the tint of the sky.

"Answer me," Jacques begged.

"You're an egotist," she said, in a calm voice.

That appreciation surprised him.

"An egotist, me? Why?"

"So egotistical that you think you're sincere. You love all the women you desire."

"You're mistaken!" he protested. "I know I'm in love, because I'm suffering."

"What romanticism!" Jeanne mocked. "You, suffering? You?"

"I'm suffering confusedly. It's not a simple desire that pushes me toward you. I respect you; you've disposed of your life..."

"No!" she cut in. "One doesn't dispose of one's life. It's a property of which we only have the usufruct."

"Anyway, you're engaged, and you love the man who will be your husband. You can see that I have no hope, no illusion. I'm a *bon viveur*. I've had, and will have, mistresses, but I don't have one at present."

"Precisely," said Jeanne. "That's why you love me."

He rebelled. "Oh! No! Don't imagine that..." He dared not finish.

Serenely, she concluded: "I don't imagine anything."

The bells of Soulac chimed. The vibrations of the angelus flew over the waves like birds.

"I'm sure that I love you," said Jacques, as vehemently as his dandyism permitted. "But have no fear, I won't harass you. I'll cure myself of that love. Yes, I'll cure myself..."

"Soon," Jeanne prognosticated. "Tomorrow, you won't experience any malaise."

198

"Tomorrow, I'll have departed!" he declared,

"And I'll still be here. I adore traveling, though."

Jacques murmured: "I'd certainly offer to take you with me…"

"Shut up!" she murmured, neither annoyed nor astonished.

He obeyed. The silence seemed to last for centuries.

"Jeanne…," he finally began. "I can't, any more! I can't, any longer!"

Madly, he embraced her knees, and buried his face in the hollow of her skirt.

The young woman shivered, but made no effort to pull away.

"Get up," she said. "This isn't reasonable…"

This time, he did not obey. Then, with two hands, she took him by the temples. Their faces were very close to one another. It was her who drew him toward her, and their lips met.

Jacques was so shocked that he was only able to translate his gratitude in a further kiss, but she pushed him away firmly.

"Let's go back," she said. "They'll be astonished by our absence."

He followed her, as if drunk, wondering whether he had not been dreaming. He heard the young woman's profound respiration, as she marched over the sand, out of breath. Very close, the windows of the villa cut out orange rectangles.

"We can't part like this!" Jacques stammered.

"Ssh!" she replied. "We must."

"When shall I see you again?"

"At eleven o'clock. I'll open my bedroom window."

And they crossed the threshold, she extraordinarily calm, he utterly bewildered.

The invalid was already in the dining room, in the company of Gastal and Madame Villaret. "To table!" he cried, on perceiving the young people. "I'm as hungry as a wolf!"

"While you were out walking," said Gastal to Jacques, "I've reviewed the majority of the contractors' accounts. They're riddled with errors."

"You're making yourself useful!" mocked Legrand.

"Orderly men are necessary," remarked Madame Villaret, stupidly, her bleached hair flamboyant in the lamplight. "You're wrong to be so scornful of numbers, Monsieur Legrand."

"Me?" said the invalid, ladling out soup for himself. "I'm not scornful of numbers! I admire account-books. Titles in rounded capitals, subtitles at a slant, irreproachable addition. It's superb! Let's eat!"

"You're caustic," riposted Gastal, vexed. "It doesn't affect the fact that one can't keep an important enterprise going without accountability."

"Not even one's heart," said Legrand. "The ins and outs have to equilibrate. You're made for Jeanne, she for you. Your life will be devoid of surprises."

"Oh, surprises," sighed Madame Villaret. "We know where they lead…"

"We shall be bourgeois," Gastal affirmed. "That's the whole of our ambition, isn't it, Jeanne?"

"Yes, my love," conceded the young woman

"You'll follow the crowd, then!" said the invalid. "After the upheaval I'm preparing, all the world will be bourgeois. I'm crossing out a formula that seemed eternal: gold for love. Who can tell whether we'll suppress the war of the sexes by suppressing the comedy of false passions and only allowing animal desire to subsist?"

Madame Villaret became indignant. "Won't there be any more difference between beasts and humans?"

"Bah!" grunted the invalid. "Do you think that in the norm, affection is confounded with amour, such as we understand it today? People remaining close to nature make two distinct sentiments of them, to such an extent that a savage of Hawaii or the Moluccas offers the body of his wife or his daughter to a visitor he honors, as simply as we would offer him lunch."

"Poor women!" exclaimed Madame Villaret, hypocritically.

"It's no different in Europe," Legrand continued, "but our conventions constrain us to ignore it. And when we're forced to see it, our indignation bursts forth magnificently."

"Papa," Jeanne interjected, "Don't be so talkative, and occupy yourself with your guests. Monsieur Gellé isn't eating anything."

"I'm not hungry," the young man replied.

"You're not ill?" asked Madame Villaret, alarmed.

"Not at all. I'm marvelously well, but I have no appetite this evening."

"At your age," said the invalid, "when one has no appetite, one is either ill or in love."

"I prefer being in love," Jacques confessed, cheerfully.

"Personally," said Gastal, "I'm in love and I have the stomach of an ostrich. I'm remarkable well-balanced, aren't I, Jeanne?"

"You're aggravating, above all," she said.

"Oh, pardon me," Gastal apologized, without taking offense. "There's electricity in the air. We're going to have a storm tonight."

Every five minutes, Jacques Gellé took out his watch, furtively.

She's damnably strong, he thought, contemplating Jeanne. *Who is she deceiving, her fiancé or me?*

The invalid was now talking about the factory. He feared surprises during the heating of the furnaces. He thought they were too high, and the walls too thin.

Jacques made a real effort to take an interest in the conversation. Then, as she did every evening, Jeanne sat down at the piano. She played Chopin for her father, and a foxtrot for Gastal. In her turn, Madame Villaret requested *Roses d'Automne*, to which she listened while squeezing the invalid's hand tenderly.

At about ten o'clock, they separated.

"Until tomorrow," Jeanne said, extending her hand to Jacques.

He then made her a discreet sign, to which she made no response.

He went as far as the sea shore in order to kill time. How would the adventure finish? Was it not already over? He felt devoid of power, devoid of strength, before that robust young woman who never surrendered her soul.

Thick clouds rolled by. The breeze swelled the waves, some of which were breaking like cannon-shots. An invisible giant hand shook the pines. As Gastal had predicted, a storm was rising.

Jacques circled around the villa. All the windows were dark. He leaned back on the wall and waited.

A flash of lightning split the shadows, but the clap of thunder was only a dull rumble on the horizon. A few raindrops fell; then, immediately, there was rain, warm and profuse.

Jacques took shelter as best he could, which did not prevent him soon being drenched by the downpour.

Finally, the window opened; in the frame he divined Jeanne's silhouette.

"Are you wet?" she whispered, in a slightly mocking tone.

"To the bones!" he replied, "but I don't regret it, since..."

"Give me your hand, and don't make any noise," she commanded.

He climbed over the sill. In the room, he bumped into a chair, and groped his way forward.

"Clumsy!" breathed Jeanne.

He heard her close the window, and a second later, she was pressed against him, bold and tremulous.

She was wearing a light peignoir. Her lips parted, she abandoned herself silently, and the bewildered young man repeated: "Darling...darling...darling..."

He became audacious without her resisting. She weakened under his caress. He thought her ready for the embrace, and tried to draw her into it.

"No!" she said, her voice cold and curt.

There was a veritable struggle, savage and merciless. He might perhaps have vanquished her, but she bit his hand cruelly. They remained face to face, unable to see one another, both breathless and exhausted.

"Go!" she ordered. "Go!"

He staggered, because she pushed him violently.

And he found himself outside again, stupid, beneath the diluvian rain.

XIII

A delirious folly was agitating the world. In all countries, riots were breaking out, and the most futile differences had tragic outcomes. In the newspapers, there was nothing to be found but protests, maledictions and threats against Legrand, accused of having unleashed the worst instincts.

The invalid did not make anyone party to his impressions and sentiments. Increasingly somber and sullen, he had crises of silence. Often, late at night, Madame Villaret heard him stirring, and found him sitting up in bed. He claimed not to be suffering physically, but he almost never used his crutches, and preferred to have himself pushed by Ali in his armchair with castors.

He went to the factory twice a day. The manufacturing process was progressing regularly, without the yield ceasing to be mediocre.

Meticulously, Legrand carried out all the weighings personally. In spite of Duret's surveillance, however, many of the furnaces were failing, only giving a metal gilded internally, brittle and friable, which was not gold, and with which nothing could be done, because it had no commercial value.

There were other, equally grave, disappointments. The radium incomprehensibly lost its power after a dozen experiments. Furthermore, the lead was impure, with the result that it had to be carefully refined before being employed.

These difficulties irritated the invalid, because the price of the ingots was effectively equal to that of the cost of the raw materials and manufacture.

Legrand, whom a dispute would have delighted, tried to provoke reproaches, or at least observations, from Jacques Gellé, but the young man had other things on his mind, because Jeanne's distant coldness afflicted him. He spent his days seeking a tête-à-tête and never succeeding in being alone with her. That covert duel was prolonged without the quotidian witnesses perceiving it.

One morning, the concierge, Minois, reported that the previous evening, while making his rounds, he had surprised a worker trying to break into the building where the gold ingots were stored. The guilty man was a young southerner with a bold gaze, who did not seem to be aware of the gravity of his action. He bore Duret's reproaches without flinching, and was undisturbed by the appearance of Legrand,

"You'll be sent to prison," said the engineer.

"I'll be released," said the thief, with a sly smile. "What we're manufacturing is for us, isn't it? I was only serving myself before the others.

"You're arguing, wretch!" growled Duret. "Oh, if I were the master...."

"Damn!" said the other. "It's necessary to be logical. Either you've been having us on, or you won't send me to prison."

"I'll have you condemned!" Duret threatened.

"It'll delight the audience!" riposted the man. "I'll talk, and the newspapers will do the rest."

Legrand intervened then. "The man was wrong," he said, "but I don't want him to be punished for a peccadillo. Give him two ingots and let him go."

Duret made a gesture of angry impatience. "If you treat him like that we'll have fine results."

"Give him two ingots," the invalid repeated.

"Thank you, Monsieur," said the man, before emerging from behind the engineer. "You're very generous, but I won't be catching up with Rockefeller like that..."

Everyone criticized Legrand for his forbearance. Duret accused him of fomenting anarchy and Minois was not embarrassed to tell him he passed by, without stopping work on his net, that he would henceforth sleep tranquilly instead of making his nocturnal rounds.

At six o'clock a delegate of the workers demanded to be received. His name was Legaye and was reputed to be a troublemaker.

Legrand was confronted by a determined fellow, visibly intelligent, who said to him: "Monsieur, my comrades have charged me with transmitting their protests to you. They disapprove of your generosity. By letting off, and even recompensing a thief, you've acted against the general interest."

"It's you who are presenting that argument?" retorted the invalid. "It seems to me, however, that you're a libertarian?"

"Certainly," agreed Legaye, "but libertarians worthy of the name are inflexible about discipline."

"Assuming that I was wrong…it's necessary, then, that I accept your reprimand?"

"Our warning," Legaye rectified. "If something similar happens again, we'll do justice ourselves. We don't want to be cheated by rogues. We'll hang them high and short."

Once he was alone, Legrand meditated. Then he summoned the engineer.

"I accept the remonstration," he said to Duret. "I'm an imbecile. I don't understand anything. Work quickly, that's all I ask of you. Henceforth, I'll be content to submit to events."

They were precipitate, those events. There was little information about the American strikes, but disorder was increasing in Europe.

The English Labor Party demanded the immediate nationalization of all industries. The Germans were slaughtering one another conscientiously in mining regions, and the French were arguing intensively before coming to blows.

The Confédération Générale du Travail, obedient to governmental suggestions, strove to calm minds, but people did not want to be calmed. They wanted nothing more than to rise up, to fight, and to overturn everything. Under the pretext that the social system was about to collapse, they already wanted guarantees for the future.

The dock-workers of Marseilles set fire to a transatlantic liner, a costly and magnificent distraction that they wanted to repeat the next day—but that time the gendarmes intervened, and there were a few cadavers in the old harbor, La Joliette and L'Estaque.

There were consequences. The north did not remain quiet. People were shot in Lille, without any plausible reason, and the mines of Lens were the theater of fratricidal battles. Miners killed and were killed in hundreds. Professional orators hurrying from Paris poured oil on the fire, and a veritable civil war broke out.

"There'll always be enough survivors!" Legrand sniggered, without daring to look his interlocutors in the face.

During lunch, shouting was heard in the garden at Le Grapon. Gastal went out to see what it was. It was a woman who, having climbed over the gate, was ranting incoherently.

She planted herself in front of the open window of the dining room. She was ugly and dirty, bundled up in mourning-dress whose veils rendered her tragic.

"Where is he?" she said, leaning through the window. "Where's the sorcerer? I've come from Lens to tell him what I think of him."

Around the table no one budged.

"Ah! I see him!" the woman continued, pointing at Jacques Gellé. "That's him, I recognize him!" She clenched her fists hatefully. "Wretch! You've caused the death of my man! He came out of the mine with the others. You've made them all crazy with your nonsense! From one day to the next, starvelings thought they were millionaires. It ended up with drunken sprees. They fought, and they picked him up with his head bashed in, dead! A man I loved...a man who gave me five kids...all alive! All of them!"

There was affectation and rancor in that cry. Five children, five dolorous maternities, which had now crushed her forever.

Gastal, who had made his way surreptitiously along the wall of the villa, grabbed the woman by the shoulders.

"Come away, Madame...."

"Me, come away? I've crossed France to avenge my man, and you think I'll go away without having obtained justice?"

Gastal recoiled, thinking that she was hiding a weapon, but she only had her fingernails, which she waved under his nose.

"What are you promising us? Gold...gold? Who asked you for it? Let us live, poverty doesn't scare us...we're used to it. Who'll give us back our men? What will we do without them?"

And, thrusting her body forward, haggard, she shouted: "Murderer! Murderer!"

Gastal and Rosita seized her from behind. Madame Villaret had the courage to close the window, but through the panes, she was still heard clamoring: "Murderer! Murderer!"

Legrand was livid. He propped himself up on his crutches, and disappeared into his bedroom.

XIV

Duret had scarcely been in his office for ten minutes when someone came to look for him on the part of Monsieur Legrand. He immediately went to the villa, where the invalid was waiting for him, with Gastal and a third solemn individual that he did not know.

Legrand introduced him: "Monsieur Dupuy de Grelière, chief of staff of the Minister of the Interior."

Duret observed immediately that they were serious, as if annoyed. The invalid's agitation was considerable, and he was ruffling his hair incessantly.

"Monsieur Duret," he began, "something essentially absurd has happened."

"Heart-breaking," Gastal put in.

"Shut up!" snapped the invalid, ferociously. "I say that it's ludicrous. It appears that we're inconveniencing the Government."

"Not the Government, France," Monsieur Dupuy de Grelière rectified, with dignity.

Legrand continued, in an indignant voice: "Although collective folly is the sole cause, we're being held responsible for the riots in Marseilles and the butchery in Lens. It's ridiculous!"

"Monsieur," said the chief of staff, "I represent the President of the Council here, who has a right to every respect."

"Monsieur," riposted Legrand, "I'm in my own home here, and I have a right to the free expression of my ideas."

"So be it!" Monsieur Dupuy de Grelière bowed coldly. "I have, in any case, no intention of debating."

"So," said Legrand, "we're guilty. We merit being thrown in the pokey, while awaiting the guillotine. I'm laughing!"

"No, Monsieur, you're not laughing," observed the chief of staff, with a small gesture of denial.

"I'm laughing!" shouted the invalid, suddenly furious.

But his interlocutor was not easy to dominate. "You're not laughing!" he repeated. "You're well aware of your responsibility. At the beginning of your experiment, you didn't hide your intention of disrupting the world. That fine project has begun. We judge it dangerous to let you continue any longer your work of mortal demoralization."

"In short," Legrand concluded, "I've become an undesirable?"

"Yes, Monsieur. We admire the scientist in you, but we are standing up against the agitator."

"Do you hear?" said Legrand to Duret. "The solution of the problem is that they're demanding that we close the factory."

"When?" asked Duret, without raising any opposition to that decision.

"Immediately," replied the chief of staff.

"And if I refuse?" said Legrand.

Dupuy de Grelière parted his arms and let them fall. "We'll have the regret of acting ourselves. Our dispositions are made. We're reluctant to use violence, but we won't hesitate for a second to use force."

Legrand uttered a terrible laugh.

"Well planned, Monsieur! If I resist, if blood is shed, I'll be responsible again, won't I?

Monsieur Dupuy de Grelière contented himself with staring thoughtfully at the ceiling.

"After what we've promised our workers," Duret suggested, "there'll surely be a squabble."

"You hear, Monsieur?"

"I hear clearly," replied the other, without departing from his extreme correctness, "but I can't do anything about it."

"Oh! They would have left me in peace if I'd agreed to work exclusively for the Republic!"

"I consider that that would have been your duty," the Parisian immediately riposted.

"You're insulting me, Monsieur!" Legrand vociferated, his fist raised.

"Not at all. I'm giving you my opinion. I regret that you find it insulting. It's said that it's only the truth that hurts."

"I'll have you thrown out by my Arab!"

"That's quite possible," said Monsieur Dupuy de Grelière, sitting down. "I'll come back, that's all. And if it isn't me, it will be someone else."

He was a man. The Minister had not chosen his spokesman at random.

And then, *zut!*" vomited Legrand, white with anger, his eyes bulging. "I've had enough! People have been tormenting me for months. You're all around me like jackals. Do what you want and leave me in peace, peace, peace!"

And with his open hands he crushed his eyes, as if to cause darkness in his skull.

"I'll go away," he went on, in a low voice. "I'll begin again elsewhere, until death strikes me down. The task is gigantic, but nothing will discourage me. I'll go to Russia…yes, that's it, to Russia. There I'll find men…true men, fashioned by poverty…"

"I'll go with you!" said Gastal, nobly.

"I don't need you," growled Legrand. "I don't want anyone. Get out, all of you!"

He chased them out of the room with grand gestures, beyond his horizon..

"What should I do?" asked Duret.

"Don't talk to me anymore! You've heard everything, like idlers at a fairground. Pay off the staff, tell my brave comrades that I'm being forced to sack them. And distribute the gold…all the gold. Let them be happy, those who have helped me, who have perhaps loved me and believed... You understand me?"

"Your orders will be carried out," replied Duret, without a muscle in his face quivering. And, standing aside before the chief of staff: "After you Monsieur…."

Monsieur Dupuy de Grelière bowed to Legrand with a respect that was not feigned.

Gastal, who was the last to leave, turned round. "Is it necessary to give them all the ingots?"

"Whatever you like. I just want peace…peace…peace…"

The roses were embalming the garden. Beyond the gate, the road was dazzlingly white in the sunlight.

They marched in silence to the factory. Duret had already decided that he ought to do his job.

At the entrance to the courtyard, Minois was patiently fitting a few more meshes to his interminable net.

"Sound the alarm," Duret said to him, without preamble.

The concierge thought he had misheard. "If you please, Monsieur?"

"Sound the alarm," repeated Duret.

"Very well, Monsieur."

Without further ado, Minois headed for the bell and sounded loud, precipitate chimes. Curious heads emerged from the windows and shouts of "Fire!" were heard. Then a few workers emerged, bare-headed, with their sleeves rolled up.

"Should we man the pump? Where's the fire?"

"Assemble!" ordered Duret.

Soon, the entire personnel was there, intrigued but anxious. The engineer, standing on the concierge's chair, dominated the crowd. He made a sign and silence fell.

"My friends," he shouted, without preamble, in a voice that carried to the furthest ranks, "I have bad news to give you. By order of the Government, the Le Grapon factory is closing its doors today."

Amazement was painted on all the faces. The Spanish laborers who did not understand French very well interrogated their comrades. A short dark-haired man raised his arm.

"And what did the Master say?"

"He's weeping!" put in Gastal, in a piercing voice.

"Then why submit?" the same man went on. "Who cares about the Government?"

"It appears that measures have been taken, that resistance is impossible," Duret continued. "I advise you to obey."

"And the gold?"

At that question, all individual conversations stopped dead.

"It will be distributed to you," said Duret.

An enormous "Ah!" of satisfaction rose up.

As the engineer leapt down, Monsieur Dupuy de Grelière leaned toward him.

"You see? You were wrong to be pessimistic. There won't be a squabble."

Duret looked him up and down contemptuously. "Do you think it's finished?"

Followed by the cohort, they headed for the building where the gold was stored. Gastal closed the door in the faces of the most eager.

"How are we going to proceed?" asked Dupuy de Grelière.

Little white sacks were heaped around them. Already the windows were obscured. The workers climbed up on the sills to try to see through the iron bars what was inside.

"Give one sack to everyone, Duret proposed.

But Gastal immediately protested. "Ten kilos! Never on your life. Half a sack each. That's amply sufficient."

Monsieur Dupuy de Grelière, stupefied, tried to ferret through the heap with the tip of his cane.

"So all this is gold?" he said.

"Yes, Monsieur," Duret replied, brusquely. "There are billions. It's not fake."

"That's extraordinary!" the chief of staff admitted, placidly. "I didn't expect so much wealth."

"If you want, don't hold back," Duret added. "You have only to help yourself, like everybody else."

Monsieur Dupuy de Grelière blushed. "In truth," he said, with a weak smile, "I won't refuse…I have three children."

"Go on, go on!" said the engineer. "It's more honest than the secret funds…"

Monsieur Dupuy de Grelière weighed a sack in his hands. "It's heavy," he murmured.

"Bah!" said Duret, ironically. "All the same, you could carry two?"

"Oh, yes!" said the envoy of the Ministry, naively.

"And you regret not being able to take three," the engineer continued. "Everyone has your mentality. That's why there'll soon be a riot."

"If we open the door," said Gastal, "we'll immediately be submerged, invaded, pillaged. It's better to pass the ingots through the window. The bars are solid."

"And if the workers want second helpings?" objected Monsieur Dupuy de Grelière.

"Have no fear of that," Duret replied. "They'll police themselves, and woe betide the greedy! Have you seen crowds unleashed, delivered to the worst instincts?"

"For twenty years," said the Ministry delegate, phlegmatically, "it's always been me who attended major strikes."

"Then I have no need to insist. It'll go swimmingly! Let's get on with it, Gastal."

And the improbable distribution commenced.

The first served was a young Catalan. His dirty fingers with thick nails clutched the one-kilo ingots.

"One...two...three...four...and five!" Gastal counted out. "Next!"

The worker's eyes were gleaming with cupidity.

"*No ay demasiado!*" he said.

"What, that's not enough!" said Duret, indignantly. "Would you like to get out of the way?"

"Yes, yes!" howled his neighbors. "Enough for him! Our turn!"

There was a kind of eddy, and the Spaniard disappeared with his ingots. Other hands were extended imperiously, just as dirty and just as avid.

And Gastal counted out, unhurriedly: "One...two...three...four...five!"

"Next!" said Duret, synchronically.

Soon, they were streaming with sweat. To make himself useful, Monsieur Dupuy de Grelière untied the sacks and emptied them on to the floor. And still hands passed through the bars, ten at a time, beneath nightmarish faces with flamboyant eyes.

Exhausted, Gastal wanted to sit down, but there were such vociferations that he carried on.

"One…two…three…four…five…!"

Suddenly, Monsieur Dupuy de Grelière tugged Duret's sleeve. "Look out! Something's going on outside."

"What?"

"I don't know. I think they're fighting…"

Raising himself up on tiptoe, they perceived beyond the crowd, in the middle of the sun-bathed courtyard, a compact and turbulent mob.

"So much the worse for them!" concluded the engineer. "If you're not too tired, Gastal, carry on."

On the other side of the building, however, violent blows shook the door.

"Hmm! It's going bad already!" said Duret, with a bitter smile.

"They won't break down the door," said Gastal. "I've set the bars."

They did not understand what was happening outside.

Meanwhile, someone shouted: "Silence! Silence!"

But those who were piled up near the window, on the point of being served, did not obey. Then, savagely, fists struck out. An old man, seized around the waist, was hauled away from the bars, and a voice dominated the decreased tumult.

"Com…rades! You're being robbed! You're being given five ingots when they ought to be distributing five times as much. You hear? Five times as much!"

"That's Legaye," announced Duret.

"A ringleader?" asked Monsieur Dupuy de Grelière.

"He has a lot of influence over them. They'll do whatever he wishes."

"We have rights," continued the vehement orator. "It's only up to us to exert them! Remember what Monsieur Legrand said. All the gold here is ours, even the factory belongs to us. After all, we're only demanding what's ours!"

Duret went to the window. "Legaye!" he shouted, "I forbid you to talk like that!"

An enormous jeer was the crowd's response. Those who were waiting at the head of the queue took against the engineer with a sudden hatred. "We have a right to two sacks! Thief!" You want to keep the rest for yourselves."

Legaye's powerful voice thundered: "What isn't given to us is ours to take!"

In the tumult, Duret turned to Monsieur Dupuy de Grelière. "We're there," he said. Our career is over. Have you made your will, Monsieur?"

The chief of staff was pacing back and forth feverishly. "If I could just get out!"

"What, you want to miss the best part of the fête?" mocked the engineer.

"I could run to the station. There's a company of infantry there, and a platoon of dragoons."

"Well," proposed Gastal, "open the door suddenly and run."

"They'll tear me apart!" groaned Monsieur Dupuy de Grelière.

Emphasizing his words, Dupuy pronounced: "They'll either do it now or later!"

Outside, the agitation was increasing. The psychology of crowds is special. It is asserted that a hundred reasonable beings, grouped by hazard, are capable of all crimes if they are excited by an agitator. The varnish of civilization cracks, and the madness is propagated irresistibly, transforming the calmest into unleashed brutes.

"Gold! Gold! Gold!"

"When will you behave yourselves?" Dupuy replied, to those who could hear. "Until then, you won't have anything!"

Jostling with his elbows, Legaye had reached the first rank. "Don't be awkward, Monsieur Duret," he said, taking hold of the bars. "We're the stronger."

"Do you think you frighten me?" the engineer replied, with his arms folded.

"No...you're brave. We're determined to..."

"To steal?"

"If you wish," Legaye ratified. "We need all the gold."

"You won't touch the ingots while I'm alive," Duret declared.

"They you'll die," someone growled.

More conciliatory, Legaye went on: "No one wants to murder you. You've always treated us right. Open up, and I swear that no one will do you any harm."

"Shut the window, Gastal!" ordered the engineer.

"Don't push us to the end, Monsieur Duret!"

"Shut the window!"

The account obeyed, passively. In order to close it, he drew closer to the bars. He was grabbed with extraordinary rapidity.

"To death! To death!"

He braced himself to resist, but in vain. Half strangled, suffocating, he clawed and bit the hands that were holding him like pincers.

"Help!" he croaked. "Help!"

Duret and Dupuy de Grelière grabbed him from behind, hoping that his garments would tear, but they felt him go limp, and, suddenly let go by everyone, he collapsed, his arms crossed, a knife embedded to the hilt full in his heart.

"They've killed him," said Duret, slowly. "Our turn now. You see how simple it is."

Terror maddened the chief of staff. "Help!" he shouted. "Murder!"

The engineer snapped at him: "Don't yap—that's no help. Look! They're demolishing the roof."

217

In fact, the assailants, weary of exhausting themselves against the door and the bars, had gone to fetch ladders, and were smashing the tiles.

Devastated by anguish, Monsieur Dupuy de Grelière grabbed Duret by the wrists. "Monsieur," he begged, "I have three children."

"I know—you've already told me," replied the engineer, sourly.

"Save me!"

"I'm not God! After all, it's you that's responsible for the catastrophe!"

Monsieur Dupuy de Grelière knelt down, his hands joined.

"Protect me, Lord!"

"Don't fall back on religion," Duret mocked. "As our resistance is henceforth futile, we'll try to get our carcasses out of it."

"Yes, yes!" stammered the other, immediately on his feet.

"I can only see one means. We open the door, and flatten ourselves against the wall. The madmen will hurl themselves on the gold. We'll let the hurricane pass, and we'll make ourselves scarce, if possible. Fundamentally, they don't care about us; we still have a slim chance..."

Things happened exactly as he had foreseen. When the door was open, the fanatics rushed in, and then the door was free. In the dust, Duret made out Monsieur Dupuy de Grelière, fleeing with a white sack under each arm.

The engineer headed for his office. A man was sitting on the doorstep, his hands at his temples.

"You don't want gold, then?"

But the man showed his face, and Duret shivered in horror. The unfortunate had an eye torn out, which was hanging down frightfully.

Passions were unleashed. Within an hour, the workers had descended to the level of ferocious beasts. They fought in twos, in fours and in twenties. Anyone who succeeded in taking possession of an ingot in the battle was immediately assailed by ten adversaries.

Peasants were arriving at the gallop along all the roads. Men, women and children, the entire region flooded toward the factory. The majority, forewarned, were armed with pitchforks and scythes; they were carrying baskets and sacks of all dimensions. A few were even pushing wheelbarrows.

And the dragoons plunged forward, followed not far behind by the infantry.

Seized by panic, the workers and the peasants barricaded themselves in the buildings. Then the dragoons wandered through the deserted courtyards, and the foot-soldiers waited, silently, weapons in hand.

The calm lasted until two o'clock in the afternoon, under a leaden sun. Finally, the captain made a decision. He advanced, followed by a drummer. After a long drum-roll, the officer spoke, but his voice was feeble and no one heard anything. He stood still for a long time, hoping for a highly improbable capitulation.

He drew his saber energetically, and gave his orders. A squadron headed for Building C, the door of which the soldiers attacked with vigorous blows of their rifle butts.

A click interrupted their work. A sergeant shook his bloody hand. He had just been hit by a bullet from a revolver.

That was the prelude to the battle. Rifles were raised; the first salvo crackled. Perhaps there were a few wounded, and a great many broken windows. And smoke rose placidly, straight up, into the blue sky. The factory was on fire.

Those who were in the burning building did not take long to come out, in disorder. At hazard, the dragoons charged. Those fleeing fell, letting go of yellow ingots.

"There's the gold!" shouted a soldier.

Then there were no longer soldiers or workers, besiegers or besieged. The ranks broke, and the horses reared up, suddenly riderless. The madness was unlimited, and death reigned, while the fire took possession progressively of all the buildings.

When Duret, hirsute, his features distressed, rang at the door of the villa, Rosita was alarmed.

"Merciful heaven! A misfortune?"

"The factory's burning," he said, brusquely. "The Boss?"

"He's just gone to sleep."

"Wake him up."

The fat maid agitated her sausage-like arms. "He's already in such a state! 'I'm the demon!' he kept repeating. 'The demon vomited by Hell! A curse upon me and mine!'"

"That's agreed," breathed Duret, pushing her aside unceremoniously. "Let me pass, you old magpie!"

Sitting in his armchair, Legrand was asleep. Ali put his index finger over his lips to invite the intruder to respect the silence, but Legrand's sleep was shallow; the bright eyes shone.

"What is it?"

"The factory's burning," the engineer told him, simply. "The savages have looted everything. I've saved the radium."

"Blood?" asked Legrand.

"Alas."

"And the representative of the government of the Republic?"

"Fled like a zebra."

"Everything normal," said the invalid. "Thank you, Duret. I'll resume my siesta."

"But the factory's burning! They've killed Monsieur Gastal!"

"So much the better…so much the worse…I don't know any more…"

Legrand let his head slump on to the back of the chair. "I'm weary of all that, you understand. It's idiotic, my dear. Society doesn't merit anyone occupying himself with it. It's necessary to be content to eat, drink and sleep, like Rosita. I regret that Jeanne, Madame Villaret and Gellé are in Bordeaux. They'll be so content! It's the triumph of their ideas.

Everything is finished, Duret, and not too soon! Me, I want to sleep. Leave me alone."

Until the evening he remained prostrate, his eyelids obstinately closed. Then he ordered the Arab to take him to the factory.

They stopped under the last pines. Sparks were springing in sheaves toward the celestial sparks, and thick smoke was hanging over the blaze like titanic foliage.

"What an apotheosis!" murmured Legrand.

And, lost in the ruddy night, under the aegis of the great Arab, as motionless as a block of stone, he watched his life's work collapse.

XV

Patrols with bayonets fixed were circulating in the vicinity. Every train brought dozens of journalists and photogra-
phers. They had no difficulty visiting the smoking ruins of the
factory, but none of them succeeded in forcing Legrand's
door.

The invalid seemed to be in an excellent mood. He talked
to his Arab with perfect lucidity, confessing his satisfaction at
leaving the country for the city as winter approached. Ali,
mute as ever, conserved his hereditary impassivity.

All the newspapers published long articles about Le
Grapon. They reported the fire, the riot, the intervention of the
troops, with details that were mostly invented, either by the
correspondents or witnesses who had not seen anything. They
insisted on the ignorance of the role played by Monsieur
Dupuy de Grelière, to whom the President of the Republic
would probably give the rosette of an officer of the Légion
d'honneur.

The number of dead, varying from one hundred to three
hundred depending on the paper, permitted the composition of
enormous headlines. The majority of the articles contained a
regulation character assassination of Legrand. His attempt was
compared to that of all known libertarians, for the most part
died of their utopia, and satisfaction burst forth everywhere
that society was still what it had been the day before.

The bankers were triumphant, albeit a trifle belatedly by
their standards, but in an indisputable fashion. They bluntly
demanded the arrest of Legrand, responsible for the blood-
shed.

The situation of the *Echo* was naturally not excellent. In
the absence of Jacques Gellé, Peyrebrune had not hesitated to
take a stand against the government. His attack, direct and
violent, had immediate effects. As usual in such cases, the
Prefect of the département was put on the spot. He chanced to

be hunting with friends in Sologne. He was accused of having deserted his post, and demands for interpellation were lodged on the fashion on which the functionaries of the Republic understood their duty.

Before the session, the Minister of the Interior unloaded ballast. Starting from the principle that the absent are always wrong, he sacked the prefect, and that action permitted him to present himself before the Chambre without fear. The old parliamentarian knew how to defend himself. He agreed entirely with the interpellators, shed tears at the tribune for the soldiers who had died on the field of honor, boldly moved a vote of confidence as soon as the movements of the session proved that he would hold a majority, and confided the sequel to the affair to the Minister of Justice, who accepted it without enthusiasm.

The Head of State went to the hospital in Bordeaux to which the wounded had been transported in cattle-wagons: men, forty; prostrate horses, eight. The Minister of War accompanied him. They distributed military medals, and a subscription was organized in favor of the widows and orphans.

All that only took twenty-four hours, but caused a lot of ink to flow. Interpellations, presidential journeys, handing out of decorations and opening subscriptions are automatic triggers: gestures made a thousand times, which were remade with the same solemnity and the same difference, and to which the same worldwide publicity was given.

One morning, an automobile stopped outside Legrand's villa and three men got out, all in frock-coats, all carrying morocco-leather briefcases. Of Rosita, who received them, they requested Monsieur René Legrand.

"He isn't visible," declared the stout maid, peevishly.

"He will be for us," replied the tallest of the visitors.

"Tell him that it's the Parquet[24]…yes, the magistrates of Bordeaux, for the investigation."

He counted a great deal on those entitlements, but Rosita, whose conscience was clear, was untroubled.

"Monsieur Legrand is very tired, Monsieur. The cerebral commotion has been so strong that he can't see anyone today."

The tall gentleman buttoned up his frock-coat and tugged it with a curt gesture.

"Madame, I demand that you inform your master of our presence."

"Monsieur Legrand isn't at your orders," riposted Rosita, sharply. "He isn't a malefactor, that man. I'll go fetch Monsieur Gellé, you can explain yourselves to him."

She withdrew in a dignified fashion, without them bowing to her.

"Hmm! This doesn't look good," said the tall gentleman. "But for the moment, we have orders not to arrest him. What weakness! What weakness!"

Jacques Gellé soon appeared, in a dove-gray pajama suit, his monocle screwed beneath his frowning brow.

"Bonjour, Messieurs," he said, haughtily. "What do you desire? I'm Jacques Gellé, director of the *Echo*."

They bowed. The tall gentleman coughed to clear his throat.

"Antoine Belloc, public prosecutor."

"Delighted, Monsieur," Jacques replied, simply, examining the prosecutor's frock-coat as if it were a museum piece.

"We've come for the investigation," Monsieur Belloc continued.

"In this house, Monsieur, we know nothing. I was absent, and Monsieur Legrand did not budge from the villa during the riot."

"I must interrogate him nevertheless."

---

[24] In France, the Magistracy is known, portentously, as the "Parquet." I have retained the word here, because the inevitable pun is brought into play when the term is repeated.

"Why, since he doesn't know anything?"

"Oh, we often interrogate people who don't know any-thing," said the prosecutor, subtly. "It's sometimes from them that we learn the most. It's painful for me to insist, but justice demands it."

"You don't want to collect your displacement fee for nothing?" Gellé riposted, insolent and imperturbable.

Monsieur Belloc teased his pince-nez. "I didn't expect this kind of obstruction, Monsieur. My task is already delicate enough..."

"So be it, Messieurs...you shall see René Legrand..." The entrance of the hirsute invalid, more emaciated and paler than usual, pushed by the Arab, surprised them

"These Messieurs are carrying out an investigation," Gellé explained. "It appears that they have an urgent need to interrogate you."

"Ah!" said Legrand, in his hoarse voice. "Interrogate away, Messieurs, and hurry."

The clerk opened his briefcase, and Monsieur Belloc asked: "You are Monsieur René Legrand?"

"I am," said the invalid.

"Your place and date of birth?"

"What does it matter to you? Assume that I've forgotten those superfluous details. Get to the point, Messieurs."

The prosecutor was momentarily nonplussed. "Mon-sieur," he said, "there are formalities that I'm obliged to re-spect."

"That's no reason for me to share your ridiculous obliga-tion," said Legrand. "I warn you...I'm not patient. You won't make me believe in the importance of the place and date of my birth. What do you want with me?"

That abruptness disconcerted Monsieur Belloc, whose discomfort visibly amused Jacques Gellé. He attempted to react, and attacked in his turn: "Monsieur, the tone you're em-ploying is intolerable. I represent the Minister of Justice here..."

"Oh, no!" growled Legrand, in his hoarse voice. "Don't flatter yourself with that! I know what they're capable of, the representatives of ministers! Don't waste time with phraseology empty of meaning, and explain the reasons for your intrusion."

"Monsieur! Intrusion is harsh!" protested the prosecutor.

"How else to qualify the casual behavior of three men I don't know who introduce themselves into my home almost by force? You're wasting my time. Question me!"

"Let us proceed in order," said Monsieur Belloc, whose forehead was moist with sweat. "You refuse to tell us the place and date of your birth?"

"Those details are of no interest to anyone, not even you," said the invalid, stubbornly.

"Note that response," said the prosecutor. "Now, what do you know about...about..."

"About what?" interrupted the invalid, increasingly sullen

"The affair...?" the magistrate concluded, tamely.

"Nothing."

The public prosecutor took out his handkerchief. "I beg you, Monsieur Legrand. This is very serious. You might be arrested...charged..."

The other started in his armchair. "Accused? But you don't know, Monsieur! Yes, note down my replies...I want everyone to hear them."

"They'll appear tomorrow morning in the *Echo*," said Jacques Gellé, phlegmatically.

"Pardon me!" said Monsieur Belloc, alarmed. "Nothing of what happens here must be repeated. To my regret, I must ask you to leave."

"If he leaves," cried Legrand, impetuously, "you won't get another word out of me!"

"And if he stays, you'll talk?" demanded the prosecutor, clutching at that branch.

"I'll make my deposition as it pleases me to make it." The invalid rubbed his hands. "I'll speak. Let's recapitulate a little. I was an industrialist perfectly in regulation with the imbecilic authorities of my country..."

"Shall I write *imbecilic*?" asked the clerk.

"Listen! Listen!" said Monsieur Belloc. "We'll prune later."

"I had a prosperous factory, where workers who were satisfied with their lot were working," Legrand went on, his eyes fixed. "They were not fatigued, working an eight-hour day, the English week, and were paid handsomely. In addition, the products they manufactured belonged to them. In truth, it seemed to me that my factory constituted a model of the genre!"

"Model of the genre...," muttered the clerk.

"One day, a certain Monsieur Dupuy de Grelière, envoy extraordinary of the Minister of the Interior, presented himself in this house. He was a charming gentleman. He ordered me bluntly to close my factory immediately and sack my staff. And when I dared to protest, he told me that soldiers were waiting, ready to impose the will of his superiors upon me, doubtless in the name of liberty. What could I do but acquiesce. I therefore closed my workshops. I yielded to despotism..."

"To despotism...," the scribe repeated, mechanically.

"So, for my part, I acted as an extremely docile citizen. After that, I did not budge from this villa. It was here that I learned from my engineer that my stores had been pillaged, my furnaces destroyed, my buildings burned, and my son-in-law killed. Because of these misfortunes, which I deem undeserved, and to which I can offer no other comment except those you've just heard, I have the intention of pursuing in the French courts the Minister of the Interior and his accomplice the Minister of War. I have nothing more to say, Messieurs. If it's necessary to sign anything, Monsieur Gellé will do it for me. I bid you bonjour and wish you a safe return journey. Ali, take my back to my room."

He had gone before the prosecutor had uttered a word.

"What do you think, Messieurs!" Jacques Gellé jeered. "The affair is taking an unexpected turn, isn't it?"

"Indeed," admitted Monsieur Belloc, thoughtfully.

"I believe that Monsieur Legrand's argument is quite strong...."

"Evidently, but..." He slipped his pince-nez into a lather case. "Oh, this affair is truly deplorable! In the end...I'm limited to fulfilling my mission. The annoying thing is that it was Monsieur Legrand's workers who fired the first shot. Captain Herchel's report is formal on that matter."

"Why were they besieged?"

"I don't have any mandate to reply to you," said Monsieur Belloc.

"I any case, Monsieur Legrand's responsibility in the matter cannot be legally established."

"That's possible. Excuse me for importuning you further, but it's necessary that we go to the scene of the disaster."

"I'll go with you," Jacques Gellé replied. "Just give me a minute to put a coat on."

A cordon of sentinels was isolating the smoking ruins of the factory. Crews were prudently excavating the rubble, under which cadavers were completing their consumption. A few fragments of walls, blackened and tottering, marked the places where the elegant buildings had stood.

"Can it be determined where the fire started?" asked the prosecutor.

"In truth, no, and that's a pity for your report. Was it in the south? Was it in the north? We still don't know..."

Jacques Gellé's irony turned the functionary's cheeks crimson.

"The essential thing," Jacques went on "is that everything is destroyed."

"And the gold?"

"Disappeared. Volatilized. Monsieur Dupuy de Grelière was seen decamping with two sacks. It's regrettable that the looters didn't leave a single ingot. I'd gladly have offered it to you as a souvenir."

The clerk, his briefcase under his arm and his hands crossed over his abdomen, was moved. "It's the abomination of desolation! Not one stone remains atop another."

"Pardon me," said Jacques. "There's still the morgue."

He pointed at the concierge's hut, which had been transformed into a mortuary depot in spite of Minois' protests.

"The charred bodies of a few victims are there," said Jacques Gellé. "They're being conserved with jealous care, awaiting the arrival of some official medical examiner or other. The families don't have the right to touch the remains of those they're mourning. Those are the orders! I spent the night in there, Messieurs, for the funeral vigil of Raoul Gastal, Mademoiselle Legrand's fiancé."

Minois was still working on his net. His fingers brushed the visor of his cap.

"Salut, Messieurs. Have you come to give orders to empty my poor house?"

"Not yet, my worthy Minois," said Gellé.

"Damned Government!" sighed the amputee, resuming his work.

The cadavers—or rather, the debris of the cadavers— were all over the place, on stretchers covered with white sheets. They were in every room, and a low-ranking soldier was sleeping his final slumber on the kitchen table.

Gastal's body occupied Minois' bed. The room had been transformed into a chapel of rest, and for want of church candles, all the tallow candles in the house had been assembled there. A black cat was asleep on the threshold.

Madame Villaret was telling her rosary. Jeanne, still calm, was meditating or praying.

"The Parquet," Jacques announced.

Instinctively, Madame Villaret looked at the floor. "What parquet?"

"The public prosecutor," added Monsieur Belloc.

"My God!" said the yellow-haired woman, horrified. "Have these Messieurs come for the autopsy?"

"No, Madame," said Monsieur Belloc, precipitately. "I'm not a medical examiner. Excuse us…we'll withdraw…"

Outside, he sniffed the sea breeze with satisfaction. "Oh, it does one good to breathe…"

"Do you have any more need of me?" Jacques asked.

"Thank you, Monsieur. Although I'm desolate to have disturbed you, you see me, by contrast, entirely charmed to have been introduced to you…"

He became bogged down in his compliment. Jacques shook his hand limply. But the third person, who had remained completely mute until then, drew the young man to one side.

"Pardon me, Monsieur…I'm literally dying of thirst…where can I get a glass of beer?"

"But…in the village, Monsieur."

"Thank you. I'm very thirsty because I'm slightly diabetic."

The three gentlemen drew away pompously, at a solemn pace.

"Have they said when they're going to get out of my house?" asked Minois.

"Soon…don't worry."

"Oh, I've seen others at Verdun…one sleeps on that…but in my home, it's annoying…"

Since he had learned of Gastal's death, Jacques Gellé had made every effort not to manifest a joy that would not have been in good taste.

Jeanne had started at the revelation of the murder of her fiancé, and then had immediately turned her beautiful eyes to Jacques. He had thought that he read a formal promise there, but whatever haste he was in to acquire a certainty, he could not decently question the young woman. He reproached himself for his intimate delight, and affected a sadness by which only Madame Villaret was duped.

He occupied himself with the obsequies when the official medical examiner had certified that the charred victims were really dead. It was necessary for Jacques to protest energetically and threaten to make a scandal in the press to avoid an autopsy being carried out on Gastal. They wanted at all costs to know which organ had been perforated by the murderer's knife.

Duret was interrogated for hours on end. He was all but accused of having killed the accountant himself. He was made to recount the scene a hundred times over, and the finest sleuths of the mobile police amused themselves looking for the guilty party. They never found him.

Legaye had been killed during the affair. All responsibility could therefore he heaped on him, and he could be convicted of all sins. It was clearly established that he had fomented the riot, presided over the pillage and commanded the battle with great tactical skill. Only Monsieur Dupuy de Grelière was not troubled, but in spite of his indignant denials, several minor opposition newspapers spoke insistently of the two sacks of gold that he had carried off.

One morning, Duret presented himself to Legrand in traveling costume.

"I've come to shake your hand before my departure," he said.

"You're leaving me?" queried the invalid.

"I have so much need of repose! I'm depressed, annihilated. I'm going home, to the Jura. I'll rest while looking after the cattle."

"Will you be willing to collaborate with me again later?"

The engineer shook his head silently.

"Why?"

"I've had enough of bad work," Duret replied, with his customary frankness.

"What bad work?"

"We have so much blood on our hands," the engineer murmured.

The invalid swore to hide his trouble. "Be fair, Duret! It's not my fault if I wasn't understood..."

"No one can understand you," said Duret. "You wanted to impoverish people, when they thought you wanted to make them rich. Instead of making them better, you made them worse. I'm not criticizing, I'm observing. So I'm not going any further. I'm changing direction. When I'm at peace, I'll go into some factory or other, where I'll manufacture no matter what. I prefer producing to destroying."

Legrand closed his eyes.

"Another one who's abandoning me! You've doubtless made your pile too. How much do your trunks weigh?"

"Monsieur Legrand," said Duret, without raising his voice, "I forgive you, because you're happy. If not, I'd cram those words back down your throat. I'm an honest man, but not very patient."

The invalid plunged his hands into his hair. "Excuse me, Duret. I don't know, any more…I don't know, any more…"

"You'll never have enough gold to corrupt me," the engineer insisted. "By suspecting me, you're causing me unnecessary chagrin."

"I beg your pardon," said the invalid. I'm going a little bit madder every day…but I don't want you to leave here as poor as you were before…"

"And I insist on it!" riposted Duret.

"Since I don't have any more gold, I'll give you the radium you saved."

"No thank you."

"You refuse? In your turn, you're causing me unnecessary chagrin."

"Then I accept," said Duret. "I'll give it to the hospitals of my département. There are many cancer patients in the Jura."

Legrand's visage brightened.

"Embrace me, Duret. You're a man!"

After the accolade, they were embarrassed, for neither of them was accustomed to effusion.

"Adieu, Monsieur Legrand," said the engineer. "I'm afraid of missing the train."

"You'll need to hurry," the invalid approved.
And it was thus that they went their separate ways.

XVI

The cemetery was square. The waves of the tide gave the appearance of wanting to drown the tombs, but they stopped a few meters from the stone wall and retreated meekly, as if regretfully.

Gastal was buried there. They had buried him at Le Grapon until Legrand had had a mausoleum constructed in Bordeaux.

"We owe him that," the invalid had said, in a melancholy fashion.

The funerals had been hasty. The remains of the soldiers had departed by railway; the bodies of workers and peasants had been buried at daybreak, to avoid a demonstration whose effects the government feared. As for Gastal, he had been honored by a rapid low mass, at the exit from which the coffin had been transported to the necropolis on a handcart.

A black cross extended its desolate arms.

Here lies Raoul Gastal
Died at the age of 31. R. I.P.

And the funeral painter, signing his work like an artist, had designed a heart surmounted by a little spark.

The fading and rotting flowers spread a powerful odor of humus. Jeanne and Madame Villaret took away the most decayed bouquets. The young woman hid her features under a crepe veil, but nothing in her attitude betrayed a genuine grief.

By contrast, Madame Villaret did not spare her tears, and spoke in a constantly whining voice.

"There's Monsieur Gellé," she revealed, lugubriously. "Oh, Monsieur Jacques, it's very sad..."

Jacques removed his felt hat, uncovering an impeccable parting.

"You're wrong to stay here for such a long time," he said to Jeanne. "You'll make yourself ill."

"She isn't reasonable," murmured Madame Villaret.

"Besides which, the sun's blazing."

"If that could revive the dead..."

"Come for a walk in the forest instead."

"Go with her, Monsieur Gellé. She isn't eating anything, perhaps it will give her an appetite. I'll pick up the dead flowers..."

The eternal whisper of the innumerable pines was son overhead. They walked at random. Heads bowed, distractedly crushing the purple heather.

"Your father," said Jacques, "intends to go back to Bordeaux at the end of the week."

"I know," said Jeanne. "And when are you going back to Paris?"

"Soon...but I'm the master of my time..."

Resin was running in bright drops from long vertical wounds in trees bleeding to death.

"Why are you asking me about the date of my return?" Jacques asked.

He divined a little enigmatic smile beneath the veil.

"To know..."

"So it's all the same to you when I go!" he said.

She did not reply.

"You take pleasure in torturing me!" he sighed.

"Me!" she said, pretending surprise.

"Yes, you. You're toying with me. Since the evening when..."

He did not finish. She waited, to be sure that he would not carry the memory through.

"I advise you not to talk about that evening," she said.

"You don't want me to talk about it?"

"Never."

"So," he said, "I'm absolutely nothing to you?"

Jeanne's large eyes became even wider. "Oh! You think you're something to me? What are you hoping for, then? You don't even dare to admit it?"

Forgive me," Jacques stammered. "You're incomprehensible. I thought for a moment that..."

She drove him to his last retrenchments with a tranquil malevolence. "Go on, then! I challenge you to make your thought precise."

"What's the point, if you don't love me?" he said, in a suddenly defeated tone.

"Yes, of course I love you," Jeanne replied, with a redoubtable simplicity. "But I'm not a prostitute. I'm free—marry me."

"Certainly! Certainly!" Jacques approved, without overmuch conviction. "That's my intention, you know...."

She smiled again under her mourning veils.

"That's what you desire, isn't it?"

"All is for the best, then. The moment isn't propitious to speak to my father about our project. It's necessary to wait with confidence."

"Won't you give me a token...?" he implored.

She held out her hand, but he seized her almost brutally, and kissed her on the lips through the crepe. She did not resist.

"Be reasonable," she recommended, as she pulled away.

They went back to the villa.

Jacques Gellé thought: *She never loses north, that one. She's still stronger than I imagined. She's going to be my wife. She's very beautiful, very decorative, but do I love her sufficiently?*

Preparing for the departure, Madame Villaret was filling the house with parcels. Legrand remained grimly shut away in his room, only consenting to become almost sociable at meal times. Then, from the soup to the dessert, it was always the same bitter dissertations on human stupidity and the insupportable tyranny of the government.

"They're content now! I haven't destroyed anything, it's them who've demolished me...their house of cards can remain

236

standing, I won't blow on it to make it collapse. Everything's fine. I'm still being treated as a madman in a few papers, but most of them are talking about other things. They're right. I ask no more than to die quietly in my corner."

Every day he searched the papers for articles about the failure of his endeavor. He found fewer and fewer, and understood with a muffled exasperation that forgetfulness was forming around him. Momentarily, he had cruelly shaken the apathy of the world, and the world was now taking its vengeance, in its fashion. The invalid preferred the most unjust attacks to silence, but it was the silence that was falling. Even the *Echo* was no longer talking about Le Grapon. Legrand's actions and concerns wearied its readers. The judicial investigation had petered out, and within a week, two at the most, the final period would be put on his story.

It was the Friday when Legrand had decided to leave Le Grapon. He was about to climb into the carriage that was to take him to the station when Rosita, astonishing in a bright pink hat, announced Monsieur Lévy-Durand. And the financier came in immediately, obsequious and cordial, his eyes duller than ever.

"Am I disturbing you?"

"Yes, Monsieur," growled Legrand, without amenity.

Lévy-Durant appeared contrite. "How I regret it! But I wanted to be the first."

"The first to what?"

"Firstly to congratulate you on being safe and sound. In riots one never knows who will live or die. It could have finished much worse for you." And, addressing Gellé: "What a loss that would have been for science!"

He looked at them alternately, in quest of encouragement, but he found them undeniably hostile—without being disconcerted by it, however.

"I know," he went on, with his most engaging rictus, "that you've renounced your original project. You're a thousand times right. It's better to work for Society…for progress.

We're builders, not destroyers. I'm in haste to affirm to you that my friends and I are still in the same disposition..."

"Me too," said Legrand.

Lévy-Durand became agitated. "Favorable, no? Favorable?"

"Hostile," replied the invalid.

"That not possible! Try to understand us, Monsieur. I assure you that our intentions...."

Legrand interrupted him dryly. "Don't waste your saliva, Monsieur. Your intentions aren't mine. I won't march with the others any more than with you. Let that be a consolation to you. Above all, don't insist, and don't come back. It would be heart-breaking for you, for I'll have you thrown out."

"You wouldn't do that," the financier protested. "Permit me to explain..."

"I won't permit you anything!" shouted the invalid. "You're aggravating me!"

"No? It would be very favorable, though...we'll constitute a kind of super-trust..."

"You're annoying Monsieur Legrand," Jacques Gellé interjected.

"All right, all right," said Lévy-Durand, precipitately. "The hour hasn't yet sounded. I'll go... I'll write to you...I'll write to you... You'll read my letter with a calm head..."

"I shall throw it in the bin!" said the invalid.

"If you desire, one day...I hope you won't address yourself to others... You have my address? Excuse me, and *au revoir...au revoir...*"

Bows, a viscous hand offered.

"*Au revoir*...and once again, forgive me..."

"He's disgusting!" declared Legrand.

"He has no self-respect," said Madame Villaret."

"If he had, he'd sell it. He's only accessible to the voluptuousness of the belly or commerce. Fundamentally, he takes me for an imbecile, and he's not wrong. I'm no longer in my right mind. You ought to have me locked in a padded cell!"

He was hoisted into the vehicle.

In order to reach the station it was necessary to go past the ruin of the factory. Children were playing in the rubble. They were naively reenacting the tragic scene. One of them shouted: "You don't have the right to kill me! It's me who's the soldier!"

Legrand stopped the carriage.

"Let me look one last time..."

He absorbed himself in contemplation, and then rebuked himself: "Bah! The grass will have grown back there tomorrow..."

XVII

The door creaked on its hinges. It was a little shrill plaint that drilled into the opaque shadow.

Like all those who have suffered a great deal, Legrand was a light sleeper.

"Who's there?" he said, immediately.

In spite of the absolute silence, he divined, and was certain, that there was someone in the room.

"Who's there?" he repeated, in his hoarse voice.

With his hand he sought the electric switch suspended above his bed, and with a flick of the thumb he made light.

In the sudden dazzle of clarity he scarcely had time to see Ali standing on the threshold, his arm raised, running toward the bed. Then there was the flash of a blade.

"Well?" said Legrand, extraordinary calm.

For the blade had not come down.

"Master, Master...," the Arab stammered.

"Strike, then," said the invalid. "You'd be doing me a favor."

Ali's arm fell, lifelessly.

"Go on, I'll restore your courage," said Legrand.

He switched off the light.

Nothing could be heard but the Arab's halting respiration. That went on, and on...

"It's not easy, then, to be a murderer?" said Legrand, softly.

He switched the light on again. Ali had stepped back. The knife lay at his feet.

"You!" murmured the invalid. "You too!" And in those words there was an indescribable pain.

Overwhelmed by shame, Ali sought the door with his gaze.

"Don't go!" Legrand ordered. "Your exploit ought to have its recompense. I know what you want; I'll give it to you."

He meditated momentarily, his eyes riveted to the Arab, whose face was ashen gray.

"It's to arrive at this," Legrand murmured, "that I've given the best of myself..."

"Forgive me!" exhaled the traitor. "I was mad...."

But Legrand shook his head pensively.

"There's nothing to forgive—you're only human. It's me who should beg your pardon for having submitted you to the temptation, and for having believed in your fidelity. The most imperious temptation to which Satan submitted Jesus was that of wealth..."

The Arab's legs buckled; he knelt down. "I won't do it again...ever..."

"Why did you wake me up?" Legrand meditated. "I would gladly have passed from sleep to death. I'm so keenly aware of having failed in my superhuman task. Why didn't you murder me?"

The Arab's forehead collided with the carpet.

The invalid continued thinking aloud. "And above all, wretch, why didn't you tell me you wanted the gold, like all the rest?"

He extended his arm toward the coffer. "Take it, my friend, it's all yours. You didn't understand, then that the metal doesn't belong to me? Take it. I give it all to you!"

Ali shivered, but did not raise his head.

"You'll be rich," Legrand went on. "That will be my only vengeance. Go, laden with gold...that will be your expiation. You must have struggled atrociously against yourself. You've destroyed the best you had. Nothing more remains in your soul and your heart. You've sacked everything, pillaged everything. What a pity you haven't cut my throat! It seemed that your thought was only a reflection of mine, and your confidence in me protected you from weakness. Once more, I was mistaken!"

"Forgive me!" said Ali, whose eyes were fixed on the coffer.

"God alone can forgive," sighed Legrand. "Men remember, and their pardon is the cruelest form of hatred. I don't want to see you again. Go away."

"Master," the Arab begged, "let me go on serving you..."

"Open the coffer," said Legrand. And when the other hesitated: "Obey, I demand it...."

The Arab literally crawled to the coffer. As he put his hand on the key he looked at the invalid.

"Open it!"

Ali tipped back the lid and waited,

"Take it!"

The Arab plunged his hands into the coffer and brought out a small handful of little scoria.

"Take it! Go on, take it all!"

Then Ali lost all constraint. Contact with the metal had made him another man. He took a canvas bag out of his pocket that he had stitched himself, and feverishly, greedily, with a sickening haste, he took the gold.

Legrand was laughing now, terribly.

"Take it, insensate! Take misfortune with both hands! Take your punishment! You're too old, my friend. That burden will crush your shoulders. Ah! You're putting it in your pockets too?"

He raised his voice, and the Arab was afraid of his cries. One more handful—the last—and he fled, engulfed by the dark staircase, bumped into the woodwork of the corridor, tumbled on to the quay and galloped away into the icy fog.

Out of breath, exhausted, he stopped. A rictus tugged at the corners of his mouth. Rich! He was rich! And he had neither killed not stolen! That heap of gold was his, really his!

An atrocious thirst dried his throat. He set out again, as weak as a convalescent.

A few steps away there was a drinking-den, whose iron curtain was half drawn. He went in. A tin-plated counter striped the back of the room. Behind the counter there was a tall thin virago.

"Coffee!" said the Arab.

She reached for a thick glass and filled it with a black steaming liquid.

"Ten sous," she said.

The Arab paid. He drank the drug, made of moldy brandy and bitter chicory, in small sips.

Nearby, a negro was drawing tearful sounds from an accordion. In one corner, two louts were playing cards. Two drunken sailors were arguing striking the table, which made the empty bottles with which it was laden shiver. Tobacco smoke rendered the air almost unbreathable.

A small woman came to stand to the Arab's left.

"What'll you offer me?" she asked.

She was so thin that he took pity on her. Prodigality was not one of his faults, but this evening, was he not fabulously rich?

"Whatever you wish," he replied.

She scented possible prey. "Suppose one sat down?" she proposed. "You must have finished your *croissance*."

To follow her, he picked up his sack.

"What are you carrying?" the whore asked. "Beans?"

"Not even close!"

Face to face, they drank. The prostitute had put her chin on her palms, and she studied him with half-closed eyes. He, thinking himself superior, affected a distant attitude.

"You're an arbi?" she queried.

"Yes," he said.

"Where've you come from, so late?"

He did not judge it useful to satisfy the prostitute's curiosity.

She went on: "Where do you work?"

"Nowhere."

"You don't look like a rentier, though," she appreciated.

"Possibly," he said.

She stretched herself like a cat. "Are you going to offer me a second glass?"

"If you like," he said.

"I don't like drinking alone. But your religion forbids you to drink rum?"

"Oh, I drink it!" the Arab exclaimed

"Two tafias," the prostitute ordered.

The proprietress served them, lazily.

"Why don't you fill the glasses to the brim?" observed the whore, peevishly.

"If you aren't content, go elsewhere," she said, recorking the bottle.

The Arab drank the tafia in one draught.

"Wow!" the prostitute joked. "You lift your elbow well. Me too, look!"

She drank as he had, and they started to laugh, stimulated by the crude alcohol.

"I'd gladly have another," said the whore.

They had several more. Patiently, she got him drunk, and he, habitually prudent, fell into the trap. The alcohol comforted him, and gave him a dangerous confidence. His gaze was swimming slightly, but he kept his head high and his gestures curt. Increasingly, he experienced the need to be admired; even so, he was suspicious of those surrounding him, especially his companion. He continually verified the presence of his precious sack, which he had set between his legs. That alerted the attention of the prostitute.

Slyly, she launched a few kicks; she had the impression of collided with coke.

"What are you lugging around in that sack?" she asked.

With great mystery, Ali put a finger over his lips and winked. "It's a secret," he whispered. "If you knew…but you shan't know…"

As she extended her neck, curiously, he tipped himself back in his chair to laugh at his ease. The prostitute suppressed a gesture of impatience, and thought that he was not yet drunk enough to talk.

"Anyway, I don't care!" she said, lighting a cigarette.

But the Arab was happy to tease her. "Ha ha! You'd care if you suspected..."

At the next table, the two louts had stopped playing. The prostitute darted an expressive glance at them.

"Oh, if I wanted to," she said, "I could guess what there is inside it."

"Never!" the Arab exclaimed.

The sound of his own voice alarmed him; he lowered the tone. "You'd never guess. It isn't possible!"

"It's coal?" said the whore. "No? Let me feel the weight."

"You can't," he said. "It's too heavy."

"Let's see?"

Under the table, she tugged at the sack, which rendered a metallic sound.

"Well!" said the prostitute astonished. "What can it be? Scrap metal?"

Ali drank the contents of his glass in slow sips. All the pride of his race was stagnant in his eyes. Solemnly, he deployed his enormous height, and opened his arms.

"I've made my fortune," he said, with the bombast of a preacher. "Tomorrow, I'm leaving for my homeland. I shall have a cool house where the water sings night and day. My life will no longer be anything but a dream...my wives..."

"Sit down and drink," the prostitute interrupted. "Let it go."

They only exchanged a few more words. The Arab struggled confusedly, instinctively, against the drunkenness that was numbing him. His head bobbed for a long time, ever ready to fall asleep, staying awake—but the bad alcohol had reckoned with his resistance. He finally collapsed, his arms dangling, his forehead on the dirty wood of the table.

One of the louts made as if to stand up,

"Wait," whispered the prostitute. "He isn't drunk enough."

They waited a little longer. When she was certain that he was asleep, she took possession of the sack herself.

"Is it heavy?" asked the lout.

"Yes…get out with the parcel…"

"What about you?" asked the lout.

The prostitute had her plan. "If I stay, he won't suspect me, but if I hop it, he'll denounce me."

"You're right," the thief approved. "We'll meet up later. Until tomorrow, and good luck."

He went out with his comrade. Standing behind her counter, the thin woman had watched the scene impassively.

"I don't much like those tricks," she complained.

After a few moments, the girl clapped her hands noisily.

"Oh, damn it!" she said. "We've dozed off. We were drunk. Pay, and let's go. It's late."

The Arab straightened up painfully, rubbing his eyes.

The two thieves walked rapidly and silently. The fog resolved into a fine drizzle, which soon soaked through their thin garments.

"Where are we going?" said one.

"To the docks," the other replied. "We won't be disturbed."

The heels of a belated passer-by rang on the sidewalk.

"Look sharp!" said the first. "We mustn't be recognized."

They pulled their caps down over their eyes. The precaution was unnecessary, because the pedestrian went past them without turning his head.

"Necessary not to run into the cops," said the one carrying the sack. "They'd ask us too many questions about our bundle."

"Especially the cyclists," the other said. "They fall on you from behind without you hearing them coming."

"It's damnably heavy," breathed the first. "Perhaps we've gone to a lot of trouble for nothing…"

"What if we took a look now?"

"We're nearly these. It's sharp, it's digging into my shoulder enough to draw blood..."

The cranes loomed up in their thin legs with the appearance of phantoms. The docks stretched out, dirt under the harsh light of electric pylons. After the strangulation of the sluice-gate the first basin widened.

"Here!" said the first. "No need to cart it any further."

Without overmuch haste, they untied the cords of the sack. They dug into it together and then examined the brownish spongy scoria. They dug in again, down to the bottom.

"No error, it's just copper," said the first.

The second laughed. "We're idiots!"

Disappointed, but not desolate, they looked at one another.

"We'll hardly get twenty francs offer it.

"I'm not risking getting caught for fool's parsley," the other protested. "I'm liable for transportation."

"What are we going to do with this rubbish, then?"

"Into the water!"

The lout seized the sack with both hands in order to swing it. He let it go. The sack disappeared into the water with a dull splash. Droplets sprang forth.

One of the thieves sneezed. "Good! Now I'm catching cold!" he said, anxiously. "Let's go have a grog."

Their thin shoulders drooping, with a trailing tread, they crossed the road and disappeared into the night.

Early in the morning, while Rosita was carefully twisting her hair in order to compose a small chignon pinned on top of the head, the bell of the entrance door rang with an unusual persistence. The racket went on and on, and dull thuds shook the door.

Rosita was not nervous. She put on a flannelette peignoir, put on her shoes without doing up the laces and went downstairs.

When she was in the corridor she shouted: "I'm coming, savages!"—for she was nurturing the intention of giving the impatient supplier a scolding.

There were some fifty people gathered outside the house—a few laborers stopped on their way to work, mostly dock-workers, shipwrights and carters, noisy and loquacious people whose voices were confused in a loud hubbub.

"He's dead," said a man with a beard. And with his index finger, he pointed at a form lying along the wall.

Rosita could only make out two feet. She advanced, already white with fright.

"He's even cold," added a crouching woman.

Ali was laid out on the cobblestones, in the mud. His sodden clothing was stained. But what terrified Rosita most of all was the purple, horrible face, with the tumefied tongue protruding ignobly from the mouth, and the bulging eyes, translating an unspeakable horror. Hair was stuck to the forehead and temples in long black wisps, from which water was dripping.

"We found him hanged," explained the bearded man. "Yes, Madame, hanged from that iron pole, which you must use when you put up flags for the fourteenth of July..."

"You shouldn't have taken him down!" decreed a plasterer, severely. "You're obliged to wait for the police. That's the law."

The bearded man declared, nobly: "When it's a matter of the life of one of my fellows, I don't care about the law."

"You're wrong," riposted the other.

"Wrong or not, I cut the rope, and I don't regret it."

"It didn't resuscitate him!" said the plasterer, stubbornly.

"I did everything possible...respiratory movements...tractions of the tongue..."

Rosita was not yet very emotional. She was only just beginning to comprehend that Ali was really dead."

"Why did he kill himself?" she asked.

"We don't know," replied the bearded man, whose authority the crowd tacitly accepted. "He really is your domestic? He does live here?"

"Yes, Monsieur," stammered Rosita,

"Then it's necessary to take him inside."

Rosita shivered at the idea of the hideous cadaver being about to come into the house. But the plasterer intervened.

"Pardon me! It's necessary to wait until the police arrive."

"The police! The police again!" The man with the beard got carried away. "You have no other word in your mouth!"

"Exactly. And then he'll be taken to the morgue for autopsy."

"You're stupid!" said the bearded man.

"You're an idiot!" said the plasterer.

People got between them, for fear that they might come to blows. The plasterer went off, shrugging his shoulders, with the result that the bearded man remained the master of the terrain.

"Here come the police!" someone said.

Rosita took fright. "What about Monsieur? I need to tell Monsieur!"

Breathlessly, she went into Legrand's bedroom. The invalid, sitting on his bed, was leafing through a large book.

"Monsieur!" gasped Rosita "It's terrible! Ali's dead! He's hanged himself outside the door."

To the great amazement of the maid, the invalid's emaciated face relaxed, and Legrand burst out laughing.

"Bravo!" he exclaimed.

"My God! My God!" she said, recoiling, frightened by that joy.

And she filled the house with cries:

"Help! Monsieur has gone mad!"

XVIII

The sequence of days was monotonous, and existence with Legrand became truly impossible. The invalid had crises of silence that frightened that disturbed the tender Madame Villaret, or burst out into imprecations at the slightest provocation. Slumped in his armchair, curled up like a sick cat, he had hallucinated eyes, the gaze of which was insupportable.

He no longer worked, no longer read, even refused the newspapers. His unopened mail piled up on his table. People still wrote to him from all over the world, but he no longer had enough curiosity to open the envelopes.

He was only kind to his daughter, in whose regard he displayed an affection more fervent than ever. The young woman, indulgent to his changes of mood, heaped him with cares and remained minutely attentive to his needs and desires. She spent hours by his side, without saying a word if he did not speak, listening with an untiring patience if he rambled.

Sometimes, the invalid summoned her in a low voice in order to kiss her. He took her head in both hands, studied her for a long time, and wept.

"What's the matter, Papa?" Jeanne said, with solicitude.

"Nothing…I'm bored."

"It's unnecessary. Don't we have everything we need to be happy?"

"Oh! You think so?" murmured the invalid.

The wound inflicted on his pride had not scarred over. He could not console himself for his failure, even though he never neglected any opportunity to prove to himself that his work had not been futile, since the changes were leveling and the big banks were no longer the masters of the world.

The director of the *Echo* spent more time in Bordeaux than in Paris. His love for Jeanne had increased, and yet he still seemed to consider her as an adversary. There is, in any case, often no better ally than a vanquished adversary.

That day, alone in the empire drawing room, they were chatting. He was asking her, once again, to set a date for their marriage.

"Wait," Jeanne replied. "You're too impatient."

"Wait for what?"

She indicated her mourning-dress.

"Propriety?" Jacques exclaimed. "Don't give me that reason, for you don't care about that, and neither do I."

Fundamentally, he was jealous. He was not sure that Gastal's death had left her completely indifferent.

"Then again," said Jeanne, "you know that immediately after my marriage, I want to leave…"

"But we shall leave!" Jacques approved. "We'll lift anchor whenever you want. My yacht is ready."

She wanted to roam the seas, visit Scandinavia, get to know Insulindia, live under other stars.

She shook her head. "I can only go when Papa's entirely well. I can't leave him at present."

Jacques Gellé, cracked the knuckles of his fingers, whose nails were varnished, impatiently. "He'll never be entirely well!"

The young woman leaned toward him. "Yes, Jacques…but he isn't yet sufficiently recovered for us to ask him…you know what..."

The secret, the famous secret. They both thought about it relentlessly, although the invalid seemed to have forgotten it. He aggravated them by repeating to them that money doesn't bring happiness and that Rosita put into practice the wisest doctrine: eat, drink and sleep.

Jacques wiped his monocle, unnecessarily, with a multi-colored silk handkerchief.

"I'm still calm," he said. "I have confidence in you, but I'm experiencing infinite pain counting the wasted days. I love you, Jeanne. If I had to choose between the secret and you, I wouldn't hesitate."

"You'll have both," she promised, very close.

He only had to tilt her head for their lips to join. When they separated, Legrand was in front of them, looking at them without anger.

"Children!" he said to the young couple, who bowed their heads. "Why are you alarmed by my presence? What have you to fear from me?"

"Monsieur," said Jacques, decisively, although his voice was quavering slightly, "I have the honor of asking you for your daughter's hand."

The invalid sat down painfully and looked at him with a smile.

"You've had her heart for a long time. I'll gladly grant you her hand. Love one another. Love consoles, love is the savior. I'd like to unite you myself, following the example of the patriarchs, but I don't want Jeanne to be excluded from the imbecile society that she's so avid to penetrate..."

In one of her rare moments of expansion, Jeanne pressed herself against her father's shoulder.

"It's necessary for you to get married as soon as possible," Legrand said. "It will be my last joy, for I'm much older than my age, and no longer hope for time to come. When you leave me, I'll give you my secret...the secret that I once wanted to give to everyone! It will be in a fragile envelope, which I'll give to you, Monsieur Gellé...you can open it later...when I'm dead. I beg you not to open it while I'm alive."

"I swear!" Jacques declared.

"Thank you. The best thing would doubtless be to slip a blank piece of paper into it, but I won't do that, even though humans have already been punished enough for having wanted to equal the gods. You shall have the secret of gold. I'll confide it to you because you have no need of it. Because of that, perhaps you'll utilize it more skillfully than another, when I no longer exist...soon, no doubt...and you'll quickly weary of being the richest people in the world. That's not a very consoling verity: life isn't worth very much when one no longer desires anything..."

He uncovered his daughter's features.

"She's very beautiful," he said, proudly. "She'll give you children in her image, and your race will be strong."

Taking Jeanne's hand, he put it into Jacques Gellé's.

"My dear Jeanne…," stammered the young man, confused.

"I give her to you," Legrand continued. "Look after her preciously, be jealous of all those who approach her. Be obstinate in remaining alone. You will thus diminish the chances of misfortune and suffering."

"We'll always be happy," Jacques affirmed, drawing his fiancée to his heart.

"I render you responsible for her happiness. That happiness is my sole excuse. My effort will not have been entirely in vain, if it permits my daughter to have the husband of her choice. Love her, Jacques. On your love, the entire future depends. Obey the most irresistible force of nature. I have not loved; that was what caused my weakness. If I had loved, and if I had been loved, I would have triumphed."

"Ingrate!" sighed Madame Villaret, who had come in a few seconds before.

"Why?" riposted the invalid. "I'm not accusing you of anything. You've offered me all that you possessed. It's neither your fault nor mine if it wasn't sufficient. These children are rich, first of all in their beauty and their youth…and then, the secret that I shall give them tomorrow. I repeat that they won't have need of it, but the certainty that they possess it, that they could exploit it, will multiply tenfold their joy in living."

He paused for thought.

Madame Villaret said, lamentably, to Jeanne: "He dares to confess that he doesn't love me!"

"No recriminations!" replied Legrand, impatiently. "You have the best part. The essential thing is not to be loved but to love oneself. Let's go into the dining room. It's better to leave these children; they have eyes full of dreams."

In the other room, Madame Villaret seized the invalid's fleshless hand theatrically. "René, once again, you're breaking my heart!"

"You always exaggerate," said Legrand, caressing the yellow hair of his humble mistress.

"You don't love me!" sobbed Madame Villaret.

"Yes, I love you, dearly. Am I not faithful to you? Now, according to you, fidelity is the supreme manifestation of love..."

"If you had deceived me, I would have been able to forgive you," she declared.

"One always forgives for one's own satisfaction," said Legrand, "just as one often does wrong in order to savor thereafter the voluptuousness of remorse. Those children will suffer because of one another, which will be normal and consoling. They won't go astray, like me, in the mists of a stupid philosophy. They'll spend their years loving one another, always happy, but always anxious to be so, for our morality is so corrosive that bliss appears to us an implausibility..."

XIX

Legrand got back from the station at six o'clock. He had accompanied Jeanne and Jacques there, married that day with the minimum of fuss, who were leaving for Marseilles, where their yacht was waiting for them. He had not wanted Madame Villaret to keep him company that evening. All alone, dogged and silent, with infinite difficulty, he hoisted himself up to the first floor. Rosita heard him open the drawing room door.

"Why didn't you call?" she reproached him.

She had red eyes and a shiny nose. She blew abruptly into her handkerchief with a noise like a trumpet.

"I'm upset," she said. "When I think that, at this moment, Mademoiselle is heading for the other side of the world, and that we won't have news of her for days on end..."

The invalid let himself fall into an armchair next to the window."

"Leave me alone," he said.

"Life is badly made," said Rosita. "The good God should never separate people who love one another. Me, I left my mother at seventeen, and never saw her again. When she died, I arrived after the funeral, at lunch time. There were forty at table. That's the custom back home, because some people come a long way..."

"Leave me alone!" repeated Legrand, exasperated.

"Monsieur doesn't want anything?"

"I want to be left in peace."

Rosita beat an immediate retreat.

Night tranquilly took possession of things. The sky descended upon the city, and the shadows seemed to emerge from the corners where they had been hiding. A line of yellow dots stretched out, indicating the bank of the river. In the water, brilliant caterpillars trembled, and the tumult of the port gradually decreased, dissolving in the buzz of the city. The peace of the evening reigned.

Legrand meditated, his gaze fixed, his body as motionless as stone.

Rosita found him as she had left him. "It's dinner time," she said.

The invalid passed his hands gently over his forehead. "I'm not hungry," he replied.

"Monsieur," replied the maid, firmly, "that's all the same to me. You have to eat. You have an omelet and a chicken-wing. It's not a matter of drinking the sea. Let's go."

Legrand suppressed a gesture of impatience, but did not attempt to argue. Perched on his crutches, progressing in graceless hops, he went into the dining room.

The icy aspect of the room chilled his heart. He swallowed a few mouthfuls, with difficulty, in order to avoid the reproaches of Rosita, who was watching him with a reproving expression. The meal did not last long. Legrand soon went back to the drawing room in order to resume his obstinate meditation there.

The quays were now almost deserted. The heaped-up bales took on apocalyptic forms. A goods train puffed and snaked along the bank with a metallic racket, flanked by men brandishing red lanterns, as if they were censers. To the left, the Garonne flowed away into the tunnel of the hermetic night.

A clock chimed ten times. A whistle sprang from one horizon to the other. A loud siren replied to it, the last roar of which ricocheted from the facing hills. Then silence fell again.

Legrand pricked up his ears. Rosita must have gone to bed, because he could not hear anything. He dragged himself on to the landing, as discreetly as possible, but a question descended from the floor above.

"Do you need something?"

"Nothing. I'm going to bed."

"Good night, Monsieur."

"Thank you. You too."

In his bedroom, he waited patiently for a long time, perhaps an hour. Finally, he made up his mind and, in order not to awaken any echo in the sleeping house, he let himself slide from one step to the next, crouched on his dead legs, carefully dragging his crutches behind him.

He went out into the street without thinking of closing the door behind him, he was in so much haste to get away from his home.

"Psst! Psst!"

He shivered with a veritable anguish, but it was a prostitute who accosted him. She planted herself in front of him, so close that he could feel her warm breath.

He looked at her. She was tall and thin, with voluminous breasts suspended like beggar's wallets. Her boldly staring eyes were sad, and her mouth seemed to be bleeding, wounded by the rude kisses of brutes who had poisoned her with their caresses.

In a low voice, she proposed: "Are you coming, handsome lad?"

He jibbed, thinking that it was an insult, but she was placid, smiling, almost maternal. For simple commercial reasons, she found all men young and handsome.

"Another time," said Legrand.

To acquit her conscience, and without the slightest conviction, she persisted: "Why not this evening?"

He became suddenly excited, and struck the sidewalk with his crutches. "Because I have other things on my mind. Such as you see me, I've lost the kingdom of the world."

The prostitute laughed, mocking without malevolence.

"The kingdom of the world? You're off your head."

He seized her by the wrist, so hard that she was frightened, and nearly fell over pulling free.

"Yes the kingdom of the world," he went on. "The secret of gold belongs to me. What's a million to me? If I wanted to, I could make you the most envied, the most hated creature...but it's necessary not to upset the social order! The social order, do you understand? Society! It's an admirable machine, which the smallest grain of sand throws out of order. Now, it's necessary that it works regularly. It needs the rich, the dirty idiots who scratch the soil, and starvelings like you on the lookout for drunken sailors. Without those inequalities, we'd no longer have the ideal, and that would be a misfortune! Do you follow me, child? Rejoice in your misery—it's as necessary as my pain."

The prostitute recoiled, fearfully.

"He's completely crazy, this brother!"

She disappeared into a narrow side-street whose single street-lamp made the damp cobblestones gleam.

"Go get yourself locked up!" she shouted, from a distance.

Walking slantwise, as laborious and maladroit as a huge crab, he crossed the road. A customs-officer sitting in front of his hut turned his head in order not to see him. He saw many go past every evening, those poor fellows who slipped under the tarpaulins, and whom the police dogs sometimes drove away. He allowed them to defend themselves again the night, that steadfast enemy of the hearthless.

Legrand reached the bank of the river. Above his head, an arc-lamp rounded out its diaphanous moon. Level with the flagstones, for the tide had finished rising, the oily water splashed, agitated by its millenarian frisson. Over all that, very low, the black veil of the night was thrown.

The quay was cluttered with barrels. Rigorously lined up, they were grouped in sections like an army. They were hogsheads from Spain. Pot-bellied and debonair, full of the thick and treacherous wine whose drunkenness is devoid of joy.

A shadow was outlined—that of a small man enveloped in a reefer jacket, whose nose and thick gray moustache could be vaguely distinguished beneath the hood.

"What are you doing here?" he demanded, severely.

Mechanically, Legrand replied: "Taking a walk."

There was a long pause.

"Me," said the other, "I'm the night watchman." After a few seconds, he added: "I'm responsible for these barrels."

"Oh?" Legrand murmured.

"That's how it is," said the man in the reefer jacket. And after a further pause, he added: "You can't stay near my wine."

"Oh, I'm not a thief," Legrand protested, "And your wine isn't at risk."

"No one's a thief," sniggered the watchman. "Theft is a joke one plays on someone."

"That's true," said Legrand.

"I know what it is," the watchman continued sententiously. "They wait until I turn my back. All right, I turn my back. Crack! There's a dry click, the bond's broken, and they drink with a straw. Then, the next day, the wine's missing and I get a mouthful. As I'm paid to guard, I guard. You have to go."

He shook his head, and twisted his thick fingers, which cracked like dry woof.

"How much do you earn?" asked the invalid.

"That's my business," riposted the other. "I earn plenty."

"If it's a secret, I won't insist."

"Union rate, five hundred francs a month," the guard revealed, with an ingenuous vanity."

"And you're content?"

The watchman spat, rubbed the ground neatly with his hob-nailed shoe, and went on: "That makes six thousand francs a year. You'll respond to me that there are risks. All métiers have risks. Mine has advantages, damn it! Such as you see me, I sleep till noon and then I play my game of manilla. There are lots worse off. We're sworn in!" And, returning to his preoccupation: "You aren't going to stay here all night, I suppose?"

Legrand leaned over on his crutches.

"Would you like to be a millionaire?"

The guard stated laughing. "For sure!"

"What would you do with your money?"

"I'd buy a watch," the man replied.

"Well, you'll be a millionaire. I want you to be. Tomorrow, you'll have your million. It will be my last folly!"

But the guard tapped him on the shoulder in a familiar fashion. "You wouldn't by chance, be a little drunk?"

Legrand did not hear him. He followed his train of thought, imagined the realization of his dream.

"Yes, of a pauper, I'll make a Croesus. A million? That's not sufficient, you'll have ten. Beautiful women will humbly request your favors, and handsome Messieurs will prostrate themselves before you. You'll be the golden calf!"

"What a joke!" The guard guffawed. "Me, a calf?"

"Ha ha! That will be amusing!" the invalid continued. You won't know how to make use of your fortune, you'll multiply stupidities, so much they'll call you an eccentric. I only ask one thing of you: be ferocious! Crush the intellectuals with your scorn, mock the beauty of science, of laws, of everything! I'll make you so rich that your monstrous wealth will devour the world!"

"Listen," the guard interrupted. "You need to sleep. Further along, on this side, you'll find bales of Australian wool. It's warm and soft."

"Oh, you doubt me? You too?"

"Don't get annoyed, we'll talk about it another time," the other conciliated.

Legrand clenched his fists. "They all doubt! I no longer have anything to hope for. It's been proven to me that I'm too dangerous a man."

The guard took a step back. "Dangerous?" he said. "Don't be an imbecile—I have a revolver. I'll drop you just like that!"

"Dangerous to humanity! If I'd been allowed to act, I'd have turned the world upside down. Why not? What proof is there that the new society wouldn't have been better? But no…forbidden to try! I was begged…I was cowardly enough to swear."

The man in the reefer jacket spat on the ground again. "You're wrong to get wound up. Go to bed, that would be better. You're annoying me with your nonsense, Adieu."

He drew away with a heavy tread. The nails of his shoes clattered on the flagstones.

Legrand fell silent. Dazedly, he stared at the electric lamp, the barrels, the black water flowing at his feet.

He drew closer...and closer...and closer...

When the watchman had covered twenty meters, he looked round.

As far as the eye could see, the quays were deserted.

SF & FANTASY

Adolphe Alhaiza. *Cybele*
Alphonse Allais. *The Adventures of Captain Cap*
Henri Allorge. *The Great Cataclysm*
Guy d'Armen. *Doc Ardan: The City of Gold and Lepers; The Troglodytes of Mount Everest/The Giants of Black Lake*
G.-J. Arnaud. *The Ice Company*
André Arnyvelde. *The Ark; The Mutilated Bacchus*
Charles Asselineau. *The Double Life*
Henri Austruy. *The Eupantophone; The Olotelepan; The Petitpaon Era*
Barillet-Lagargousse. *The Final War*
Cyprien Bérard. *The Vampire Lord Ruthwen*
S. Henry Berthoud. *Martyrs of Science*
Aloysius Bertrand. *Gaspard de la Nuit*
Richard Bessière. *The Gardens of the Apocalypse; The Masters of Silence*
Chevalier de Béthune. *The World of Mercury*
Albert Bleunard. *Ever Smaller*
Félix Bodin. *The Novel of the Future*
Louis Boussenard. *Monsieur Synthesis*
Alphonse Brown. *City of Glass; The Conquest of the Air*
Émile Calvet. *In a Thousand Years*
André Caroff. *The Terror of Madame Atomos; Miss Atomos; The Return of Madame Atomos; The Mistake of Madame Atomos; The Monsters of Madame Atomos; The Revenge of Madame Atomos; The Resurrection of Madame Atomos; The Mark of Madame Atomos; The Spheres of Madame Atomos; The Wrath of Madame Atomos* (w/M. & Sylvie Stéphan)
Félicien Champsaur. *Homo-Deus; The Human Arrow; Nora, The Ape-Woman; Ouha, King of the Apes; Pharaoh's Wife*
Didier de Chousy. *Ignis*
Jules Clarétie. *Obsession*
Michel Corday. *The Eternal Flame*
André Couvreur. *Caresco, Superman; The Exploits of Professor Tornada* (3 vols.); *The Necessary Evil*
Camille Debans. *The Misfortunes of John Bull*
Captain Danrit. *Undersea Odyssey*
C. I. Defontenay. *Star (Psi Cassiopeia)*

Charles Derennes. *The People of the Pole*
Georges Dodds (anthologist). *The Missing Link*
Charles Dodeman. *The Silent Bomb*
Harry Dickson. *The Heir of Dracula; Harry Dickson vs. The Spider*
Jules Dornay. *Lord Ruthven Begins*
Alfred Driou. *The Adventures of a Parisian Aeronaut*
Sâr Dubnotal *vs. Jack the Ripper; The Astral Trail*
Odette Dulac. *The War of the Sexes*
Alexandre Dumas. *The Return of Lord Ruthven*
Renée Dunan. *Baal; The Ultimate Pleasure*
J.-C. Dunyach. *The Night Orchid; The Thieves of Silence*
Henri Duvernois. *The Man Who Found Himself*
Achille Eyraud. *Voyage to Venus*
Henri Falk. *The Age of Lead*
Paul Féval. *Anne of the Isles; Knightshade; Revenants; Vampire City; The Vampire Countess; The Wandering Jew's Daughter*
Paul Féval, *fils. Felifax, the Tiger-Man*
Charles de Fieux. *Lamékis*
Fernand Fleuret. *Jim Click*
Louis Forest. *Someone is Stealing Children in Paris*
Arnould Galopin. *Doctor Omega*; *Doctor Omega and the Shadowmen* (anthology)
Judith Gautier. *Isoline and the Serpent-Flower*
H. Gayar. *The Marvelous Adventures of Serge Myrandhal on Mars*
G.L. Gick. *Harry Dickson and the Werewolf of Rutherford Grange*
Raoul Gineste. *The Second Life of Doctor Albin*
Delphine de Girardin. *Balzac's Cane*
Léon Gozlan. *The Vampire of the Val-de-Grâce*
Jules Gros. *The Fossil Man*
Edmond Haraucourt. *Daah, the First Human; Illusions of Immortality*
Nathalie Henneberg. *The Green Gods*
Eugène Hennebert. *The Enchanted City*
Jules Hoche. *The Maker of Men and His Formula*
V. Hugo, P. Foucher & P. Meurice. *The Hunchback of Notre-Dame*
Romain d'Huissier. *Hexagon: Dark Matter*
Jules Janin. *The Magnetized Corpse*
Michel Jeury. *Chronolysis*
Gustave Kahn. *The Tale of Gold and Silence*
Gérard Klein. *The Mote in Time's Eye*
Fernand Kolney. *Love in 5000 Years*
Paul Lacroix. *Danse Macabre*

Louis-Guillaume de La Follie. *The Unpretentious Philosopher*
Jean de La Hire. *The Fiery Wheel; Enter the Nyctalope; The Nyctalope on Mars; The Nyctalope vs. Lucifer; The Nyctalope Steps In; Night of the Nyctalope; Return of the Nyctalope*
Etienne-Léon de Lamothe-Langon. *The Virgin Vampire*
André Laurie. *Spiridon*
Gabriel de Lautrec. *The Vengeance of the Oval Portrait*
Alain le Drimeur. *The Future City*
Georges Le Faure & Henri de Graffigny. *The Extraordinary Adventures of a Russian Scientist Across the Solar System* (2 vols.)
Gustave Le Rouge. *The Dominion of the World* (w/Gustave Guitton) (4 vols.); *The Mysterious Doctor Cornelius* (3 vols.); *The Vampires of Mars*
Jules Lermina. *The Battle of Strasbourg; Mysteryville; Panic in Paris; The Secret of Zippelius; To-Ho and the Gold Destroyers*
André Lichtenberger. *The Centaurs; The Children of the Crab*
Maurice Limat. *Mephista*
Listonai. *The Philosophical Voyager*
Jean-Marc & Randy Lofficier. *Edgar Allan Poe on Mars; The Katrina Protocol; Pacifica 1, 2; Robonocchio; Return of the Nyctalope;* (anthologists) *Tales of the Shadowmen 1-12; The Vampire Almanac* (2 vols.)
Ch. Lomon & P.-B. Gheuzi. *The Last Days of Atlantis*
Xavier Mauméjean. *The League of Heroes*
Joseph Méry. *The Tower of Destiny*
Hippolyte Mettais. *Paris Before the Deluge; The Year 5865*
Louise Michel. *The Human Microbes; The New World*
Tony Moilin. *Paris in the Year 2000*
José Moselli. *Illa's End*
John-Antoine Nau. *Enemy Force*
Marie Nizet. *Captain Vampire*
Charles Nodier. *Trilby and The Crumb Fairy*
C. Nodier, A. Beraud & Toussaint-Merle. *Frankenstein*
Henri de Parville. *An Inhabitant of the Planet Mars*
Gaston de Pawlowski. *Journey to the Land of the 4th Dimension*
Georges Pellerin. *The World in 2000 Years*
Ernest Pérochon. *The Frenetic People*
Pierre Pelot. *The Child Who Walked on the Sky*
Jean Petithuguenin. *An International Mission to the Moon*
J. Polidori, C. Nodier, E. Scribe. *Lord Ruthven the Vampire*

P.-A. Ponson du Terrail. *The Immortal Woman; The Vampire and the Devil's Son*

Georges Price. *The Missing Men of the* Sirius

Edgar Quinet. *Ahasuerus; The Enchanter Merlin*

Henri de Régnier. *A Surfeit of Mirrors*

Maurice Renard. *The Blue Peril; Doctor Lerne; The Doctored Man; A Man Among the Microbes; The Master of Light*

Jean Richepin. *The Crazy Corner; The Wing*

Albert Robida. *The Adventures of Saturnin Farandoul; Chalet in the Sky; The Clock of the Centuries; The Electric Life; The Engineer Von Satanas*

J.-H. Rosny Aîné. *Helgvor of the Blue River; The Givreuse Enigma; The Mysterious Force; The Navigators of Space; Vamireh; The World of the Variants; The Young Vampire*

Marcel Rouff. *Journey to the Inverted World*

Marie-Anne de Roumier-Robert. *The Voyage of Lord Seaton to the Seven Planets*

Léonie Rouzade. *The World Turned Upside Down*

Han Ryner. *The Human Ant; The Superhumans*

Frank Schildiner. *The Quest of Frankenstein*

Pierre de Selenes: *An Unknown World*

Angelo de Sorr. *The Vampires of London*

Brian Stableford. *The Empire of the Necromancers (1. The Shadow of Frankenstein; 2. Frankenstein and the Vampire Countess; 3. Frankenstein in London); Eurydice's Lament; The New Faust at the Tragicomique; Sherlock Holmes and The Vampires of Eternity; The Stones of Camelot; The Wayward Muse.* (anthologist) *News from the Moon; The Germans on Venus; The Supreme Progress; The World Above the World; Nemoville; Investigations of the Future; The Conqueror of Death; The Revolt of the Machines; The Man With the Blue Face; The Aerial Valley; The New Moon; The Nickel Man; On the Brink of the World's End*

Jacques Spitz. *The Eye of Purgatory*

Kurt Steiner. *Ortog*

Eugène Thébault. *Radio-Terror*

C.-F. Tiphaigne de La Roche. *Amilec*

Simon Tyssot de Patot. *The Strange Voyages of Jacques Massé and Pierre de Mésange*

Louis Ulbach. *Prince Bonifacio*

Théo Varlet. *The Castaways of Eros; The Golden Rock.; The Martian Epic* (w/Octave Joncquel); *Timeslip Troopers* (w/André Blandin); *The Xenobiotic Invasion*
Pierre Véron. *The Merchants of Health*
Paul Vibert. *The Mysterious Fluid*
Villiers de l'Isle-Adam. *The Scaffold; The Vampire Soul*
Gaston de Wailly. *The Murderer of the World*
Philippe Ward. *Artahe ; Manhattan Ghost* (w/Mickael Laguerre); *The Song of Montségur* (w/Sylvie Miller)

MYSTERIES & THRILLERS

M. Allain & P. Souvestre. *The Daughter of Fantômas*
A. Anicet-Bourgeois & Lucien Dabril. *Rocambole*
A. Bernède. *Belphegor*; *Judex* (w/Louis Feuillade); *The Return of Judex* (w/Louis Feuillade); *The Shadow of Judex* (anthology)
A. Bisson & G. Livet. *Nick Carter vs. Fantômas*
V. Darlay & H. de Gorsse. *Arsène Lupin vs. Sherlock Holmes: The Stage Play*
Séamas Duffy. *Sherlock Holmes in Paris*
Paul Féval. *The Black Coats (The Parisian Jungle; Heart of Steel; The Sword-Swallower; 'Salem Street; The Invisible Weapon; The Companions of the Treasure; The Cadet Gang); Gentlemen of the Night; John Devil*
Émile Gaboriau. *Monsieur Lecoq*
Goron & Émile Gautier. *Spawn of the Penitentiary*
Paul d'Ivoi. *Around the World on Five Sous* (w/Henri Chabrillat)
Rick Lai. *Shadows of the Opera: Retribution in Blood; Sisters of the Shadows: The Curse of Cagliostro*
Steve Leadley. *Sherlock Holmes: The Circle of Blood*
Maurice Leblanc. *Arsène Lupin vs. Countess Cagliostro; Arsène Lupin vs. Sherlock Holmes (1. The Blonde Phantom; 2. The Hollow Needle); The Island of the Thirty Coffin; 813; The Many Faces of Arsène Lupin* (anthology)
Gaston Leroux. *Chéri-Bibi; The Phantom of the Opera; Rouletabille & the Mystery of the Yellow Room; Rouletabille at Krupp's*
Richard Marsh. *The Complete Adventures of Judith Lee*
William Patrick Maynard. *The Terror of Fu Manchu; The Destiny of Fu Manchu*
Frank J. Morlok. *Sherlock Holmes: The Grand Horizontals; Sherlock Holmes vs Jack the Ripper*

Jean Petithuguenin. *The Adventures of Ethel King*
Antonin Reschal. *The Adventures of Miss Boston*
P. de Wattyne & Y. Walter. *Sherlock Holmes vs. Fantômas*
David White. *Fantômas in America*
Pierre Yrondy. *The Adventures of Thérèse Arnaud*